GORGEOUS Lies

BRITTANY TAYLOR

 Created with Vellum

DEDICATION

To those who have ever questioned their worth.
You have a seat at the table.
You are enough.
You are more *than enough.*
You. Are. Worthy.

Hello dear reader!
Gorgeous Lies is a high angst, emotional read. **Please be aware** this book contains scenes and topics which may be sensitive to some. Topics include alcohol addiction, drug addiction, pregnancy loss and scenes of drug use.
I sincerely hope you enjoy Victoria and Jude's story.
Thank you and happy reading!
Xoxo,
Brittany

VICTORIA

THERE HAS ONLY EVER BEEN A HANDFUL OF THINGS I'VE been certain of ...

My passion for dancing.

My obsession with reading.

My first love.

And the moment I realize I no longer want to marry my fiancé, Greg Bailey.

Who is not, in fact, my first love.

No. He's the man standing across from me with the expression one would have if they just realized they'd drank an entire gallon of spoiled milk, with his sweat covered forehead, and a look of regret buried deep within his golden-brown eyes.

I swallow and stare at the bead of sweat dripping down his forehead as he utters the words *I do*.

Confusion. It's the only emotion to settle in my bones as the bead of sweat migrates from his temple to his cheek.

"And do you, Victoria Jean Monroe, take Greg Henderson Bailey to be your husband?"

I shift my attention to the Justice of the Peace standing between us. His eyes are wide, and his forehead crinkles as he pretends to patiently wait for my answer. Deep down, I know he's aching to get this over with. He's longingly and silently pleading for us to wrap this up, hoping we don't drag this out past his thirty-minute lunch break.

Every. Minute. Counts.

I swing my gaze back to Greg's. His face is just as unsettled as before, even though he'd casually recited his vows and allowed the words *I do* to spill from his mouth as if he was reading the instructions off the back of a box of cake mix.

But this time Greg's eyes aren't on mine. They're on the woman standing behind me. My sister.

I guess I should be clearer, actually. My *step*sister.

The tension between Greg and my stepsister Amy is a weight pressing down on me over my right shoulder. If it weren't for the text message I'd received a mere ten minutes ago, I wouldn't be thinking too hard about the heat of regret building in Greg's eyes, or how he is silently wishing and begging that it were Amy standing in front of him instead of me.

I wonder why in the hell he's going through with marrying me when it's clear I'm not the one he truly wants. In the past six months he's never given me any indication that he *didn't* want to go through with marrying me. Not until I read the text message he mistakenly sent me—the one intended for my sister —right before I'd shuffled into the courthouse with Amy by my side.

> Greg: I know we said we would forget what happened between us, and you want me to fulfill my obligation to Victoria, but I can't marry her without letting you know something first, Amy. I will never forget last night. We will always have Benedict's.

Fulfill. I replay the word in my mind a million times over. He used it as if we were in some sort of arranged marriage. But we aren't. I met Greg six months ago when Amy forced me to create one of those online dating profiles. She said it would help me to get out of my dating slump and move on from the life I'd left behind. At first, I didn't think too much about the profile. After scanning through a hundred men who didn't catch my attention, I'd given up. Months passed before I bothered to open the app again, and then there was Greg. He'd swiped right on me. His profile picture had been of him sitting at a table, shoving a piece of Texas toast in his mouth. He had a kind smile and warm eyes.

I fell for it and sent him a message. All it took was three dates and for Greg to stay at my place two nights in a row before he was moving in and asking me to marry him. We were the typical online dating success story. Now, six months later, here we are.

"Well?" The Justice of the Peace asks.

I blink and look to my left. "What was that again?"

He clears his throat. "I asked you if you wanted to marry . . ." He pauses long enough to glance at the sheet of paper in his hands. "Greg Henderson Bailey." He nods with pride, satisfied he got the name right again. He probably performs dozens of marriages a day.

I give him a weak smile. It's all I'm able to offer. 'A' for effort.

I realize I already know the correct answer to the Justice's question the second I finally turn back to look into Greg's eyes. I already know my choice. In fact, it dawns on me I've known all along. I've lived in a constant state of denial for the past four years, on a mission of people pleasing. I should marry Greg. I should *want* to. But I don't. I just hate that I didn't see it until now.

I should hate him for what he's done. I should allow shame to fill my gut for not catching on to every little sign I must have missed. I should feel embarrassed for being sandwiched between my fiancé and my stepsister, knowing I have proof of their affair burning in the pocket built into my white minidress.

But I'm not.

There's no anger. No jealousy. No heat simmering in what should be my shattered heart. There's nothing. What does that say about my relationship with Greg?

"Why?" I ask him. "Why are you still marrying me when you and Amy will always have Benedict's?"

"Benedict's?" He blinks, caught off guard with my sudden question. "I'm not sure what you mean." He nervously wipes his hand across his mouth, then smiles, as if his smile will erase the uncertainty inside him.

He inhales a deep breath, and his neck contracts with his nervous swallow.

Benedict's is one of the local restaurants here in Austin. The only time Greg and I have ever been to Benedict's was the night we celebrated our engagement. With Amy.

I replay that night in my head, pinpointing the moment Greg must have been talking about in the text. Then I remember I'd left early in a cab because my landlord had called telling me my pipes had burst in my apartment. Greg hadn't even offered to go with me. He'd stayed behind with Amy. Maybe they'd created a tradition out of it. Maybe that's the place they would meet up, without me knowing. Maybe they'd fucked in the bathroom of Benedict's more times than Greg and I have in our own apartment since living together.

I cock my head to the side and wait for Greg's answer. My question sits heavy between us like a wet towel.

His face pales, and Amy coughs behind me, breaking her silence. She catches Greg's attention. He looks over my shoulder for the hundredth time. I don't bother turning to look at her. We've never been terribly close, considering she didn't enter my life until after I'd already moved here. I was barely twenty, and heartbroken. I won't deny the pin prick to my heart, remembering how she'd played the part well. She played me like a fool. She pretended to care for me, sympathizing on all the reasons I'd left home behind and moved to Texas. But now, I'm certain it was all bullshit. It was nothing but an act. Every word. Every hug. Every smile.

The prick in my chest is brief, fading before I give it too much thought.

"Why are you marrying me?" I ask Greg again.

"I, um..." He clears his throat. "What do you mean? I'm marrying you because I love you."

"No," I disagree. "If you truly loved me, you wouldn't have sent Amy a text minutes before coming here."

His lip twitches. "I do love you."

"No. You don't." I quickly slip my engagement ring off my finger and turn around. I'm standing face to face with Amy for the first time since we walked into this room.

Her eyes are lined with tears, but she hasn't shed a single one. Her cheeks are flaming bright red, and her hand is pressed against her stomach. Her blonde hair is curled around her face, and her painted red bottom lip quivers. Not because she's heartbroken for having a hand in breaking my heart. She's nervous and ashamed for having been caught.

"Vic, I..." she starts.

"Stop." I sigh. "I don't need or want your excuses. Every word out of your mouth since I moved here has been a lie. I wouldn't know what to believe."

Amy shakes her head and steps forward. "I never intended to hurt you." It's not like I haven't heard that lie a million times. It's always the ones you love the hardest who hurt you the most with their lies.

She reaches for my hand, but I pull it back.

"There might be truth to what you're saying, but I'll never

be able to tell. You know I can't get married to him after this, and something tells me you don't want me to." I turn back to Greg and drop the ring in his hand. "If you two love each other then you deserve each other. I wish nothing but the best for you."

I look back at the Justice of the Peace. He's watching this entire scenario unfold in silence.

"You're in luck," I tell him. "You might still be able to perform a wedding before your lunch break. It just won't be mine."

I take a step back and trade glances between Greg and Amy. They are both looking at me the same way: slight regret, slight relief. I see it in the way their eyes widen.

Greg doesn't move. He doesn't follow or fight for me. He stays with Amy.

I don't want their pity. I may have only just realized I don't love Greg the way I thought I did, but it doesn't make the sting of their betrayal any less painful.

A betrayal is a betrayal no matter how sharp it is.

I spin on my heels without another glance in their direction and push through the two wooden doors leading out of the courthouse. The second my face hits the Texas heat, I know I've made the right decision.

Marrying Greg would have been a mistake, and even if we'd still gone through with the ceremony, it wouldn't have lasted. My love for Greg wasn't deep. It wasn't the kind that burrowed itself into my soul. It wasn't the kind that had the ability to shatter me into a million pieces at the snap of a finger.

I know because four years ago I experienced that kind of love. It crashed into my life without warning. Consumed me. Nestled into every bone and muscle in my body. It made me weak at the knees. It made me feel alive. Then it destroyed me.

It left every muscle shredded, and every bone broken. It chewed me up, spat me out, and left no crumbs.

Now, it's all led me here.

My foot lands on the concrete steps, carrying me farther away from Amy and Greg, where they have no doubt already started to recite their vows, and the Justice of the Peace is thrilled, relieved to know his lunch is only minutes away.

As for me, I'm once again left figuring out how to pick up the pieces of my life and where to turn next. At least this time I'm nowhere near as broken or bitter as I was the day I moved here four years ago.

No. The memory of that pain will always be reserved for him. The man who told me lies as gorgeous as his midnight blue eyes.

The man who made a home in my heart, then destroyed it.

CHAPTER ONE

VICTORIA

Seven months later

"Five, six, seven, eight." Riley snaps her fingers as she scans the room with narrowed eyes. "That's it, girls. Remember to watch your arms with your pliés."

The four girls lined up on the dance floor lift themselves up on the ball of their foot and spin around, wrapping their arms around themselves like Riley instructed. Their faces are hardened in concentration as they bend, flawlessly moving on to the next step in their routine.

"Yes, perfect!" Riley shouts over the music. She glances down at me with a reassuring smile before turning her attention back to her students.

I stay where I am on the floor beside her and stretch my legs out into a perfect 'V'. I grind my teeth, preparing for the sensation I know is coming, and point my toes. Both hamstrings constrict and swell with the motion. I flex my foot back and forth, hoping the pain will magically go away simply by me willing it to disappear. It doesn't. If anything, it gets worse.

The pain rolls in waves, radiating across my hamstrings

down to the back of my knees, then my calves before stopping at my ankle.

"Are you okay?" Riley asks above me. The girls on the dance floor are still dancing in unison without her instruction.

"Yeah." I swallow and give her a grin, closing the book I've been burying my nose in for the past thirty minutes. I set it down beside me. "Sometimes the pain is worse than other days. But today isn't bad. It'll fade."

"Oh." My aunt chews on the inside of her cheek, hesitating. "Did you maybe want to join them?" She holds her hand out to the group of girls.

I follow her gaze with a sigh.

The girls are beautiful. They're her younger class. None of them can be older than ten, but they step and bend across the dance floor effortlessly.

The way I used to be able to.

Pressure builds behind my fingertips as I massage my knee. "Not today." I shake my head.

I tell her as if I might decide to dance tomorrow. Or the next day. Or the next. But the truth weighs heavily between us.

I haven't danced in four years, since I first left Boston before heading out to Texas.

I don't plan on trying or have any plans to change my mind. Even if I did, we both know it wouldn't be the same. My body is simply too fractured to move the way it once did before the accident that quite literally changed my entire life.

"Okay." Riley nods in reluctant agreement. She presses her mouth into a thin line and plants her hands on her hips. The corners of her lips lift, and her eyes sadden when she looks down at my legs. Her sympathy tugs on my heart.

My Aunt Riley has owned this studio for as long as I can remember. Set in the heart of Boston, I used to spend hours after school and endless days in the summer on this same dance floor. Riley has taught me everything I know. It's where I fell in love with the art. It's where I decided dancing was all I ever wanted to do in life. At least it was then.

But the shadow of the accident that tore it all away still hangs over this studio like a heavy, looming dark cloud.

Riley remains standing above me with her hands planted on her hips and a distant look in her eyes. The memory of that night is clearly playing in her mind, also.

Two broken bones, over a dozen torn ligaments, and a loss only I and one other person in this world know about since the day I left Boston and moved to Texas. Even my aunt doesn't know about the hurt that took my already shattered heart and crushed it.

Riley continues with her class without asking about me joining in again. I'm thankful she's dropped the subject of me dancing, but I can't ignore the hollow feeling carved out of my chest.

I do miss it, but I don't have the courage to start again. Not now, at least. It's been years, and the distance has allowed me to pursue another passion I refuse to let go of.

"All right, girls." Riley claps her hands and picks her phone up from the stool set near the front of the studio. Her blonde hair bounces with her every step. It's a wonder we're related considering my hair is a dark shade of brown.

I watch the reflection of the girls' faces in the long mirror stretching from one side of the room to the other. They all have smiles on their faces, which isn't surprising considering my aunt's studio has been a local favorite here ever since she opened it when she was eighteen. Like me, dance has been a passion of Riley's.

She taps her finger against her phone, and the music playing immediately stops. The studio quietens, allowing Riley's voice to echo across the space.

"You did a great job today. I want you to remember to point your toes when you do this move." She sticks her leg out, pointing her toes down. In one swift motion, she sweeps it out in front of her and drags it across the floor, stopping at her right. She points to her foot, showing them what it should look like. "Like that."

The girls nod in understanding.

"Now," Riley says. "I'll see you all next class, and be sure to practice when you can." She lifts her finger and narrows her eyes at each of the girls. "But of course, not before you finish your homework and anything else your parents want you to do. Right?"

I can't help but laugh. The girls chuckle as well. "Yes, Ms. Riley."

She grins in satisfaction. "Great. I'll see you next week."

The girls disperse and cross the room to grab their bags. Within seconds, Riley and I are by ourselves.

I pull myself to a stand, wincing when a sharp pain shoots down the back of my leg. It's quick, disappearing when I take my first step away from Riley.

"So," she says behind me. "What are your plans for today?"

I keep walking until I reach the other side of the room. I left my phone sitting in Riley's office. I reach in and grab it, checking for any missed messages, but there's nothing except an email.

"I'm not sure," I mumble.

"Did you apply in time for next semester?"

I click on the email and nod, answering Riley's question. Ironic that she asked when I finally have my reply sitting in my inbox. I quickly read the first line of the email and snap my head up. Riley's gathered a pile of dirty towels and is tossing them into a laundry bag.

My stomach somersaults.

"What is it?" Her eyebrows slant, and she takes a step forward, leaving the laundry bag. Her tan skin crinkles between her pale green eyes.

I exhale. "I got accepted."

"You did?" She stands on her toes and clasps her hands in front of her, somehow holding in her excitement, waiting for me to repeat what I've already confirmed.

Nerves bundle inside me. "I did." I feel the tears already welling behind my eyes.

"I'm so proud of you." She squeals and wraps her arms around me, squeezing all the air out of me.

I can't help it. I let the tears flow. One slides down my cheek when Riley pulls away. Her smile stretches from ear to ear.

"Are you happy you finally get to finish what you started years ago?" she asks. Riley rolls her eyes, pausing when she realizes what she said. She waves her hand frantically in front of her, wincing. "Well, sort of started. You know what I meant."

Attending Boston College has been a dream of mine since my childhood. Growing up in Boston, I always envisioned enrolling in their dance program, following in my aunt's footsteps, and opening my own dance studio after graduation.

My dream did come true when I was accepted into their dance program on a full scholarship before I'd even graduated high school. Then it was destroyed before the end of my sophomore year.

But after I left Greg and Amy standing in the courthouse the day he and I were supposed to get married, I've worked to get my life back on track. Seven months later, I'm back in Boston, and now I've been accepted to the school I left behind.

This time is different than the last. I'm four years older. I'm a different major. I've saved every penny possible to afford this class.

In certain ways, it feels like a step backward, but my gut is telling me this is the only way for me to march on and take control of my life. One semester with one class. It's all I need to make up if I want to move forward.

I couldn't control the accident and how it stole my passion and career from me. I couldn't control Greg and Amy's secret affair. But *this* I can control. I can take back my life.

"Honestly," I confess to Riley. "I'm shocked they took me back considering I started as a dance major and now I've switched to literature."

"That shouldn't be a big deal." She frowns, disagreeing. "Your courses transferred from Texas, and that's all that matters."

"I'm just nervous, that's all." I consider her answer, sighing heavily.

"Why?" She weaves her arms beneath her chest and tilts her head to the side.

Riley is my mother's sister, and while my mother and I don't have a close relationship, Riley and I always have. Ten years older than me, Riley was constantly around when I was growing up. I'd spend days in the studio with her after school, avoiding going home until I absolutely had to. My mother was kind and caring, but she was also absent most of my childhood. Even now as an adult, she's still absent. My stepfather and her quickly retired once they'd cashed in their stock investments, claiming they'd done so at the perfect time. Now they live on some boat sailing around the Mediterranean. Or so they say. I only hear from them maybe every six months. I never even told them about Greg, and I doubt my stepfather even knows what made the headline news in our family. His daughter Amy was having a full-blown, scandalous affair with my fiancé. Riley was the only person I knew I could go to when I needed to leave Greg and Texas behind.

It took several months to tie up loose ends between school

and my job, but now here I am, a week later, crammed into the studio apartment above her dance studio, struggling to reclaim the city I once called home.

I wipe the tears from my face, my nerves taking over, once again.

"I don't know why I'm worried," I lie. I know the biggest reason out of the two, opting to give her the lesser of them. "This last writing class is incredibly selective. I'm surprised I even got in. There are times when I wonder if I made the right choice switching careers. At least, picking this one. Dance used to be all I ever knew. Now I don't even have that."

"You may not have dance." Riley steps forward, swiping her thumb across my cheek. "But you have your writing and your books. That's what's important. Boston should be grateful to have you back."

"True." I nod, sniffing. "It's just one class, though. It might have been a different story if it were more than that."

"Victoria Monroe," Riley scolds. "Don't doubt how incredible you are. Boston is lucky to have you. I don't care if it's one class or if it isn't the dance program. You've earned your place. Own it."

I give her a reassuring smile. Her encouragement warms my chest.

But once the warmth of Riley's enthusiasm wanes, the reality sets in. My stomach twists into another impossibly tight knot. I bite down on the inside of my cheek, letting my other unspoken worry slip away: seeing the man who single handedly broke my heart and crushed it until there was nothing left for me to do but leave him behind.

Now I'm at risk of seeing him again. I think.

I haven't spoken to him since the night our lives shattered, but I'm not ashamed to admit to a little social media sleuthing.

The last post he made was months ago... wearing a Boston College sweatshirt.

Then again, part of me hopes he finished college. He must have by now. I've been gone for four years, and he was already ahead of me by a few classes.

"Are you sure you're okay?" Riley places her hand on mine and gives it a gentle squeeze. "Is your leg still hurting?"

"I'm fine." I inhale a shaky breath. "I think I'm just more nervous because I took a couple semesters off."

"Well, it's still your dream to become a writer, isn't it?" Riley asks, sensing the hesitancy in my voice.

"Definitely." I nod. "I'm hoping to write my own book one day, but I don't necessarily need to finish college to do that."

"No," Riley agrees with a light smile. "But it helps." She drops her hand to my shoulder and gives it a gentle squeeze. "You are going to kill this final class. When does it start?"

"Next week. Monday."

My nerves settle slightly. At least I have a few days to come to terms with the possibility of seeing my ex again.

I turn my head and look out at the tall floor-to-ceiling windows running along the entire front of the studio. The sun has begun to set, flooding the room in a warm, golden glow. I sigh and tuck my phone into my back pocket. Dance was my first dream. Writing is my second. I know writing wasn't what I envisioned for my life, but it doesn't feel like settling. It feels as if I'm simply following another passion I didn't know existed until I'd lost the only one I'd spent my life focusing on.

"Monday is perfect." Riley giggles, pulling my attention back to her. "That still gives me time to take advantage of your help around here. Starting with this load of laundry." She twists around and grabs the bag, dropping it in front of me, and letting out an exaggerated breath. "You'll have to take it to the laundromat down the street. I don't have a washer and dryer here."

"Really?" I widen my eyes.

Having just moved back here a week ago, Riley's offered to wash my laundry with hers up until now. I always suspected she took it downstairs to a laundry room I assumed existed. But I guess she's been carting it down the streets of Boston to the laundromat instead.

"Yeah." She waves me off. "I've been meaning to buy a set, but they're always so damn expensive."

"With how many loads you do a week and with how long you've been using the laundromat, you've probably spent the same amount in quarters that you could have spent on a new set." I wrap my hand around the handle of the bag and give her a knowing smirk.

She rolls her eyes. "You're probably right, but saying it out loud makes me sick."

"Of course, I'm right." I grin, grunting as I lift the bag and hitch it over my shoulder.

"I usually take mine down to Village Laundry," Riley says. "It's about a block down that way." She lifts a hand to shield her eyes from the bright afternoon sun, using her other to point in the direction of the laundromat.

"I'm sure I won't miss it." I start to carry the bag out of the studio, but she stops me before I make it too far.

"Oh, wait." She disappears inside her office, then pops back out with a small black bag in her hand. "The washing machine takes eight of these, and the dryer will probably take about the same depending on how many cycles you need to use."

I eye the bag in her hand. "You're kidding." I laugh in disbelief. The worn fabric droops down with the weight of the quarters inside. I can see it now. Walking down the streets of Boston when the bag suddenly breaks and quarters spill everywhere on the concrete.

"I've had this bag since before you were born."

I lift my eyebrows, amused. "Clearly."

Riley ignores me. "It used to hold all the makeup I would use for my recitals. This bag hasn't let me down, and I'm sure it won't let you down, either. There should be just enough to get you the one wash and dry."

"Okay." I take the coin bag from her.

"I'm going to get this place cleaned up, then get ready for tonight." Riley grins.

"What's tonight?"

"Your celebration." She laughs. "You didn't think you'd get accepted back into Boston College without us having a little bit of a celebration now, did you?"

"We don't have to go out." I shake my head, my smile fading.

"Of course, we don't *have* to. But we should. After all the shit that's happened this past year, you deserve it."

"I don't know." Though, I know I won't convince Riley to not celebrate my re-admission to Boston. That's a battle I've lost before it's even begun. It's the odd sensation growing in my chest at the thought of celebrating anything in my life. It's difficult to celebrate your achievements when all you've ever known is loss. Good things simply don't happen to me. One way or another they get lost or ruthlessly stolen from me.

Riley claps her hands in front of her, snapping me out of my thoughts. Her mouth is pulled to the widest grin I've ever seen. "We are going out, and there's nothing you can say to change my mind. Now, go. The sooner you get going, the sooner you'll get back for us to head out."

"Fine." I give her a small smile before heading through the front door.

The city air hits me the second my feet land on the sidewalk. The noise of the cars and the hushed chatter from those passing me on the street surround me. Moving from Austin to Boston hasn't been a difficult transition. Both are major cities but in their own way. Although they have completely different vibes, stepping back into the heart of Boston has felt like home, as if for the past several years, I've lived in some alternate universe. It's strange how a city can bring you comfort when it still holds so much pain.

But is it truly a fresh start when you've returned to the place you escaped from in the first place?

By the time I make it to the laundromat, sweat beads down the back of my neck. My right leg throbs when I swing open the door and drop the bag on the counter with a huff.

I rest my elbows on the hard surface and hang my head, catching my breath long enough to allow the pain to subside. Lugging this bag down here makes me realize I should have just taken it in my car.

"Fuck," I whisper.

I rest the heels of my hands on my forehead and breathe out. Pushing my hair back, I thread my fingers through the long, brown strands and look up. Thankfully, the laundromat is empty. I'm the only one here.

I slide the bag across the bright orange counter to the edge, stopping in front of the first washer I come to. A dozen of them are set in the middle of the room surrounded by two walls of dryers. Thankfully, there are chairs scattered throughout. The pain in my leg has faded enough for me to start this load before sitting down in one of the seats.

I lift the large metal lid to the washer and drop all of Riley's towels and clothes inside. Unzipping the pocket on the side of the laundry bag, I find a detergent pod and drop that in before closing the lid.

"Okay." I huff, eyeing the machine for the coin dispenser. After finding it, I dig through Riley's obnoxious coin bag and fish out eight quarters.

I drop a quarter into each of the four slots and slide the

mechanism forward. The first four quarters slide in effortlessly. I load the second set and shove the metal slide forward again. But this time, my hand abruptly stops.

"What?" I frown, staring down at the machine. I try again. It's jammed. The four quarters are stuck halfway in. "You've got to be kidding me." I groan.

Resting my hands on top of the washer, I tilt my head back and sigh. I consider what to do. I could move the clothes and try washing them in the machine next to the one I'm in, but when I look inside Riley's coin bag, I only have four quarters left—not enough to start a new wash.

I spend the next five minutes desperately trying to pull the quarters out. I try to push on the metal slide again to no avail. I pinch each quarter, somehow hoping they will pop right out. They don't.

My fingers are red and sore by the time I give up. Frustrated and feeling only slightly bitter for having two dollars worth of quarters stolen, I slap my hand against the machine and lift the lid. I'll just have to wash Riley's clothes another time.

"Stupid fucking machine," I grumble. I bend to grab the clothes out from the drum, but then I stop when someone sidles up beside me.

"Beating up and cussing at the machine isn't going to make the quarters magically pop out."

My hammering heart comes to a screeching halt. The familiar voice floats through the empty laundromat. I'm suddenly wishing there were some other noise to filter over it. Anything to drown it out. Or maybe not. My mind and thoughts are immediately scrambled. I haven't heard his voice since that night in the hospital.

I don't move. I stay facing the machine, gripping the edge to keep myself steady. Two hands reach forward and push against the metal slide beside me. Large, sun-kissed hands covered in black smudges and speckled with dirt.

They're all I'm able to see from the corner of my eye, but I don't need to see the person's face to know who they belong to. It's almost impossible to forget the same set of hands that have touched you and made you feel more alive than ever before.

"You have to put a little more pressure here." He grunts, pressing the heel of his hand to the metal slide. "Then pull back quickly to snap it back."

The mechanism pops back, clicking loudly in the otherwise empty laundromat. All four of my quarters are still sitting in the slot.

I mentally count the same rhythm as if I were preparing to perform a dance routine and finally bring myself to look at the man beside me. I know exactly which pair of eyes I will find.

"Um, well..." I swallow the heat in my throat. Yep. Familiar, cobalt-blue eyes set under dark, firm eyebrows stare back at me. Long strands of chocolate hair rest on his too perfect forehead. Then there's the same chiseled jaw, as if it were carved perfectly out of stone, and lips that used to hover above my skin, whispering broken promises and convincing lies. Every angle and line of his face tells you he's trouble but in the most subtle of ways. He's capable of deceiving you into believing he won't crush your heart to dust.

Jude may not have intended to break me four years ago, but he did.

Just when I think the sight of his face has stolen my breath, I'm proven wrong when the two large, maroon-colored words printed across the chest of his shirt catch my eye.

Boston College.

Heavy, smoldering heat simmers under my muscle and bone. It splinters, reminding me of the fear I'd considered back in Riley's studio when I'd received my acceptance email. It seems the past has caught up to me sooner than expected.

Did he finish school as planned? Did he graduate with honors? Does his fancy business degree hang on the wall of his lavish, sky-rise office of Harding Holdings?

My mind automatically votes in favor of all questions becoming a reality.

He most likely graduated on time. With honors. The Jude I knew was incredibly smart. If it wasn't for his family name or the money fueling its power, there isn't a doubt he would have made it through college on academics and merit alone. But his family most likely had a play in it. It would be nearly impossible for them not to. Their hands were dipped into every inch of this city. They probably still are.

His eyes lower, following mine, falling to the logo of his shirt. We both stare at it in silence before he lifts his gaze.

He doesn't speak a word. Neither do I.

It's been years since I've seen Jude. Years since I've stood close enough to touch him. Every bit of him is familiar, but at the same time, I feel as if I'm looking at a stranger. A man who said all the right words but never kept the promises he'd speak. Empty words. A skill Jude Harding had perfected.

I may have known him in a past life, but in the present, he's simply a man standing in front of me at a laundromat.

Wait.

My mind takes a few seconds to catch up with the fact that Jude is here in a laundromat. I thought I was alone when I walked into the space. It's as if he appeared out of thin air like some sort of magic act. Either that or my eyes are playing tricks on me. Maybe he was already here when I walked in.

"Well, what?" he asks, teetering on the edge of impatience. He reaches out and rests the heel of his hand on the edge of the washing machine, staring at me with an expectant expression.

I stare back at him in disbelief, holding back the urge to make some snide comment about how a member of the coveted Harding dynasty dare to step foot in a common place such as a laundromat, let alone this side of the city.

I decide to go for the more civilized approach instead.

"Um, thanks, I guess." My jaw clamps shut, the words edging between my gritted teeth as if I were chewing on glass.

Jude's family comes from a long legacy of money and power in Boston. His father owns and runs the largest law firm in the city. The line went as far back as Jude's great-great-great-great-great-grandfather, or something like that. Either way, the Hardings were the elite firm, working for every mayor, senator, or representative the state has had for the past century and a half. Sure, my family came from money, too. Sort of. At least not in the traditional sense. My family was considered *new* money. My stepfather played the stock market like a slot machine. He gambled, landing on his wealth with luck.

Hardings are considered inherently and disgustingly wealthy.

Even though, at one point, I knew Jude to be different than the rest of his family—or at least I used to think he was—but it's still an odd sight to see him standing in a laundromat.

Jude crosses his arms beneath his chest. His hardened muscles twitch, and his eyes narrow. I expect him to say something. Anything resembling a simple polite exchange of appreciation in return. But our history hits hard in the ten seconds we stare at one another.

I can see it in the way his eyes cloud over and his shoulders lift with tension.

"Thanks, you guess?" Jude quirks an eyebrow. It disappears under the length of hair resting above it. He unravels his arms and shoves it off his forehead with a smirk. The same fucking smirk that used to make my teenage knees go weak.

My heart races at an impossible speed. I swallow the heat in my throat threatening to devour me. It ignites like a match to kerosene.

A conversation. I guess we're doing this.

"It's been four years, Jude. Are you expecting more than just a thank you?" I ask him, zeroing in on him with narrowed eyes. The pain of our history rolls over me like a cloud of fog.

His cocky eyebrow falls. His mouth pops open, thanks to my question and jab at stating how long it's been since we've spoken to one another, let alone seen each other.

A bell chimes behind me before I'm able to get a response from him. I glance over my shoulder when Jude's eyes snap over mine, following the sound.

An elderly woman with snow white hair steps through the door, pulling a laundry cart behind her. She notices she isn't alone and gives us a small, kind smile.

I return her gesture when she lifts her finger, pointing to the machine I'm using.

"You'll want to be careful with that machine, dear. It'll eat your quarters if you don't put them in correctly."

A light chuckle passes my lips. I can't help it. "I appreciate it."

She nods, staring down at her feet as she shuffles across the room to the other row of washers. The wheels of her cart squeal, piercing the silence between Jude and me.

"Here," Jude says, pulling my attention away from the woman. He gestures to my hand, urging me to hold it open for him before he drops four quarters into my palm. "If you've already put the first four quarters in, you might as well cut your losses now. Move to a different one."

His velvety voice is laced with anger and disdain for me, shooting straight for my heart. Years ago, I thought Jude had crushed it to dust, but facing him now makes me realize it wasn't. It was simply put into a coma only to be woken up just now.

Jude raps his fingers on the washer and inhales a deep breath, unable to meet my eyes. I open my mouth again, hoping to come back with a snide comment in return, but I'm at a loss for words. I don't get the chance to respond before he moves past me. I spin on my heels, watching his back as he pushes through the front door of the laundromat, then turns and heads down the sidewalk, disappearing into the now-dark night.

"He seemed like a kind young man," the elderly woman says as she's closing the lid to her machine.

"Um." I swallow. "I guess so."

"Oh," she answers. "You don't know him?"

I look back at the front of the store, staring at the spot I'd last seen Jude before he disappeared. "Not anymore, I don't."

"I apologize, dear. It looked like you did."

The woman's words shoot straight to my newly awoken heart.

My anger and hatred toward Jude may still be alive and thriving but one truth is staring me directly in the face.

Regardless of Greg's affair with Amy, marrying him would have been a mistake, because despite the anger and hatred I have for Jude, I know at one point in my life I loved him just as fiercely. And that sort of love is incredibly hard to match.

CHAPTER TWO

Jude

It's not often I wish I had a drink sitting in front of me. The tight ball twisting in my chest is aching for the relief a glass of whiskey is sure to promise.

I flex my fingers back and forth, pushing through the double glass doors with more force than intended. It's been years since I've had a drink. The desire to have one still swells in my chest. Air fills my lungs, seeping into every corner. My lungs burn until I blow out a heavy, forced breath, shoving the sensation away. My power to be sober will always win out. Eventually.

That still doesn't stop the pull I have inside me telling me to leave this godforsaken office building and walk into one of the pubs lining the streets of downtown Boston.

"Are you ready to go?" I ask my brother Lennon the second I spot him at the end of the hallway. I storm past the firm's assistant, Jillian, bypassing all our usual pleasantries.

My brother is standing at the end of the hallway, flirting with a woman I've seen grace his office more times than I can count. I don't know her name, just her face. I don't even think she works on this floor. It's hard to keep up with the women Lennon spends his time with.

"Dude, you were supposed to change and be here thirty minutes ago." He quirks an eyebrow as he surveys me from head to toe. "You look like shit."

"I offered to help a friend who owns the laundromat a few blocks over." I hitch my thumb over my shoulder.

I swallow my rushed breaths. I doubt Lennon or the woman he's with notice. I'm hoping I'm hiding my shock well.

Victoria Monroe.

The woman I thought I'd lost years ago. The woman I thought I would never see again after our lives were brutally crushed.

I may have been nineteen and completely naïve, but I was also hopelessly and maddeningly in love with her.

For years, I was angry with the way she left. I thought after all this time that the anger disappeared. But the moment my eyes rested on her deep, chestnut brown hair and her hypnotic green eyes, every memory of how it felt when she left came rushing back.

The anger isn't as fierce as it was back then. It's a dull ache. A smoldering fire still simmering under my skin. I can still feel the sizzling of the ashes when I reach my brother and the woman he's with.

"Well," Lennon scoffs. "Dad's going to be pissed if you show up to dinner looking like you just crawled out from the sewer."

"Come on." I grin. "I'm not that bad."

"Yeah," Lennon's date chimes in. "I kind of like the rustic look he's going for." The woman reaches out and drags her long fingernail down the length of my arm.

"Hey, Madison," Lennon warns. "I wouldn't fuck with my brother."

Oh, right. Madison. I think I have heard him mention her once or twice before.

"I wasn't fucking with him." Madison giggles. "I was merely

making an observation." She leans back against the wall, humor laced in her expression. She knows exactly what she's doing, aware her attention on me is annoying my older brother. Her short, sparkling, silver cocktail dress hugs her body, the hem riding up her thigh as she drags the toe of her stiletto across the floor. She clearly isn't dressed in office attire. She's too flashy, even for corporate standards.

When Lennon doesn't respond, she swings her eyes back to me, narrowing them with curiosity. "Why should I stay away from the infamous Jude Harding?"

I don't answer Madison. My mind is still reeling from running into Victoria earlier. My body is humming and flooding with questions.

When did she get back?

What made her want to come back?

Did she wonder if I were still here in Boston?

"Because if you're planning on getting in with the Harding family and their money," Lennon answers Madison, anyway. "My little brother is the last person you should set your sights on. As far as our baby brother Micah goes, then you might have a shot. But not Jude."

"Why do you say that?" she asks.

"Oh." Lennon nods, removing his hand from the wall and pulling himself to a stand. His eyebrows arch across his forehead, and he inhales a deep, sharp breath. "You'll see why at dinner."

He tucks his long, dark hair behind his ear, then slides his hand into the pocket of his suit with a smug grin. Lennon is considered the face of the business, the next generation to continue expanding the Harding dynasty. Only not in the typical sense, one would think of when they say the word dynasty of family generations living on past my two brothers and me.

Fuck if I know if my father expects any grandchildren from Lennon, but there's one guarantee my father does gain from Lennon: security in the business.

As for the youngest Harding boy, Micah, he's already vowed to dedicate his life to the Harding way, starting with expanding the company's relations abroad. Last I heard, he was in talks with Spain to establish an office out there. Ambitious for someone who's only nineteen, and that's the privilege of having money. It allows you to grow up and do things you wouldn't normally be able to do otherwise.

Then there's me. I'm a gamble. An uncertainty. Attributes and circumstances my father despises more than anything.

"Madison's joining us?" I ask Lennon, Madison's name rolling off my tongue as if I've talked about her dozens of times. "Does Dad know you're bringing a date?"

"Does it matter?" Lennon shrugs. "If anything, the asshole will be pleased when he sees Madison walking in beside me."

"My father is the attorney general." Madison grins and raises her chin as if I'm supposed to be impressed with her family's social and political standing in this state.

I'm not.

"That's nice." It's all I can manage to say in response. I'd like to believe it's impossible to impress James Harding, but if there's anything I've learned over the past twenty-three years with my father, it's not impossible. For anyone other than me.

"Don't be a dick." Lennon shoves my shoulder with his fist, rocking me back. "Just get dressed."

The toe of my black boot drudges across the marble floor as I stumble back. I correct my footing and cross my arms beneath my chest. The last place I want to be is sitting across from my father's glare in a restaurant where one meal costs more than others earn in a month.

"By the time I head back to my place and change, I'll have missed nearly half of dinner," I say, taking a step back.

"Nope." Lennon shakes his head. "I keep a spare suit in my office. You can wear that."

I open my mouth to argue but quickly shut it. My brother and I are the same size, even though there are five years between us.

"Madison and I will wait for you downstairs." Lennon quickly wraps his arm around Madison and ushers her down the hallway.

I stand alone, watching them until they disappear behind the closing elevator doors. With a heavy sigh, I run my fingers through the length of my hair and stare at the floor. My reflection in the marble tile is a blurry mess, but it doesn't need to be clear for me to know what I must look like in this moment.

I reluctantly spin on my heels and head toward Lennon's office, bypassing mine.

I haven't stepped in my office in months. The inevitability of meeting my father for dinner has only reaffirmed my decision to keep away from Harding headquarters. It's been a temporary solution until I find a permanent one.

Once I find Lennon's spare suit in his office, I quickly change into it. I adjust the cuffs and slide on the jacket as I push through the door.

The receptionist, Jillian, is gone, leaving the entire floor empty. I'm the last one here. I stride past my office but abruptly stop. I inhale a sharp breath and push open the large glass door.

Seeing Victoria triggered me. She had her long, dark hair weaved into a braid and effortlessly pulled to the side, draping over her shoulder. The loose wisps and strands danced across her smooth skin. The color of her eyes intensified with every second she glared in my direction—a clear indication that the pain of our past is as permanent as her scars.

There's hurt and loss swelling inside me, bringing on a constant flood of memories I've wanted to forget. I've pushed them to the deepest recesses of my brain, telling myself they belonged to someone else. They belonged to a different Jude Harding.

But some memories are impossible to erase. Even I'm not a fool in believing it can simply evaporate. Love and loss are too grand for such an inconspicuous departure.

With the weight of unexpectedly seeing Victoria bearing down on me, I step inside my office. Not a single item on my desk has been touched since the last time I was here. It's apparent the janitors haven't bothered to come in here to clean, either.

I slide open the bottom drawer and immediately find the item I'm looking for. I grab the worn, leather-bound book, cracking it open just enough to make sure the lilac ribbon is still slipped inside it. Satisfied to see it there, I tuck the book into the small pocket on the inside of Lennon's suit.

My phone dings in my pocket the second I press the call button to go on the elevator.

> Lennon: You've been wearing suits since the day you were born. Taking a month off to play this charade of yours shouldn't have made you forget how to put one on. Get down here, fucker. Madison is starving, and Dad will be pissed if we're any later than we are.

I roll my eyes and groan.

For years, I secretly confided in my brother Lennon. With our five-year age gap, it made it easy for him to slip into becoming a pseudo father figure any time our father couldn't keep an eye on us for longer than thirty minutes, which was the standard time limit he could tolerate to parent his three boys. Despite the endless number of nannies he had on rotation.

Long time resentment allows me to not care about my response to Lennon. I'm twenty-three years old. He doesn't need to parent me now.

> Me: You say that like it matters what I do anymore when it comes to Dad. Tell Madison her free dinner won't be much longer.

When I slide my phone into my back pocket, something tells me my text won't go over well with Lennon.

Somehow, the idea of hurting my family seems trivial. Especially if I think about the pain and destruction they've caused me.

CHAPTER THREE

Jude

Lennon remains silent throughout the entire ride over to the restaurant. With himself wedged between Madison and me, I lean farther into the car door to keep some semblance of distance. I knew my text would piss him off, but I don't care. I adjust the jacket of the suit I'm borrowing from him, fighting the strong desire in me to rip it off and toss it out the window. Despite my frustration with Lennon and his constant pressure to bring me back into this world I no longer want to be a part of, he's still my brother and best friend. He's one of the only people I have on my side. Him and my best friend Cain.

I smooth the deep, dark red tie I'm wearing, and sigh as I stare at my lap. The book inside my jacket might as well be burning a hole in Lennon's suit. I haven't read the words written inside for years, but I can remember every single one. Every written loop and crossed line. Every ounce of ink bled into the beige paper.

The car quickly pulls to a stop in front of the restaurant, tearing me out of my thoughts. Mac, our family's driver, steps out and stands in front of the door, waiting for the usual signal that we're ready to get out.

"All I'm asking for is an hour," Lennon begs. He shifts in his seat, turning his back toward Madison to face me. "Please, just give us one hour of peace."

I knit my eyebrows together. Anger simmers under my skin. I wish I had time to get high before walking into this fucking snake pit. "You're telling me as if I'm going to be the reason this dinner ends up being a dumpster fire."

"I'm just saying... You don't exactly help matters." He reaches over Madison and knocks on the window three times. Mac opens the door, and Madison immediately steps out.

Madison bends at her waist, eyeing Lennon. I follow him as he steps out of the car to join her. She links her arm around his, and they both make their way into the restaurant. I follow behind, wishing I hadn't agreed to take one of the company cars. I should have taken my own car instead of leaving it parked back at the office.

This is the last place I want to be. Not only because I spent the entire day working hard manual labor at the laundromat, but also because my mind is still grappling with the fact I saw Victoria.

What the fuck is wrong with me? She's invading my thoughts when I saw her for a total of less than five minutes.

If I'm going to survive this dinner with my family, I need to get her out of my head.

"I'm starving," Madison says, glancing back at me. "I've heard this place has the best steak and frites."

I groan, rubbing my fingers across my chin. Lennon snaps his head back and shoots a quick glare my way—a warning to keep my mouth shut and let Madison's comment slide off my back.

The Harding family has been coming to the Eclipse since the day it opened. I think. It's hard to put a number on the years considering there's never been a time I can think of where our family didn't come here at least three times a week, at a minimum.

I keep my mouth shut, letting Madison have her moment. I've had the steak a million times.

The attendant standing at the front holds the door open for us the second he sees us. He greets us by name, bowing his head as we pass as if we're fucking royalty.

Boston royalty if we're going to get technical.

All Hardings are.

Even disappointments such as me.

No one knows the secrets and lies our family holds. Those are kept buried in our money-lined pockets. They run as deep as our family's relationship to the Eclipse.

Hush money followed by more hush money. My father and his father before him ensured a legacy of using lies and money to get anything and everything our family could ever want.

The main section of the restaurant is wide open and brightly lit. White lights and chandeliers hang from the tall, vaulted glass ceiling. Tables from the front to the far back are filled with people. They all stare as the three of us walk by. The presence of any Harding always catches the attention of every guest at Eclipse.

I give the staff a few close-mouth smiles as we weave our way to the back of the open dining area. Each server we pass nods in return, but the thoughts in their expressions are easy to read. They hate our family and the pressure it's put on the restaurant. More than likely, they hate serving our family. The owner bows at my father's feet, and the staff hide their discontent behind their fake niceties.

I ignore everyone the best I can. Once my hands are hidden inside my pockets, I curl my fingers into a tight fist. It's been over a week since I've seen my father. The last time we spoke, I was standing inside his office, refusing to meet with one of the state representatives our family has worked with for the past fifteen years. Feeling his longtime client slipping through his fingers, he attempted to persuade me to act on his behalf. When I refused, he responded in his usual pattern of silence before offering an extension of amends through dinner at the Eclipse.

By the time the three of us are halfway through the restaurant, we find my father sitting in his usual spot at the only table in the restaurant reserved for the Harding family. No other guests ever use this table. Ever.

My father is leaning against the dark red, leather booth, tapping his finger on the table. He doesn't need to speak for me to know he's irritated, impatient, and infuriated beyond measure already. His dark eyebrows are slanted in anger above his dark brown eyes. They're narrowed in a tight glare, zeroing in on me the second I move out from behind the cover of Lennon and Madison.

It isn't until I'm within ten feet of the table that I realize he's brought someone with him. And not just anyone. A woman. A woman far younger than him. She has smooth, tan skin, and bright blonde hair, as well as the same hopeful expression Madison was wearing back at the office.

She straightens her back the second she sees us. My father doesn't move.

He twists his mouth, hissing between his teeth. "You're late." It's a statement with the intention of fishing for a reaction. I know James Harding all too well.

Lennon answers first, taking his bait. "Got held up at the office finishing up some last-minute emails."

My brother's lie falls effortlessly from his mouth without a second of hesitation. He's fine tuned the art of covering for me.

I fight the urge to elbow Lennon in his side. I don't need him to lie to our father for me. I'm perfectly comfortable telling him the truth. It's a trait I've been working hard on picking up.

"Good for you, Len." My father nods in satisfaction before quickly shifting his attention to me. His bright blue eyes narrow in an icy glare. "I assumed Jude had a hand in it."

"Of course, you did." I sigh. "Wouldn't expect anything less," I mutter, matching his intensity.

I don't care if there are two other guests with us tonight. It won't take them long to learn who the real James Harding is.

My father smirks, the corner of his mouth curling. "Have a seat. I've already done the courtesy of ordering everyone drinks."

Lennon holds his arm out, allowing Madison to slide into the booth first, then he slides in after her.

"I apologize," my father adds. "I didn't realize us Harding men were going to be graced with the presence of two beauties tonight or else I would have ordered you a drink as well."

"No need to apologize," Madison is quick to reassure. "It's me who is intruding."

"Think nothing of it." He grins. "I'll have the waiter bring us whatever you'd like." He lifts his arm into the air and snaps his fingers, signaling one of the servers waiting in the corner of the room.

It isn't until I've made myself comfortable in the booth that I notice the full drinks set on the table. My father has already ordered for me, too.

Placed directly in front of me is a short rocks glass, filled halfway with ice and whiskey. Anger flares in my chest. I curl my hands into fists under the table until my nails cut into my skin.

Arrogant, fucking asshole.

Lennon elbows me, clearly catching onto my shift in mood.

I lean forward, rest my elbow on the table, and scratch at my chin. My father's eyes follow the untouched glass when I push it away from me.

"I'm sorry," Lennon interrupts the silence. "I don't believe we've had the privilege of meeting yet."

Fuck. I hate the persona Lennon puts on any time he's around our father. It's as if he's putting on a costume, hoping he'll manage to pick up more brownie points.

The woman sitting beside my father grins, a small giggle erupting from her throat. "We haven't. My name is Laurel. I'm one of the new attorneys at Branford and Branford."

Branford and Branford is the law office located in the same building three floors below our family firm.

"Wow." Lennon chuckles. "You look rather young to be an attorney."

"Well..." Laurel cringes in embarrassment. "Actually, I'm still in law school, but my uncle is Frederick Branford. He's allowing me to shadow him and take on a few cases."

"Oh," Madison chimes in. "Like Elle Woods in *Legally Blonde*."

Laurel giggles. "Exactly."

"Huh," Lennon says, bringing his glass to his mouth. He takes a sip, grinning against the rim.

"Aren't you going to say anything?" My father's eyebrows lift in anticipation. He and everyone else seated at the table are staring at me.

"What would you like me to say?" I lean back, dragging my finger across the bleach white tablecloth. Dirt and grease line my fingernails. I flick my gaze to Laurel. "Congratulations."

My father narrows his eyes to two tight slits. He examines my hands resting on the table before bringing his gaze back to my face. "Couldn't be bothered to wash up before slapping on that designer suit?"

"I did," I snap back. "I was helping a friend with his business."

"Right." He nods, shifting in his seat. "*Business*."

"It is a business." I deadpan. Dinner is already starting to fall apart. There's a heavy, weighted shift in the air.

Lennon's entire body tenses beside me. He feels it coming on. Madison and Laurel are clueless, waiting with bated breath for the show to unfold.

"A laundromat is not a legitimate business, Jude. Hardings are too important and distinguished in this city to be seen in places such as those."

"Fuck, Dad." I scoff, slapping my hand on the table. I can't hold the anger in any longer. "Just because the job doesn't require a million-dollar trust fund or a dozen investors doesn't make it any less of a business."

Snarling, he lifts his glass to his mouth and downs the rest of the amber liquid. He reaches out and grabs mine, making a show to drink it quickly. Slamming that glass down, he snaps his fingers for another.

"I'm not here to argue," he mutters.

Bullshit. That's exactly why he's here.

I bite the inside of my cheek and force myself to remain calm as he removes a small metal flask the width of a pencil from the inside of his sleeve. With the flick of his other wrist, he pops open the small top and brings his wrist to his nose. He inhales a quick, sharp breath in his right nostril, pretending as if no one knows what he's doing. But even if the entire restaurant staff and guests know he's just snorted about two hundred dollars-worth of cocaine in the middle of the fucking dining room, no one would question him. No one ever questions James Harding. The tiny vial disappears back under his sleeve, and he runs his finger under his nose and quickly rubs it along the top of his gum. When he's finished, he inhales a deep breath and pins me with daggers.

"Contrary to what you might believe, son, I truly am here to talk a bit of business. I have a client who is looking to build his portfolio."

I try looking at Lennon, but it's clear he isn't the target of this shift in topic. I am.

"And?" I ask, shoving my annoyance further down my stomach.

"I told him you would meet him tomorrow for lunch to discuss his options."

My anger flares again. "I can't."

"What do you mean, you *can't*?" he grits between his tense jaw. His cheeks flush red.

"It means I can't." I shake my head and sigh. "I promised Cain I'd help him on this new project."

My father taps his finger on the table. "By project, you mean construction."

"He didn't explain." I shake my head again, avoiding his glare.

"Of course not."

"I'm sure Lennon can do it, or you can find someone else." I immediately reel myself in. I hate throwing Lennon under the bus. I don't want him to always clean up the mess I know I make when it comes to our father. It isn't his responsibility.

"When will you stop playing around and show you are committed to this family? To this enterprise?"

Family.

I stare at my father, thinking of the meaning of the word family. He throws the word around as if he understands it.

Silence surrounds the five of us. The subtle clinking of silverware and hushed conversations fills the void... until my father decides to break it. He knows I've decided to take his questions as rhetorical.

"I invited Laurel here to dinner for a reason." He taps his

finger gingerly on the table. His shift in conversation and tone gives me whiplash. One minute he's getting on to me for not playing my part in the business, the next he's talking about the strange woman he's brought to dinner.

"I'm sure you did," I mutter. My tongue pulls from the roof of my dry mouth. I really wish there was liquid other than fucking alcohol at this table. My throat burns, begging for the relief of a drink that I won't give it.

My father runs his fingers through his hair and rests his arm on the back of the booth behind Laurel. He zeroes in on me. "Considering Laurel comes from a distinguished family such as ours, and her father is a loyal and dedicated friend, I thought you two could get to know one another."

"Get to know?" I ask.

"Yes." He nods, gesturing in front of him. "Get to know. Take her on a date. Show her what it means to be with a Harding."

What the fuck?

I swallow my shock, navigating my best response. It's been years since my father has bothered to involve himself in my love life. Most likely the distance between us has caused him to be less involved in my life in general. Not that there was much involvement to begin with.

James Harding set the bar quite low.

"No." My answer is clear and direct. To the point.

My father clears his throat and purses his lips. He shoots piercing daggers in my direction. "I apologize for my son, Laurel. He isn't himself today."

I trade glances between my father and Laurel. He has his arm draped behind her back as if he's the one who brought her on a date. He's acting as if he isn't pawning her off on me in the hopes I bring some bullshit dignity back to our family.

In reality, he's the embarrassment.

I open my mouth to snap back at him. I'm reaching inside for a comeback—one that will deliver a blow deep enough to cut my father, but not enough to ruin dinner for the other three at our table.

I shift my attention to Laurel, offering her a look of sympathy, but it's only brief. I know exactly what kind of woman Laurel is. I can't fault her for her naivety. She's a victim to this lifestyle just as much as Lennon and I are. At least, I assume she is.

"What did my father offer you in exchange for coming here?" It's a simple question, but it catches her off guard.

"Um." She tucks her red bottom lip beneath her teeth.

"Money?" I ask. "A good fuck?"

She snaps her head to her right as if she's expecting my father to give her approval on whether she should answer my question.

Lennon tenses beside me.

"I'll tell you what I think," I say, leaning over the table. I shove the glass of watered-down whiskey farther across the surface, clinking it against my father's empty one. The sound causes the table to fall silent. My father's anger-fueled eyes shoot straight for the glass before lifting back to me. "My father invited you here with the promise of introducing you to his two very rich, eligible sons. And you wouldn't pass this up because why would you? You get a free meal, a few cocktails, and shit, you might end up with the chance of fucking me or my brother here by the end of the night." I hitch my thumb to the side, pointing to Lennon. "But half the equation was shot to hell the second you saw Lennon walking in with Madison on his arm. So, that leaves me as your only option." I pause, but not long enough for Laurel or my father to cut in. "The thing is, eating here is a family ritual of ours. My father drags us out to this restaurant weekly to put on a show for the city and families like yours to give you the impression that we care. Now, we might. In truth, Lennon does have a heart behind that five thousand dollar-suit he's wearing. As for me, though, I sincerely hope I'm wrong about this whole situation. You seem like a kind woman caught in the tangled web my father has expertly weaved. Maybe you came here strictly for business, and that I can respect. But if you're looking for a good fuck with a Harding, that's the one you should be looking at." I point to my father. "You wouldn't be the first, and you certainly won't be the last."

I slide out of the booth, ready to leave. My heart is racing, and my mouth is still as dry as the fucking desert.

I eye everyone at the table. The four of them stare up at me, all with different expressions. Lennon is gulping the rest of his drink as fast as he can. Madison's jaw has dropped, her mouth forming a perfect 'O' shape. Surprisingly, a hint of a smile plays on Laurel's lips. And my father's flaming red face and cocaine fueled gaze is staring up at me.

His anger and frustration don't faze me.

Seeing Victoria standing in that laundromat earlier, slapping and cussing at the machine, made me remember how I used to walk on eggshells around my father. At one point in time, I would have done anything to please him. But that all went to shit four years ago.

Unfortunately, despite my outburst tonight, I know he won't give up. He won't write me off, but not because he doesn't want to ruin our relationship. He won't give up because it simply isn't in his blood. Giving up on me would be admitting he's a failure.

I rap my knuckles on the table. "Looking forward to our next dinner, Dad."

I inhale a deep breath through my nose and back away from

the table, knowing I need to leave. I need to get out of here before I allow the guilt to settle in my bones, convincing me to stay.

"Save yourself the trouble," I say to Madison before walking away. "The steak and frites are shit."

September 8th

Dear J,

They were the shade of midnight blue.

I didn't intend on meeting you tonight. Kate dragged me to the party after our dance practice. My feet were sore and aching from the endless hours in the studio. My toes were still bleeding from my shoes, with varying shades of purple dotting the skin on all sides of my feet. The last place I wanted to be was in that building, in that room.

Stuffy. High class. Hundreds of rich college frat guys shoved into a few hundred square feet. Kate insisted it was the place to be. Especially when you're new to Boston College.

Apparently, attending Kappa Sigma parties is an essential rite of passage for the freshman dancers. Some bullshit about an unwritten tradition.

The second we walked into the party, Kate dragged me inside before heading off on her own. I lost her in the crowd. I didn't bother calling or texting her. I knew how important this was to her. As for me, I grabbed a shot, downed it, and snatched up another before heading down the hall. Parties weren't for me, no matter what advantages it might have handed me as far as joining the social circles were concerned. I swiped a drink from the kitchen and slinked my way through the party, searching every corner until the comfort of solitude radiated over me. Thankfully, the farther back I went, the quieter it became, until I found a small, random staircase leading up onto the roof.

I pushed through the old wooden door and allowed it to close behind me. There was immediate solace and quiet. The busy streets of Boston were far down below, yet I still felt calm. I reached inside my bag and pulled out the book I'd been trying to read for the past three days. Between dance and class, it doesn't leave much time for my favorite pastime. I found carrying my book for occasions such as this one made a perfect escape. At least until Kate came and found me, dragging me back to the party.

But the safety of my quiet was stolen when I heard the squeal of that wooden door opening behind me. I shoved the book back into my bag with a groan.

You stumbled through the door, tripping on the gravel. Your shiny black dress shoes slid across the tiny rocks. You eventually caught yourself and paused long enough to rest your hands on your hips.

You didn't see me at first. All I could think was how gorgeous and unreal you looked. You didn't belong there. At least, I didn't think you did. It was as if you'd stepped out from one of the magazines my mother poured over when she found out how much money my father had earned on his investments. Lifestyles of the obnoxiously rich and privileged.

You stood in the middle of that roof in silence. I held my breath.

You stared up at the blanketed sky, and when you finally looked back down, you saw me.

They were the shade of midnight blue. Your eyes caught the golden, sparkling lights strung around the perimeter of the roof. You stole my breath.

Literally.

I coughed a few times, and your alcohol-soaked eyes softened. You asked me if I was okay.

I nodded once.

You asked me again.

I choked out a yes.

You rubbed your too perfect fingers on your clean-shaven jaw, seeming satisfied.

It was all it took for you to move on.

You stumbled across the gravel in your half-buttoned collared shirt. Your gold watch clicked every time you swung your arm, the flawless metal glinting in the city lights.

You leaned on the three-foot cement wall with

your large hands before turning around. You rested your back against it and eyed me from across the roof.

"I've never seen you here before," you said.

"I've never been here before."

"I would have noticed you if you had." Your words rolled off your tipsy tongue without hesitation.

My heart fluttered. "No one notices me."

"Somehow, I don't think that's true," you answered back.

"You look like the kind of person everyone notices," I said honestly. Maybe too honestly. I threw your words back at you.

"I might be." You slid your hand effortlessly into the front pocket of your black pants.

I dragged the toe of my worn sandal across the gravel, wondering why in the hell I'd decided to wear them. The evidence of my dedication to dance was on full display for you to see.

My entire body ignited into flames knowing you were staring at me. I knew you were drunk and clearly out of my league. A man doesn't wear a shirt like yours unless his pockets are full of money and secrets.

"You're a dancer," you said, matter of fact.

I curled my lip in a smile. The one drink I'd had downstairs was firing on all cylinders. I never drank, so the alcohol was loosening me up before I even realized it. "That obvious, huh?"

You nodded toward my feet. I immediately felt self-conscious.

"The bruises and cuts don't lie," you said.

I smiled brighter for the first time in what felt like forever. The stress of starting my dream school with a full ride on dance scholarships had had me stressed. But I wasn't stressed with you.

"They don't," I agreed. "Are you one of them?" I asked, stepping closer to you. You didn't look like one of them. Sure, you reeked of your family's wealth, but you weren't obvious about showing it off in the traditional sense. At least, I hoped you weren't. My judgment might have been impaired considering the drink I'd had on an empty stomach.

I found myself hoping you weren't one of them.

You were still several feet away, but your scent was all around me. Beer and pine.

"One of who?" you asked with a laugh.

"Kappa whatever…" I waved my hand. I couldn't remember the name of the fraternity throwing the fucking party.

You grinned, and your midnight eyes sparked with amusement. "Not yet. But I'm working on it."

"Hmm." I won't deny the subtle sinking

disappointment like a weight in my alcohol-laden stomach. I didn't want you to be one of them. My mind immediately started coming up with the person you were. Self-absorbed. Cocky. Endless money. Privileged.

"What's your name?" you asked to my surprise.

"Victoria," I answered. "You?"

"Jude."

You smiled and quickly closed the gap between us. I held my breath this time, forcing myself not to choke on it again.

I opened my mouth to tell you your name was unexpected. It's not that your name didn't suit you, but it was one of those moments where I didn't realize how much it did suit you until it spilled from your mouth.

"My mother was a huge Beatles fan," you explained, as if I'd asked the reasoning behind your name.

The corner of my mouth lifted again, and I giggled. Maybe you weren't as much of a lost cause as I thought you were.

You towered over me in the Boston moonlight. I held my hands at my sides, clenching my fingers. I didn't know what you were going to do. There we were. Two drunk college students standing on a rooftop alone.

"Have you ever met someone and just known?"

you asked me.

This time I think I did lose my breath. My heart beat impossibly faster. "Known what?"

"Known you would rather be close to them than the hundreds of people downstairs. That you wanted nothing more than to taste them and feel them because you've never felt more alive than in that moment," you clarified.

"You're drunk," I answered, finding humor in your deep, philosophical question.

"I am," you said.

You were polished and clean, but the way your eyes twisted in thought made me think there was more to you than the shiny image you effortlessly portrayed. There was a reason you wandered and escaped up to the rooftop.

I found myself staring at you, wondering what your story was. Every few seconds, your mouth bent to the ghost of a frown, breaking whatever barrier the alcohol had built.

You raised your hand beside my head. You fingered the purple ribbon I'd forgotten to remove after dance practice. Fuck, I felt lame.

Blood drained from my face. My heart sank into my stomach.

You were proudly spouting off the same words you had spouted to hundreds of girls before me.

I knew nothing about you other than your name

and that you were hoping to get into the fraternity throwing the shitty party booming beneath us, which meant you must at least have gone to Boston College as well. But how long and what major was a complete mystery to me.

"I asked if you ever just knew." You watched your own fingers slide down the length of my ribbon. It unraveled under your touch, the strip relaxing in between each of your fingers. "Do you know what I mean?"

It was crazy, but I did.

I knew exactly what you meant.

I stared up at you. Your eyes swirled with alcohol and torment.

"You shouldn't get mixed up with someone like me," you added, your voice cracking.

"Why?" I gathered up the courage to ask.

"Because where I come from, we thrive off the innocent."

"Do I look innocent to you?" I asked. A fire sparked in my belly.

You nodded. "Yes, and that's what worries me."

"I'm not as innocent as I look." I didn't know if it were true. I just knew in that moment that I wanted you to stay. I didn't want to give you a reason to head back downstairs and join the mass of party goers.

Because in those few seconds you were standing

in front of me, all I wanted was for you to touch me. I wanted you to push me against the cement wall and grind your hips into mine. I wanted you to make me forget the pulsating pain in my bruised feet. I wanted you to press your hands into my flesh just to feel how strong they were. I wanted you to unapologetically slam your mouth to mine. I wanted you to bury yourself in me before Kate or one of the other guys from Kappa Sig-whatever came searching for us.

And that's exactly what you did.

You and your midnight blues consumed me without regret.

CHAPTER FOUR

VICTORIA

My stomach is begging for food, but my brain stubbornly refuses to allow me to eat. Or it could be the restless humming sensation pumping through my veins as my nerves remain at an all-time high, prickling across my skin.

I'm sitting in a small booth at a small bar. Riley's sitting across from me, waving her hands dramatically in the air, immersed in the same story she's been raving about for the past ten minutes.

I watch her, though I have no idea what or who she is talking about. Every few seconds she utters the words *leap* and *yoga*.

How can she sit here and make small talk?

Does she not know who I ran into back at the laundromat?

No. She doesn't.

I didn't tell her.

After seeing Jude at the laundromat, I quickly moved all of Riley's towels to the next washer, shoved the quarters in, and sat in one of the chairs lining the wall, facing the sidewalk outside.

Unable to move, I sat with my hands laced in my lap until I heard the buzzing of the machine that would tell me my load was finished. My body was made of stone, refusing to move from the only piece of reality keeping me tethered to it. I zoned out, reluctantly replaying every moment of my interaction with Jude. The buzzing of the machine suddenly yanked me out of a daydream.

Before I knew it, the old woman who walked in on Jude and me was gone. Riley's towels were tumbling in the dryer, and I returned to the slippery mustard chair.

I sat quietly until the dryer was finished, then I started back to Riley's dance studio.

Now, I swallow the thick, dry sensation in my throat, and pinch the tip of my straw. I take a long sip of my cocktail—an incredibly sweet drink Riley insisted on buying me to celebrate my recent acceptance.

"You've barely touched your food." She points to my plate of shrimp. "If you don't eat, that drink will hit you a lot faster and a lot harder."

"Let it," I grumble, eyeing her across the table.

"What is with you?" she asks, her eyebrows pulling together.

"Nothing." I sigh and straighten my back against the worn, wooden booth. I try to give her a reassuring smile. Either she buys it, or she doesn't believe me, allowing my lie to pass.

"Are your nerves getting the better of you again?" She scrunches her nose.

I think it's sweet that she suspects my anxiety is caused by something as trivial as returning to Boston College after losing my full scholarship, then running off to Texas without realizing how terrible of an idea it turned out to be.

"You could say that." I nervously laugh.

I hate that my small interaction with Jude has caused my stomach to flip completely upside down. I haven't been able to sit here and enjoy my celebratory dinner without thinking about him and his stupid, gorgeous face.

It's been four years. Four years since he ruined everything. Four years since I lost everything that ever mattered.

This isn't how my return to Boston is supposed to go. Running into Jude isn't supposed to be how I start my life over, once again.

Leave it to him to still somehow slip his way into my life and hijack anything good that comes out of it.

"No." Riley shakes her head. "Something isn't right with you."

"Stop." I laugh her concern away. "I told you it's nothing."

"Sure." She blinks. "Then, why haven't you answered my question?"

"What question?" I stab a shrimp with my fork.

"The one where I asked you what your plans were."

Huh. I must have missed that when I was caught up thinking about Jude again.

"Oh." I shove the shrimp in my mouth and force myself to chew it. It's delicious, but my appetite has disappeared. "You have to be a little more specific."

"I was." She turns her head to the side and eyes me with suspicion. "I asked what you planned on doing about your living situation now that you're back in school."

"Right." I nod. I'm thankful Riley is allowing me to stay in the small loft above her studio, but I know it isn't a permanent solution.

"Now..." Riley wipes her mouth with a napkin and weaves her arms, resting them on the edge of the table. "I know you don't mind living with me above the dance studio. The space is just big enough for the both of us, and it serves its purpose. But my studio is also a good distance from the college."

"That's okay." I shrug. "I can grab an uber or ride the T. I'll figure it out."

"You can, but why would you when you could live only a few blocks away?"

"What do you mean?" I drop my fork, clearly confused where she's going with this.

She digs inside her purse beside her on the booth. Keys dangle from her fingertips before she drops them on the table.

I pick them up. "What are these?"

"Keys to a building I own three blocks from campus."

"Um..." My jaw drops. "I didn't know you owned another building."

"I bought it years ago with the intention of turning it into another dance studio, but I never got around to it. Honestly, I think I'm content right where I am. Taking on another studio would be too much for me to handle."

"Okay." I drop the keys back onto the table, confused, then I stab another shrimp.

"The place is yours," she blurts out. "If you want it, of course."

"What?" I drop my fork again; the shrimp still freshly speared. "What do you mean it's mine?" My heart falls into my stomach.

"It's yours." She pushes the keys toward me with the tips of her fingers. "It was meant to be a studio, but it doesn't have to be. You can turn it into whatever you want it to be. Want a bookstore? Make it one."

"No." I shake my head. "I can't take this, Riley."

"Yes." She hardens her stare. "You can."

Emotion fills my body, threatening to drown me. "I don't know."

Liquid pools along my eyelashes. Returning to Boston and

running into Jude unexpectedly seems to have made the emotions in me swell by one thousand percent.

"You can, and you will." She nods, then sighs, taking my silence as some form of acceptance for her incredibly generous offer. "There's an apartment on the second floor for you. It isn't much. Basically, the same as the apartment I have now. But it's something you can finally call your own."

I open my mouth to speak, but Riley continues.

"I also hired a renovation team to come out and fix up the place."

"Well, shit." My back hits the hard wood of the booth. I stare at Riley, stunned.

"I know." Riley holds her hands up. "They'll mostly be coming over tomorrow to clean up the place and then I figured you could go from there. They're starting with the floors and walls, anyway. Plenty of time for you to come up with whatever you want to make of it and then you work with them."

"Riley." I hold up the keys and close my fingers around them. "I don't know what to say."

"Look," she starts, her eyes lining with tears like mine. "I'm sure you have enough on your plate, especially now with getting accepted back into Boston College. Honestly, I had planned to gift you this place before I knew you had reapplied. If it's too much on your plate, I understand. It will be waiting for you when you're ready, though." She shrugs. "It's yours whatever you decide."

I quickly wipe a tear from my cheek and step out of the booth. I slide in beside Riley and wrap my arms tightly around her, resting my chin on her shoulder, and squeezing my eyes shut. "Thank you," I mumble, forcing myself to stay calm.

I have no idea what this place looks like or the condition it's in. Living in a construction zone for months on end while trying to finish my degree at a school I practically begged to take me back sounds daunting, to say the least. But, considering I left Texas with no plan in sight, I can't pass this opportunity up.

Riley's basically given me a fresh start. A blank canvas to paint.

When I pull away from Riley and sit back on my side of the booth, reality starts to hit me in waves.

Moving to another new place sounds overwhelming. Deciding what to do with it is a whole other ball game in itself.

But it's a challenge I'm willing to accept, no matter how hard it might be.

"I still don't know what to say." I laugh.

Riley laughs with me. She takes a long sip of her drink and slams it back down on the table. "Now you know why I was insistent on celebrating tonight."

"I do."

There's something to be said about a fresh start. At one point in time, I thought moving to Texas was the perfect example. But is it truly fresh if you're still carrying a broken heart?

When I left Boston the first time four years ago, I was crushed. Then when I left Texas, I almost lost faith. But the fresh start Riley is giving me is different than either of those situations.

This time I'm not running from something. I'm running to it.

CHAPTER FIVE

VICTORIA

I decided what I wanted to do with the space Riley gave me before we finished dinner last night.

A bookstore.

It's hard for me to imagine that there was a time in my life when I thought of nothing but dance. it used to come as easily to me as breathing. But after the accident, my body simply didn't move the same. My toes couldn't hold my weight. My legs couldn't keep up with the pace of routines I'd done a thousand times. It's amazing how your mind and body can erase what you've known for almost your entire life in a matter of minutes.

After the accident, I attempted to dance again. In my mind, it was as if I was re-learning how to walk. Every doctor insisted it would take time and patience. More time than I was willing to give. Patience I didn't have. I knew it was practically impossible for me to get to the level I was by the time I needed to be.

Not only did dance come with time and patience, but it also brought pain, and not just the physical kind.

Dancing reminded me of Jude and what I'd lost.

It's challenging to dance when pieces of you are broken, inside and out. For months, I'd hoped to find the glue that could put me back together, but there was no amount of glue that could fix me.

Instead, I leaned into my writing. I leaned into reading. I buried myself in worlds that weren't mine.

That's where I found my love of books.

Dance brought pain. Books brought healing.

This is my true fresh start. A place I can call my own. A place where I have one hundred percent control over every decision made. I might be crazy for thinking I can pull this off all while going back to school, but I convince myself I can do it. Aside from it only being the one class, my love and passion for this new adventure drives me to want to pull it off.

I stand in my new apartment and drop the box of books I carried with me from Riley's apartment. The books inside bounce when the cardboard hits the wooden floor, echoing in the small space.

Riley wasn't joking when she said it isn't much different than her place. If I stand in the middle of the room, I can see every wall. I peek into the bathroom, checking to see what needs to be done.

Four folded purple towels have been neatly stacked onto the shelves above the toilet. A square bath mat sits in front of the shower.

I step back into my living room, slash bedroom and stare down from one of the two windows facing the street.

The streets are lined with old brick, and the trees running along the sidewalks sway in the breeze. I'm imagining all the ways I will make this new apartment mine, and how I can turn downstairs into a bookstore, when a large, blue van pulls up along the sidewalk in front of my building.

Printed along the entire side are large white letters that read:

CAIN'S RESTORATION AND REMODEL

This must be the contractors Riley hired to work downstairs.

I check the time on my phone. Fuck. My class begins in one hour. If I don't want to be late on my first day, I'll need to start heading that way soon. My nerves have been a disheveled mess all morning. The last thing I need is to show up late to my one and only class, blowing it before I've even had a chance to begin.

I quickly scoop up my bag, shoving my laptop and notebook inside. I lock the door to my apartment and bound down the stairs, hoping to catch the contractor before he knocks, and I make it just as he's standing on the other side of the glass.

My eyebrows arch, surprised to see how young he appears. He must be around my age, at least. His kind face brightens when he sees me on the opposite side of the glass, and he waves, grinning wide.

I return his gesture and drop my bag on the table set along the wall.

"Hi." I hold the door open for him. "Come on in."

"Thanks." He steps inside. "I hope I'm not too late. I got held up on another job site."

"That's okay." I wave him off. "Unfortunately, I have a class to get to in a bit, so I won't be able to stay long. As much as I would like to."

"Understandable." He holds his hand out. "I'm Cain. You're Riley, right?"

"Nice to meet you." I return his gesture. "Riley is my aunt. I'm Victoria."

Cain's brown eyes twitch, narrowing the slightest bit. It's a subtle movement, not entirely obvious. If I'd blinked, I might have missed it. He scratches at the stubble along his chiseled jaw and clears his throat. "I'm sorry. I only spoke to Riley on the phone. I assumed she was going to be here. This is the correct place, right?"

His eyes move away from me, and he plants his hands on his hips with a resolving sigh.

"It is. Riley decided to gift this place to me last minute. She didn't even tell me about it until last night."

"Wow." The corner of his mouth curls into a small smile. "You aren't kidding when you say last minute."

"I'm not." I follow him deeper into the open space. "I hope that's okay."

"Absolutely," he utters over his shoulder.

The once white paint on the wall has shifted into a pale shade of beige. The hardwood floors are covered in dirt and dust. A rusted metal, winding staircase is set back, leading up to a small loft lined with broken bookshelves.

When I first walked in here this morning, I didn't dare go up the steps in fear of what I might find, not even sure if the frail metal might be able to support me.

"Today is basically a consultation and routine clean up," Cain explains. "We'll assess the walls and floor damage as well. Then we'll clean the dirt and debris."

"We?" I ask.

"The rest of my team." He hitches his thumb over his shoulder. "I'm usually the first one to the site. They'll show up here in a bit."

"Oh." I nod and check the time on my phone again to see it's almost eight.

A knot twists in my stomach. I spent years wondering if I would ever make it back to Boston College after my unexpected drop out my second semester. Once I stepped into this space last night, I immediately began imagining the endless possibilities for this place. The idea of stamping my mark on a place filled a void in my soul that's remained vacant for years.

I frown, surveying the empty space. "I don't know if this will throw off your schedule, but do you think we could discuss the plans when I get back from class?" I ask Cain, wincing. "I should be back in less than two hours."

"Oh," he says, rubbing his hand across the back of his neck before he shrugs one shoulder. "It shouldn't be a problem." He waves his hand. "There is plenty to do here, and by the time you come back, we'll have a cleaner palette to create the space you want."

"Thank you." I grin, relief settling over me. I snag my bag from the table and hitch it over my shoulder. If I don't leave now, I truly will be late on my first day. "I haven't had a chance to explore the whole place yet, but Riley left some drinks and snacks in the small fridge in the back. There's also a bathroom." I point toward the back of the building, but Cain doesn't turn around. He simply stands, finding humor in my sudden and dramatic exit.

I'm already breathing heavily when I push through the weighty glass door and leave him inside.

I walk as fast as I can. My hamstring tenses the farther down the street I get, forcing me to square my shoulders and shove the pain in my leg aside by gritting my teeth. The Boston sun pours over me, repeating a mantra, injecting me with confidence.

As I trek the three blocks to my first day of class, I know this is where I'm meant to be.

I CLUTCH the crumpled paper in my hand as I walk back to my apartment. Anticipation bubbles in my veins.

The drawing looks like shit, and I bite down on my lip, hoping Cain and his team will look past the quality. I never claimed to be an artist.

I scribbled out the plans I've had in my head for my bookstore and hold onto them now as tightly as I possibly can. You'd think I was afraid someone was going to pass me on the street and yank them out of my hand.

But listening to my new professor drone on about social media impacts on modern texts only drove my desire to get this ball rolling even faster. I took pen to paper, drawing endless rows of bookshelves, a small coffee bar, and my favorite feature thus far: a section of blind-wrapped books.

I want this so fucking badly, my ears are practically ringing from the jolt of energy.

My leg twitches. I adjust the strap of my bag over my shoulder, briskly finishing the last block to my apartment. Cain's van is still out front, and parked parallel to it on the other side of the street is a utility truck I'm assuming belongs to one of the members of Cain's crew. A large metal ladder is strapped to the top, along with some other construction supplies tall enough to peek out of the bed.

I yank the door open, and the smell of dust and dirt greets me when I step inside.

A handful of contractors line the far wall, scooping mounds of debris into large barrel trash cans. When one is full, one of the men grabs the edge of the can and pulls it toward the front of the store. Filled to the brim with sheets of paper, dirt, and other items of trash I couldn't possibly identify, he drags the can past me. With a smile, he pushes the door open with his back, disappearing to the back of another truck parked farther down from Cain's.

"Oh, good." Cain's voice pulls my attention. "You're back."

"I am." I snap my head to the direction of Cain's voice.

"I can't believe it's been two hours already." He slides his phone from his front pocket, checks the time, then slips it back in, and he crosses the room to meet me.

"My professor didn't keep me as long as I thought he would." I grin. "How is it going here?"

"Great." He surveys the room. "We're just about finished with the initial cleaning up process. Just need to get the vacuum in here to pick up the layer of dirt and dust."

"It's looking better already." I giggle, still giddy on the inside. Riley picked a great remodeling crew. They're clearly fast and efficient. Maybe this won't take as long as I imagined it would. I hope not, considering I only have so many months' worth of savings left in my bank account, and there's no possible chance in hell I'm taking any more money from Riley, or asking my parents. I've never asked my parents for a dime. Not even when I went to Boston College the first time.

"Thanks." Cain puffs his chest out with pride, then plants his hands on his hips and twists back in my direction. "Did you get a chance to figure out what you want to do with this place?"

"I did. I drew a blueprint—" I stop speaking, immediately losing my train of thought, my fingers still crimped around the edges of my amateur drawings.

I open my mouth to speak again, struggling to remember what I was saying to Cain, but the words evaporate the second I catch another man walking through the back door.

Sweat-covered skin and muscle emerge from the hallway. Heavy, tattered leather boots beat across the floor, carrying him toward Cain and me.

"Hey, man." He sighs, his thick, gravelly voice growing closer. "There's a whole stack of wood piled against the back of the building. Do you know what you want to do with it?"

I wouldn't have guessed it were him until his midnight blue eyes... and that voice of his. A clear giveaway. My stomach somersaults, and emotion swells in my throat.

Will I ever be able to look at Jude without remembering every detail of everything I lost?

As if he just now realizes Cain isn't standing by himself, Jude looks at me.

I press my lips in a hard line.

"Victoria?" Jude clears his throat. "What are you doing here?"

"You know Victoria?" Cain asks, his voice raising an octave.

"Yeah." Jude blinks, unwilling to take his eyes off me.

Asshole.

"We knew each other back in college," he adds.

I grip the paper impossibly tighter. My nails slice through it to my palm. I add pressure to my already pressed lips, holding the anger in. Or vomit. Both options aren't out of the scope of possibilities.

He told Cain we merely knew each other, as if we were simply acquaintances. Two people meeting in passing. Two people who didn't have an entire fucking relationship. Like we weren't hopelessly and madly in love.

Knew each other.

Liar.

"Wow." Cain nods, mulling over this coincidence. "Well, Victoria was just about to tell me the plans for this place. Right?"

He reaches out, grabbing onto the paper still held hostage in my death grip. Heat and anger simmer to the surface. It's been years since Jude mercilessly broke my heart, but with the way my body immediately reacts to him, I wouldn't have known any better.

The pain of catching Greg and Amy in their affair doesn't hold a candle to every moment I've ever had with Jude. This one being a prime example.

Over the years, I must have become numb, and Jude must be the antidote. I hate how he manages to elicit this response out of me.

"Is this it?" Cain asks, tugging on the paper in my grip.

My eyes fall to our hands. I blink. "Oh, yeah, it's just a rough sketch." Heat creeps along my cheeks.

"This is Victoria's place, if you didn't already know." Cain nudges Jude with his elbow, straightening out my sketch. He glances up long enough to look at me, nodding his head toward the man beside him. "Jude is my right-hand man. I may be the project manager, but he's the guy you'll be working with."

"What?" both Jude and I ask in unison.

Cain pauses, trading glances between the two of us. "I have a few other projects I'm supervising, so I won't be able to be here all the time."

The ticking. The muscles in Jude's jaw tick endlessly in anger. It's apparent in every tense muscle and angled brow. He's just as unhappy as I am with this arrangement.

I swallow the emotion and replace it with my determination to not let this predicament ruin the high I was riding only seconds ago.

But it's difficult when Jude is around.

It always has been.

Jude

"WHY ARE YOU HERE?"

I close my eyes and count to five before picking up another slab of wood. I carry it inside and lay it beside Victoria's feet, unable to look at her. The reality of our situation isn't lost on me. I'm still trying to fucking process it.

Ignoring her question, I step back outside, deciding which piece to pick up next. Some are broken, some are intact. After Cain made sense of what Victoria called her blueprints for her new place and suggested we could repurpose the wood to build wall-to-wall bookshelves, I escaped to the back as fast as my feet could carry me.

Apparently, not fast enough.

Victoria followed me, determined to find out why James Harding's prodigal son is now working for her.

She hasn't moved from her spot in the back room, refusing to let me work in peace.

I guess parts of Victoria haven't changed. She's always driven me fucking mad.

"Seriously," she continues. "I don't get it."

I chance a look in her direction over my shoulder, and she

dramatically lifts her arms in the air, allowing them to fall back down by her sides. She's exasperating herself trying to make sense of this. Shocking, considering she couldn't muster the effort to speak to me at the laundromat. Maybe the initial shock of seeing me for the first time was enough to silence her. The second time has done the complete opposite.

I don't feed into her prodding statement. I pick up another slab of wood and hitch it over my shoulder. Victoria's eyes follow me the entire way back inside. I set the wood down on the stack I've been building.

"Is this how it's going to be?" she asks, her perfectly arched brows pulling together, and frustration turning her cheeks crimson red. "You work for me, but you get to ignore me?"

"I'm just trying to do my job." I shrug my shoulder and shake my head.

"Right." She crosses her arms beneath her chest. "You, Jude Harding, working construction. Do you not see why I might be shocked? None of this is making any sense. You live in penthouses and trade rich people's money, not—"

"Stop," I cut her off. "In case you've forgotten, it's been four years since you last spoke to me. You don't know anything," I sneer, pinning her with daggers. "Besides, between the way you left and the years of silence since, I don't think you get the benefit of my answers, much less the privilege of asking questions. I'm here for a job. To build you a bookstore. Plain and simple."

She slowly unravels her arms, allowing them to gently fall by her sides again. Her green eyes have widened, now softening. They remind me of the night we met. I was out of my mind drunk, but even when the world was hazy, she remained crystal clear. The image of her staring up at me that night has lived rent free in my head ever since. Even if our relationship has dissolved into nothing but a mere memory, they're clear as fucking day.

I ignore the knot twisting in my chest and continue working, leaving Victoria inside. I won't lie. It's difficult not to take in every inch of her and not think about the times we had together. The first time we kissed on the rooftop of that frat party. The way I pushed her back against the cement wall and fucked her among the city lights of Boston. How I touched her every day for a year after.

It's hard to watch her now, knowing how her pink lips taste and how the curve of her full hip fit easily into the palm of my hand. It's hard not to think of what we lost.

I wipe away the sweat lining my brow with the back of my hand. The sun bears down on me, but I welcome the heat it brings. It's a balm to the thoughts brewing in my head.

How am I supposed to spend the next couple months working for Victoria, renovating this place? How did this even become her place? Why is she back? Why now?

These are all the same questions I was asking myself after running into her at the laundromat.

I can't help it. Seeing Victoria standing in front of me, demanding answers she doesn't deserve, pricks at my chest. How can she demand to know why I'm here when she left the way she did?

I carry another board over to my stack inside. I expect Victoria to still be standing in the same spot, but instead I'm met with Cain.

He's squatting beside the pile of boards, inspecting the ones set on top. He picks one up and looks underneath it before dropping it, then pulls himself to a stand.

I drop the board on top of the one he just looked at. "You could have told me before I came over here," I mutter.

"Told you what?" Cain asks. His voice carries the same edge as Victoria's did.

"Told me that Victoria hired you."

I met Cain the year after I lost Victoria and everything that ever mattered to me. He never knew her, but apparently I mentioned her a few times in my sleep when we were roommates back at Kappa Sigma.

"You're kidding, right?" he asks, his eyebrows raised.

"No," I breathe out. "I'm not."

Cain rolls his eyes. "She didn't hire me. Her aunt did."

"Riley?" I ask.

"Yeah." He nods. "You never told me much about Victoria, so how was I supposed to know who either of them were?"

"I guess you weren't." I scratch the stubble lining my chin. I need to get a fucking grip.

"Asshole." His mouth lifts into a smile.

I give him one in return. "I deserve that one."

"Listen..." He leans against the wall, crossing his arms over his chest. "I didn't know this was Victoria's place. She told me this morning that her aunt gifted it to her last night at the last minute. I think she's just as shocked to see you as you are her."

"Huh." I plant my hands on my hips, mulling over what to do. My mind starts to wander from how the next few months will go to why Riley gave her this shop.

"Now that we know the situation, I need to ask you something," Cain says, pushing off the wall. He narrows the space between us, shoving his hands into his dirt and dust covered pockets. "I need to know if you still want to work this job. I already feel guilty, since you won't let me pay you the full amount you deserve for working for me."

"I don't want your money. I don't do this for the pay."

"I know." He nods. "I only pay you the minimum required

so my company doesn't get in trouble, or I won't be held liable if something happens to you on the job."

He's right. A fact I learned from the family business. A fact I told him.

When I first mentioned to Cain that I wanted to work for him back in college, he was shocked that I told him I wanted him to pay me half of what he pays his usual crew members. But I wasn't in this for the monetary gain. That isn't what I needed.

I wanted to get as far away from my father as possible.

I do this because, unlike my father, I need a constant reminder that there is more to life outside the Harding business.

"I would understand if you can't," Cain adds.

Fuck, I hate the expression on his face. It reminds me of the expressions plastered on every single doctor in the emergency room the night before Victoria left. Sympathy. Pity. Condolences.

I loathe it.

"I can do it." The words fall from my mouth before my mind catches up.

"Are you sure?" he asks, unconvinced. "I won't be able to fill in for you or show up every day, since I have those other projects going on. I know I made you supervisor for this one, but if you want me to appoint one of the other guys, I can." He points down the hall where the rest of the crew is still working to clean the area.

I turn back to Cain, straightening my back. "No, I'll stay."

There's no shot in hell I'm quitting. Not when I know my father is sitting up in his office, waiting for me to show back up and work with Laurel. I think that was her name. It's hard to keep up with the endless number of women my father tries to pawn on me or Lennon when he's deemed them unfit for himself.

I haven't spoken to him since the other night. This routine

of ours has become reliably predictable. To a degree, he's certain I'll return. Show my face to the public. Make a spectacle to drum up more talk and gossip. It's all in the Harding handbook.

My desire to stay away from the office outweighs my desire to stay on this job Cain has tasked me with. It doesn't matter if I'm working for Victoria. I'll figure out how to work around her without thinking of how it felt to be buried inside her, or the memory of how, at one point in my life, her and one other person were the only things that ever mattered to me.

It's just a shame I didn't realize it until it was too late.

"Okay." Cain nods, inhaling a deep breath. "Then, you should probably meet up with her before you leave today to go over what you're going to be doing." He slaps a wrinkled piece of paper covered in black ink against my chest. "Time to build a bookstore."

October 26th

Dear J,

You've been unexpected from the start. Unpredictable. Exhilarating. Addictive.

Is it too soon for me to feel this way? Probably.

I shouldn't be with you. I wasn't looking for you in the first place. I guess that age old saying stands. You always find the one when you least expect it. And fuck, you weren't expected.

I need to stay focused. I need to remember why and how I was able to go to Boston College in the first place. I can't forget my dream and my purpose.

But I can't help it. After meeting you on the rooftop that night, I never expected to see you again. Until I saw you waiting for me outside my yoga class the next day. You claimed you saw me through the window when you walked by. I didn't believe you. I'm still not completely convinced. I mean, how is it possible to run into the same person coincidentally within the same week? Especially on a campus as large as Boston. The odds certainly weren't in our favor for that likelihood. But something about your need to find me turned my insides to molten mush.

We might have been drunk that night, but I remembered everything about the night we met. Every touch. The feeling of your cock sliding into me. The rustic, faded red brick grating against my back with every thrust. The chills that hummed through me as you dragged your mouth across the curve of my exposed neck. I even remembered the reverberating sound your voice made against my body as you spilled inside me.

I remember it all.

You weren't my first, and you weren't my second, or even third. But you were certainly more than everyone I've ever been with combined.

I never knew my body and my heart could respond to someone the way it does to you.

It's ridiculous because I know we don't belong. We are two people from two entirely different worlds.

You took me for a ride in your car that day after yoga. I'd never seen a car like yours before. All black leather. Sleek. Small. Entirely too perfect to be anything I or my family could ever afford.

You drove me to the harbor. We stood on the edge of the pier, staring out at the water, and we talked for hours. I told you how my dream was to graduate with a dance degree, then move to Paris. It was cliché, but it was my dream. You never made me feel ashamed. Instead, you grinned, reassuring me that you knew I'd make it there, even though you'd never seen me perform even one dance move. You told me about your family's reputation in this city, and all the pieces suddenly clicked into place. Your family saw more money in a year than the average person sees in a lifetime. Me being the average person who just scrounged up change from the bottom of my gym bag to grab a cup of coffee before class that morning.

I thought we would never work. I didn't need the distraction. But then you showed up to my dorm room the following day carrying a fucking box of donuts, and the swoon worthiest mouth I'd ever seen. Thankfully, Kate was at her morning class, and we had the room to ourselves. I'm sure others in the building could have heard our ragged breathing through the walls, but I didn't give a shit. At that moment, I knew it didn't matter.

It's been one month since then, and I can't get enough of you.

As I write this, I've just gotten back to my room from spending the day in yours. I didn't want to leave. I was comfortable, tangled up in your sheets with my skin pressed to yours. I understood when you told me that you had to meet your father for your weekly meetings. I haven't met him yet, but I won't lie when I say I'm nervous for when I do. If I do.

If there's one thing I've learned about you, J, it's that you will do anything to make your father proud. Or maybe it's your family.

Either way, I see how dedicated you are to them.

I understand that sort of passion, but I can't help wondering how long we'll last in this surreal bubble of bliss we've created, and since I've come back to my room after leaving you, I can't help replaying the last conversation in my head.

"My father was a Kappa Sigma," you confessed, drawing imaginary circles around the swell and curves of my breasts.

"So?" I shivered, swallowing a breath as you dragged your finger down to my hip, pulling me into your side. "You want to follow in his foot-steps? Be a Kappa Sigma, too?"

"Yes," you quickly answered.

I smiled, resting my chin on your chest. "Sounds like you have your mind made up, then."

"Oh..." You laughed. "My life has been planned out for me from the moment I was born."

"Is it what you want?" I asked. "Is your father's plan yours, too?"

You didn't hesitate with your answer, but your eyes flashed with a momentary second of thought. "It didn't used to be."

"And now it is?" I lifted my hand and

brushed the hair away from your midnight blue eyes.

You swallowed. This time you hesitated before answering. "It is." You cleared your throat as I dragged my hand down the side of your neck to your chest, then farther down. "It's all I've ever wanted."

I didn't say anything after that. You hooked your fingers under my chin and pressed your mouth to mine like you knew I already belonged to you. And the thing is, I did. I've belonged to you since you stumbled through the rooftop door.

But I can't help the worry that's burrowed in my brain since I left you an hour ago. Maybe it's too soon in our relationship to worry. Maybe I'm overthinking it. But damn, J, it's hard not to, knowing it's only been a month and I've already fallen for you a million times over.

CHAPTER SEVEN

VICTORIA

I WAKE UP TO A SHRILL PIERCING SOUND COMING FROM downstairs. With a loud groan, I roll over and crack one eye open wide enough to read the time on my phone. It's five in the morning. Five. In the morning.

"What the fuck?" I grumble to absolutely no one, rolling back over to my original sleeping position. I gather the blankets and wrap my body around them, draping one leg over the bundle. I fist the fabric and hold it to my stomach. The piercing sound stops long enough for me to focus on my breathing. Maybe I dreamed the sound. Maybe I imagined it and I'm not fully awake. I count to ten and think about the day ahead.

I haven't seen Jude since yesterday.

Not because I can't stand to see his face. The man was cursed with obnoxiously good looks. It's part of the spell he's had on me from day one. I'm dreading seeing him for the simple fact of all the memories he brings out of me when I do.

Images and reels play in my mind like a silent movie, repeating endlessly. My body tenses, the muscles in my legs and arms growing in pressure. I squeeze my eyes shut, forcing myself to forget the memories long enough to allow me another hour of sleep. I need sleep if I'm going to be able to focus on class *and* working with Jude today. I don't know what to expect, but if it's going to be anything like it was yesterday, I'm going to need all the energy I can muster.

A heavy weight washes over my body, and I'm nearly asleep when the shrill sound goes off again.

This time both my eyes snap open. The barely-there morning sun peeks through my worn plastic blinds. It takes a few seconds for my eyes to adjust, but it doesn't matter. Before I know it, my feet are swinging out of bed and taking me out of my apartment.

"What is wrong with you?" I yell, slamming the door shut behind me. Whoever is working downstairs probably can't hear me with whatever tool it is they're using.

I stomp down the stairs, curling my hands into fists at my sides. As soon as I reach the landing, I swing the door open.

Jude is on the other side of the room. He hasn't noticed me, his focus on the work in front of him. There's a long piece of wood under a large, circular blade. His hand steadies the board as he lowers it. Sawdust flies into the air around him, floating like a cloud of powder. Tiny flecks land on his faded black T-shirt and dot his damp skin. Quickly, the sound of the saw meeting wood hits my ears again. Only this time, the ear-splitting sound is much closer and much louder.

"What are you doing?" I yell, stomping my way across the room.

The saw immediately stops as Jude lifts the handle. He slides the board out and snaps his head in my direction.

"What the fuck, V?"

Heat slams into my chest. I haven't heard him call me by my nickname in years. Was it reactionary? Was it instinct?

"You can't just come down here and yell at someone when

they're working with a saw," he bites back. "I could have cut myself."

"It's five in the morning, Jude," I seethe, anger still hot in my voice. "How did you even get in here? I made sure the door was locked before I went to bed."

"You gave Cain a key."

He's right. I did.

"Well, I didn't give it to him with the intention of you coming here before the sun has fully come out yet."

"I have a job to do, Victoria."

So, that didn't last long. His use of my nickname was reactionary.

I bite the tip of my tongue. It's driving me crazy that Jude hasn't told me why he's working for me. All the man was designed and destined to do was work for the Harding firm. I still haven't been able to make out why he's here of all places.

"You're right. You do." I cross my arms beneath my chest. When I do, Jude's eyes follow my motion, causing me to look down as well.

Dammit.

I rushed down here so quickly to scold Jude, I hadn't realized I'm still wearing the same clothes I went to bed in, which isn't much. Just a thin strapped tank top and my lace panties. I practically feel my nipples perk beneath the tight fabric.

"Fuck," I mumble, trying and failing to cover myself up. Too angry to worry about it much, I keep my arms crossed. Realizing I'm standing in view of one of the windows, I instinctively take a step back, tucking myself behind a broken, freestanding bookshelf.

Jude's perfect mouth curls into a devious smirk.

I lift my eyes and stare at him, deadpanned. "I couldn't get the air conditioner to work last night. It was hot."

His eyes roam over my body once more before he looks back

to the board he was cutting. "Nothing I haven't seen before." His smirk fades with his comment.

My expression and shoulders drop. I'm still frustrated for his unwanted and unwarranted wake up call.

"I get you have a job to do," I point out. "But you don't have to be here this early. In fact, I don't want you here right now. I have a class in three hours, and I've barely gotten any sleep. Especially with you sawing with that thing." I gesture toward the saw he's using.

"A class?" he asks, unable to break his attention from his work. Only his profile is visible from where I'm standing, but I can see the blank expression on his face. He's focused on his task, uninterested in me. He might as well be a stranger asking how I take my coffee.

"Tell me why you're working here instead of your firm, and I'll tell you what class I'm taking."

He considers me for a moment, absently dropping the board to the floor with the rest he's already cut at this ungodly hour.

He frowns and shakes his head. "No. Not worth it."

My arms are still crossed. I squeeze my hands hard enough for my nails to slice half-moon shapes into my palms. We might not be on civil terms, but Jude's jabs don't hurt any less. After all these years, his whispered promises are still stained on my skin in invisible ink. It's hard to reconcile how drastic our lives have changed in four years. How different we are with each other.

Not that I blame Jude for his anger with a dash of indifference. I left him and Boston behind without a single word. I didn't have it in me to face the truth. I was young and naïve. Heartbroken and shattered. Mind, body, and soul. All of it.

When the universe nearly breaks you for good, it's hard to face your reality. In my mind, I couldn't face Jude. Because facing him would have made our loss a thousand times greater.

I loosen my fingers, giving my palms a break from the sting of my nails and Jude's words.

"You don't have to be such a dick," I spit out. I have no reserve in me. The lack of sleep and stress of starting a new class while trying to renovate a bookstore has me sliding off the cliff at full speed. Jude's words simply gave me the last bit of energy I have left to come crashing down.

He pauses, hovering his pencil over the board he was working to mark. With one finger pinning a ruler to the edge of the wood, he releases a heavy sigh. His fingers slide down, gripping the edge of the board. The muscles on his back twitch and flex, pulsating as my words float between us.

"I'm not trying to be a dick," he forces out between clenched teeth, slowly turning his head. "I'm just trying to get these pieces cut, and that's difficult to do when you come barging down here with your nipples peaked and half your ass showing from that sad excuse for a thing you call underwear."

Heat blooms across every inch of my skin. I've forgotten Jude was famous for his smart mouth. At times, he'd make me go weak at the knees and wet in seconds from the words he'd say to me.

Standing in front of him now leaves me utterly confused on how I'm supposed to feel. I wish there were a handbook on the guide to grief and facing the one you loved who had a hand in causing it.

Because right now, I feel like a deer caught in the headlights.

"Fine," I say, tipping my chin up. I scramble to come up with boundaries. *Boundaries.* That's what we're going to need if we're to survive this co-worker situation we have going on. I move to step forward but stop myself, remembering the book-shelf currently being used as a shield from passersby. "We're going to need to lay a few boundaries, then, if you insist on staying on this project," I suggest.

"Boundaries?" Jude's eyebrows arch, disappearing under the hair that has fallen over his forehead.

"Yep. No work before six. I have one more class before I'm finally done with school. I won't give you the chance to screw it up for me."

I ignore the questioning expression transforming his face. He's surprised I haven't finished school yet. He doesn't know a single reason why or how, but I can tell my confession of still working on my degree doesn't slide off his back. This fact is difficult for him to ignore.

"If we're going to work together on this place, we can't let our history get in the way," I say.

The second I make this a point, the tone and energy in the room shifts. It's a hard pill to swallow, but the more I'm around Jude, the harder it is to pretend we don't have a sordid history. It would be difficult not to.

He drops his pencil. It bounces on the new piece of wood, rolling and falling to the floor. He leaves his workstation for the first time since I stormed down here. His work boots beat against the floor, matching the rhythm of the pounding in my chest. I hold my breath when he stops in front of me.

He's close. Incredibly close. I fight the urge to close my eyes just so I don't have to stare up into his piercing midnight blues. Jude tore my heart apart in more ways than one. He fed me false promises and lies until they broke us both.

Or maybe he wasn't broken. Maybe Jude's angry with me for the simple fact of family embarrassment. I, Victoria Monroe, have been a stain on the Harding family ever since I stepped foot into their lives. Maybe that's where his resentment toward me stems from. Maybe after I left, Jude had to deal with his family's response to the accident. Our loss. Everything. He's had to work overtime to correct the wrongs he made by choosing to be with me.

Sawdust and sweat hit my senses, surrounding me. My leg quivers, the dull ache pulsating all the way to my pounding heart.

His eyes roam over my face as if he's taking inventory of every detail that might have changed since the last time he stood this close to me. I inhale a breath and hold it, hoping it'll calm my nerves.

He tightens his glare and blows a hot breath through his nose. "Fine."

One word.

The only word he chooses to give me before he turns around and sulks his way back over to his workstation.

Satisfied with his agreement, I cross my arms over my chest. Jude was right. My peaked nipples press into my arms. My cheeks flush. My head pounds. The lack of sleep catches up with me. I move to spin on my heels, ready to head back up to the solace of my bedroom, but Jude stops me.

"Cain mentioned you and I setting up a time to go over your plans."

"He and I already talked about it," I say over my shoulder. "Maybe you should take it up with him."

The less interaction I have with Jude, the better.

"Cain isn't managing this project. He appointed me."

A knot squeezes my chest. "Okay." I chew on my bottom lip. "We can meet in the morning to talk. At six."

"Of course," Jude reluctantly agrees.

Satisfied again, I continue making my way back up to my room.

When my foot hits the first step, Jude adds, "Preferably with a little more clothing."

. . .

AN HOUR after my confrontation with Jude, I'm awake, dressed, and walking toward class. Riley met me halfway, insisting she wanted to catch up with me to discuss what I planned on doing with the place she gifted me. I took it as an opportunity to let her know the truth about the person she had hired to renovate my bookstore.

"Wait..." She blinks. "I hired who?"

"Jude," I repeat.

She comes to a stop, covering her mouth with her shaking hand. Her eyes immediately soften, and I grab her wrist, pulling her hand away to give it a gentle squeeze.

"I'm not mad at you," I reassure her, knowing her thoughts have already wandered there.

"I'm sorry." She gasps. "I swear I didn't know he worked for Cain, or else I wouldn't have hired him."

"Seriously, Riley. I figured you didn't know. Besides, I think Cain is more than just his boss." I gnaw on the inside of my cheek. The fact Jude is working for Cain is still eating away at me.

"Maybe. I can't believe Jude works in construction. Kind of strange, right?"

"Exactly." I press my mouth into a thin line.

I start back on our walk, with Riley following suit behind me. When she falls in line with me again, I bite into the strawberry frosted donut she handed me the moment we met on the corner of the street a block back.

We push our way through the thickening crowd as we grow closer to campus.

I'm chewing on my donut, surprised I have an appetite. Seeing Jude has brought a heavy weight bearing down on me. I feel hollow at the same time. There are a range of emotions consistently giving me whiplash.

"Are you going to be okay?" my aunt asks. "Working with him? I can always hire a different company if you'd like."

"No, no, no." I shake my head. "Don't do that. Cain doesn't deserve to be let go simply because Jude and I have history. Besides, he agreed to not let it affect his work when I saw him this morning."

"Okay," she agrees, clearly unconvinced. "But if it gets to be too much, let me know."

"I will." I nod and swipe my tongue across the corner of my mouth, licking up the sweet frosting gathered there.

From the corner of my eye, I watch Riley take a sip of her iced coffee. She grins with her mouth wrapped around the straw, closing her eyes briefly before opening them again. Her messy bun is piled high on top of her head, the few loose strands framing her face blowing in the breeze.

I love her, and I'm glad I have her to lean on. For mostly everything.

"I wanted to talk to you about paying you back for gifting me the apartment and bookstore," I suggest.

"Absolutely not." She immediately shuts the conversation down. We reach the first pillar signifying one of the entrances to campus, and we stop. Riley grabs my hand, squeezing it with the same amount of pressure I used on her only seconds ago.

"The apartment and store were a gift. You aren't meant to pay someone for a gift." Her mouth tilts into a smile. "Gifts immediately nullify any sort of payment."

Tears line my eyes. I don't deserve her or this fresh start. It doesn't matter how many times she says it, I'll never think I'm worthy enough. Not when my life has launched in an entirely new direction. Not when I know the man she hired to work for me is also the one who had a hand in forcing me to change my life into what it is now.

"I love you." I pull her into a hug, give her a tight squeeze, then pull back far enough to keep her at arm's length. "I'll figure out something, though."

"You can thank me by letting me be the first customer in your stunning bookstore."

I grin. "Deal."

After our agreement, we part ways. Riley heads back in the direction of her studio while I head to class. But as soon as I'm alone, Jude creeps back into my thoughts.

I was naïve to believe I couldn't face him after the accident, and for leaving Boston the way I did. But now, after agreeing to let him stay on as project manager for my bookstore, I feel like a bigger fool than ever.

CHAPTER EIGHT

Jude

Seeing Victoria that night in the laundromat was one thing. Seeing her standing next to Cain in the middle of her future bookstore was another. Then seeing her standing in front of me wearing a small tank top and her tiny lace panties was a whole fucking thing entirely.

It's been a full day since I watched her stomp her way across the room to me in nothing but her underwear and bed head. I won't deny the jolt that sight sent to my heart.

It wasn't until she stood closer that I saw the scars, though. The ones running jagged up her right leg. The scars on her chest. Her stomach. I swallowed the burn in my throat and held it together the best I could.

"Wake up." A hard object digs into my ribs, stirring me awake.

"No." I groan into my pillow. Every muscle in my body aches. Even my fingers pulsate when I grasp onto the plush fabric.

"Come on, asshole." Lennon's voice hovers above me. He jabs me again. "You can ignore Dad, but you can't ignore me."

"Try me," I mumble, rolling farther away from him.

"It's almost eight."

"Oh, fuck." I sit up, snatching my phone from my night-stand. He's right, it's eight. I fucking slept in. I told Victoria I would be there at six to go over her plans for her bookstore.

I shove my blanket off me, tossing it behind me on the bed, and swing my legs over the edge. My feet hit the floor, and I look up. Lennon is standing in front of me—my floor-to-ceiling windows behind him covered in darkness. I expected the sun to be out, blinding me the way it always does. I shouldn't have insisted on living in the fucking penthouse. I should have gone for the townhouse on the south side of the city. At least it would have been slightly easier to avoid my family. Especially my older brother. But my father reserved this apartment for me as a grad-uation gift. For all the good deeds I'd done in following in his footsteps. For all my accomplishments in following through with upholding the Harding legacy.

The moon hangs in the night sky above the building across from me. I immediately shoot Lennon a glare.

He catches it. His mouth presses into a thin line. "It's eight at night. Calm down."

"You fucking suck, you know that?" I shoot him another glare and get up from my bed. I leave him in my bedroom and head to the bathroom. Once inside, I slip a shirt I tossed on the floor the other night over my head and stay in the sweatpants I slept in.

When I step out of the bathroom, I find Lennon in my living room with his hands planted on his hips, staring out of another floor-to-ceiling window.

"I know you don't drink anymore, but it wouldn't kill you to have a bottle of bourbon. Maybe even a beer." He glances over his shoulder, his eyebrows set in a firm line.

"You say I can ignore Dad but not you. Does that bullshit rule of yours fly out the window when you say shit like that?" I sit on my couch and tilt my head back against the cushion. My eyes are heavy. "Because you sound just like him."

"What's the matter with you?" Lennon asks.

"I've been working." My brother already knows the answer to this question. He just wants me to say it out loud.

"Working on that little project of yours?"

"Seriously." I lift my head, delivering another unimpressed glare. "Now you really do fucking sound like Dad."

I refuse to tell him the woman I'm working for is Victoria. My family and Victoria go together like oil and water. Never mixing, never blending. Lennon was never as harsh on her as Dad, but the relationship wasn't exactly smooth, either.

Lennon loosens his tie on a sigh, squeezing his eyes shut before opening them again. "Sorry." He sits beside me on the couch in one exhausted heap. "I was in meetings all day, and I think the longer I'm there, the more I sound like him. We closed on three deals."

"Damn," I scoff. "Three is crazy."

"Yeah." He nods, lacing his fingers together while his hands rest in his lap. "It would have been nice if you were there with us. Maybe we could have gotten four."

"You know I can't." I pinch the bridge of my nose. A rhythmic beat pulsates, and my temples twitch. I'm exhausted. I spent ten hours working at Victoria's place. After she left for her class, she didn't come back until I was ready to head out at five. I at least had the rest of the crew to keep me company, finishing the last bit of clean up and deciding what was worth putting in a pile for Victoria to consider keeping or donating.

I figured I could bring it up to her when I showed up tomorrow. At six. Per her ground rules.

"Remind me why you can't," Lennon says, pulling me from my thoughts of Victoria and the argument we had this morning.

I pause and swallow. My throat is dry. My father has articulated the art of sucking me into the family business. He did it my entire childhood, feeding me only the good side of the business and reassuring me it was the only destiny that was in the cards for me. For a long time, I believed it, too. Until it cost me everything.

Lennon only knows the details of the price I paid for our father's acceptance. Nonetheless, he knows he isn't the saint he pretends to be, evidenced by the other night at dinner when he tried to pawn Laurel off on me.

"I don't need to remind you of anything." I move from the couch and head back to my room. I rifle through my nightstand until I find the bag of gummies I keep tucked away for times such as this. When my brother hasn't dropped the topic of my lack of commitment to our family and its business, and when I can't get Victoria out of my head. Apparently.

"You eat that shit, but you won't drink," Lennon says behind me.

Fuck, why is he following me?

"This isn't the same." I shake my head, chewing around the orange flavored taffy. "Besides, it's better to chew than to smoke it. Doesn't smell as bad."

"Still gets you fucked up."

"Nope." I shake my head again. "Still not the same. Helps with my headaches."

And it allows the pain to disappear. It's easier to numb the pain than to allow myself to feel it.

But I keep that reason to myself.

Before I quit drinking, I spent most of my time either drunk or high. More often than not, I was both. But ever since I stopped drinking, I haven't been able to give up getting high. It's the one thing I can control.

I drop the gummy bag back into my nightstand and slam the drawer shut.

"Either way," he says, "it affects your brain."

"Are you going to tell me why you're here? Or how you got in here?" I spin around, sitting on the edge of my bed. I want nothing more than to crawl back into it and hibernate under the sheets until I need to head back out to Victoria's in the morning. I still haven't come to terms with the fact we need to find a way to work together without letting our past get in the way. I just need to allow the weed to take effect. I need it to relax every sore muscle and bone.

"Your doorman let me in," he explains. "I told him it was an emergency."

"Of course, you did. Leave it to a Harding to lie his way in."

"It's tradition." Lennon chuckles under his breath. His joke makes me nauseous.

When he realizes I'm not laughing with him, his expression falls. His tie is readjusted already. He must have fixed it back in the living room.

"Dinner." One word is all it takes for me to understand what Lennon means. Harding weekly dinners.

"I'm skipping this week," I tell him. "I'll see you at the next one."

"Not dinner with Dad," Lennon says. "Dinner with Laurel."

I grind my teeth and stare at my brother. I feel like I'm in another dimension, caught in the traps my brother keeps setting, one after another.

"You're kidding," I scoff. "Why would I have dinner with Laurel? Dad was trying to pawn her off on me like he does every other fucking week. Next dinner, he'll bring up some other woman for me to sleep with so he can get his hands in their family's wallet. I'm not playing this game anymore. And you wonder why I've pulled back."

Lennon sighs, running his fingers through his thick, dark

hair before sliding his hands into his front pockets. "This has nothing to do with Dad. I think Laurel could be a great asset to the company. I want to speak to her one on one. Get in on her account without Dad. But I need you there with me."

"I don't know." I wince. I haven't completely pulled out of the family's business affairs, but it makes it more difficult to decide which cases to tackle. Which ones are the safer bet.

The path of least resistance, so to speak.

"One dinner," Lennon pleads. "Madison will be there."

Great. A double date.

Lennon crosses my room and sits down in the plush chair set between my bed and the endless glass windows. The city is wide awake below us, while I just want to hide and feel numb.

Resting his elbows on his knees, he looks up at me with pleading eyes. "I know we've been through a lot of shit with our family, but you wouldn't be doing this for him. You'd be doing it for me."

"I don't understand why you need me in the first place."

"You're a better negotiator than I am. You do an excellent job of getting all the details out in the proposal. I end up fumbling over my words or taking too long to get to the point."

"Maybe you should work on that instead of dragging me into your deals."

Lennon frowns, and I instantly feel guilty. Despite my desire to pull away from the family business, I only stick around for Lennon's sake. He may be my big brother, but he's one of the only people I can truly lean on.

Silence descends upon the room as I consider his request. Sleep begins to weigh heavy on me, but even as I sit on the edge of my bed, frustrated and sore, I still see the sincerity in Lennon's eyes. A rare sight.

His frown evens, replaced by familiar desperation.

"One dinner and that's all." I groan, reluctantly agreeing. I lay back on my pillow and swing my legs up and onto the bed. I tuck them under the blanket and turn away from Lennon. "Just let me know when and where. I have work in the morning, so see yourself out."

I'M WAITING for Victoria downstairs in her future bookstore, and I pull the plans Cain handed me the other day from my pocket. It's nothing but a crumpled-up piece of lined paper covered in black scribbles, though it isn't the worst drawing I've seen. I can make out most of the distinct parts of the store that already exist. The spiral staircase. The current death trap of a loft.

I study the page and flip it over. On the back are eight words written at the top of the page in Victoria's handwriting. Handwriting I know all too well.

Marketing in the modern age of social media.

I'm staring at the words, mulling them over as if I'm attempting to decipher a puzzle that's just been handed to me when Victoria bursts through the door leading to her apartment.

This time she's in a T-shirt and leggings. Thank God.

I'm not sure my dick can handle another surprise hard on from seeing Victoria in anything less.

Her long hair cascades around her shoulders. It's longer than I remember it being. The morning light catches her strands, highlighting the subtle streaks of red running through it.

I flip the paper back over to her rough sketch.

"Morning," she mumbles. It isn't the warmest of greetings, meaning she isn't exactly happy to see me. The feeling's mutual.

It's difficult to put my feelings into words. One second, I hate her. The next, I don't. I can't. I want to understand why she left the way she did, but another part of me doesn't blame her. At least a part of me tries not to.

"Morning," I answer back.

"Thank you for not breaking out the saw." She gestures toward my workstation with a small smile of gratitude.

"You're welcome. I was just going over your plans." I hold the paper up for her to see.

"Oh my God." She places her hand on her forehead. "I can't believe Cain gave those to you."

"Why?" I frown, looking over the paper again. "Is this not what you want?"

"No, it is." She releases a small, breathy giggle. "I just don't think you can read it very well. You can't make out what anything is." She points to the paper.

"I couldn't," I lie. "Well, at least not anything except the staircase." Not an entire lie.

"Oh." She stands in front of me, wrapping her hand around her neck. "I never claimed to be an artist."

"I never said you did." The tone in our conversation has shifted. We've traded our polite morning greeting exchange for one of slow torturing bitterness on both ends. I think back to our conversation yesterday. Victoria's ground rules. We can't let our history affect us working together. She's right. We can't. I can't allow it to affect it.

I still haven't spoken to my father yet, letting him stew on our last meeting a little longer instead. I figure I'll have to face him by tomorrow. For now, I'll stay here, in the comfort of the real world.

I close the gap between us and hold the paper out to Victoria. "Walk me through it, then, and I'll get started on figuring out where we start."

At first, she's caught off guard by my niceness. She cocks her head back, and her eyes twitch with surprise. "O-okay."

This seems to do the trick. Her mouth pulls into a smile for the first time since I've seen her. The dimple in her right cheek is still prominent. Two lines crease in the corners of her round eyes.

I clear my throat, not allowing my thoughts to get carried away again.

She takes the paper from my hand and moves to the far wall. I try not to think about the words on the back of the paper, trying to understand why she would write them.

"This is the wall I'm thinking would be great for bookshelves." She waves her hand from the back end of the space to the front. "Wall to wall."

"Okay." I shove my hands in the pockets of my jeans, walking behind her.

She stops in the middle of the space, near the back, and points to the alcove. "I would like to do a feature."

"A feature?"

"A special feature specific to only my store," she explains. "I mean, we're in Boston. There are a million bookstores. I want to find a way to bring more customers in and give them a reason to come to my place over anyone else's."

"Okay," I repeat. Warmth spreads across my chest when listening to her vision for her own store. She takes pride in her vision, and I can't help admiring it, but I hold back on digging in and asking her reasoning behind it. How did the woman who was obsessed with dance suddenly want to open a bookstore?

"What is it?" she asks.

"What do you mean?"

"I don't know." She closes the space between us. "I thought you would ask more questions. Isn't that what we're doing? Discussing and figuring this out together?"

The word 'together' falls from her like she's taken a bite of something bitter. She pauses, realizing what she said.

"We are," I reassure her, swallowing down the way her expression makes me feel.

She tips her chin, narrowing her eyes. "Well, you're the heir to the largest firm in the city. You're the one with the business degree. At least, I think you are."

"I am." I nod.

My confession flashes in front of me like a bright red warning sign. The reality of me finishing school as planned stings Victoria. I think back to yesterday morning when she said she had a class at eight, and to the backside of her rough sketch blueprints. She's taking a business or marketing class.

A hundred questions pop into my head, my curiosity piqued, but I reign them in, remembering why I'm here.

"Basically," I start. "You're saying you want my business advice." I feel my own mouth curl into a smirk. The sensation is foreign yet familiar.

"Like I said," she quips back. "You're a Harding. Aren't you considered the elite when it comes to business advice and getting a stake in the game?"

"Okay." I blow out a hot breath, thankful she's keeping a humorous tone when it comes to my family's business. Because when you've been through the shit she and I have been through with my family, it's easy to slip into focusing on only the dark, ugly parts. Which is almost all of it.

"Go ahead," I urge her. "I'm listening. What's your plan for this special feature?"

"Over here." She crosses the room. I follow. "A blind bookshelf."

"A what?" I blink, entirely confused.

She laughs, and the sound is beautiful. It's hard not to focus on her pretty little mouth when she swipes her tongue across her bottom lip, prepping herself for what I'm sure will be her version of a presentation.

She motions with her arm toward the bare wall tucked into

a small alcove near the back. "This entire wall will be dedicated to blind books."

"I'm sorry. Still not following. What is a blind book?"

She plants her hand on her hip and turns halfway to stare at the wall as if she's already imagining what it will look like. "A blind book is a book wrapped in brown paper, completely hiding the cover. You don't know the title or the author," she explains. "On the front or the spine of the brown paper are a list of tropes or themes. The buyer bases their choice on those instead of the title or the author."

"Huh." I twist my mouth, staring at the wall, envisioning bookshelves lined with brown paper wrapped books.

"What are you thinking?"

When I look away from the wall, I find Victoria standing in front of me with her lip tucked nervously beneath her teeth.

"So, the buyer doesn't know what they're getting?" I ask.

"No." She shakes her head and gives me a wide grin. "That's the fun of it."

I nod. "How do you know what to charge for each book? Are they all the same price or do you write the price on each one?" I've slipped into a business state of mind. A place I haven't been in what feels like an eternity. Part of me hates it. Part of me wants to end this conversation with Victoria and stalk back over to my workstation to saw or hack at another piece of wood. But the attention and hope in Victoria's eyes keeps me going. She's genuinely interested in hearing my opinion.

"I haven't worked that part out yet." She shrugs.

"You have some time, but I would have that figured out before you commit."

"You think it's a good idea?" She scrunches her nose, clearly afraid of my answer.

"Sure." I casually shrug and spin around to look at the rest of the place now that the clean-up is finished.

"Wait, so that's it?" she asks behind me. "All I get is a 'sure'?"

I turn on my heel and cross my arms beneath my chest with a sigh. "It's a great idea, Victoria. I don't know much about it, but I can see the appeal it would have to readers. It gives your store a feature."

Her eyes widen as if she can't believe I gave her my opinion. She grins in appreciation, but I can sense the hesitation in her eyes. She doesn't fully trust me or my judgment.

How could she when I'm still a Harding to my core?

CHAPTER NINE

VICTORIA

Thankfully, this final literature class has been a breeze... for the most part.

My professor has resigned us to listening to his seemingly endless lectures on different social media platforms and how it pertains to the accessibility of written works.

Not that spending two hours each day learning about literature doesn't interest me. It's the mind-numbing discussions in between, dissecting each word, and trying to interpret the meaning behind them. Those are the instances when I find myself focusing on other aspects of my life.

Jude's reappearance in it, mainly.

I've almost made the walk back to my apartment when I find myself still mulling over how it feels to be working with him. I shouldn't have any emotions, though. Our relationship at this point should be strictly transactional.

Business doesn't require feelings. It doesn't require emotion. In fact, most experts will tell you that business is better handled when emotions are put aside.

But how do you put emotions aside for someone you used to love? Especially when you find yourself waking up every morning to them sawing through a piece of wood or drilling in new sheets of drywall, sometimes shirtless. I'm itching to reach inside my bag and tug my journal free. Scribbling the first thoughts that come to my mind has always helped in sorting out my feelings. When I was in Texas, I stopped writing. Maybe it was Greg. Maybe it was because my life was mundane and comfortable. *Routine.*

Either way, I started writing again the second I made it back to Boston and found myself staring at the same buildings I used to stare at with Jude.

I leave my notebook in my bag, though, and wrap my fingers around the strap.

I pause outside my building and stare through the picture window in front. Jude is inside, bent in front of a white bucket. I can't make out its contents, but he dips a spatula inside, scooping a large glob of white goop. He carries it over to the wall and slaps it against the seam, meticulously dragging it from the top to the bottom near the floor. He's careful with his work, taking the time to make sure he's doing it right. Smoothing it up and down the surface, making it as level and even as possible.

I still haven't worked out why he's here. I would say it could be because of me, but I know deep down that Jude still harbors anger against me for the way I left. Despite all the lies he used to tell me when we were together, I have a feeling he truly didn't know he was coming to work on a place Riley owned. Now technically a place *I* own.

I wrap my hand around the door handle and pull it open. The smell of chemicals slams against my nose, immediately masking any sort of scents from outside. Not that the city air is much better.

I pass by a few of Jude's crew members, waving and nodding to each of them in greeting.

"Late class today?" Jude asks. He hasn't turned around, keeping his focus on the wall in front of him.

I sit back on the sawhorse propped up behind him—three pieces of wood slapped and nailed together, giving the guys a surface to work on if they need something done quickly. I only know this from watching them over the past two weeks.

"My professor likes to talk," I say.

"Most professors do." Jude glances over his shoulder long enough to eye me before turning back around. White streaks are smudged across his cheeks and nose.

I smile to myself. The Jude I met years ago would have never been caught dead covered in white plaster and sawdust. I twist my mouth in thought, wondering what shifted. Is this a temporary thing? Is this his way of indulging in his curiosity of what life is like outside the four stifling walls of the Harding firm?

"I don't know." I blink away my thoughts. "I'm ready for it to be over."

"Didn't classes just start?" he asks, laughing.

He still hasn't turned around. I'm considering how much information to feed him. We aren't exactly on a friend level yet, but I can't deny the warmth that blankets me every time we have a decent conversation. It reminds me of the first night we met. It reminds me that at one point in time in my life, Jude was the person I always went to when I needed to talk.

It's strange how I spent years without ever seeing Jude, and now I see him every day. As if he weren't the person who practically ripped my heart out. He's also the person I used to be in love with.

My lower stomach hums when he drops the spatula into the bucket and turns around. He steps forward, bringing himself toe to toe with me. The scent of whatever goop he was spreading across the walls grows stronger. It invades my senses, clouding my judgment. I grow lightheaded as the smell swells, surrounding me like a cloud of fog. Or maybe it's just Jude. His gray Boston College shirt and faded blue jeans are covered in white smudges. His skin is coated with beads of sweat. His hair isn't slicked back. He isn't clean shaven. There's no gold watch wrapped around his wrist.

He's a mess, and it's a completely foreign sight to me. I have yet to see Jude wear anything other than casual, everyday clothes.

His eyes are pinned to mine, anchoring me in place.

I gasp, and my thighs instinctively flinch when he reaches out beside me. I hold my breath, fully anticipating his touch, but instead, he grabs the rag sitting on the sawhorse beside me.

"It's only been a couple weeks into the course," I say, forcing the words out. My voice comes out hoarse. My throat is dry, and I swallow.

He rubs the rag over each of his fingers, taking his time on each one. He hasn't moved his feet, the toes of his boots touching the tips of my ballet flats. His eyes are laser focused on the end of my braid draped over my shoulder. Years of dancing made tying my hair into braids a habit I haven't been able to shake.

"Is that your major now? Business?" he asks, his mouth set into a straight line. He's serious. This is his first attempt to dig into my reasoning for still being in school.

Maybe he thinks I'm working on my graduate degree.

Well, I guess we're doing this. We're *talking*.

"It is." I nod, careful with my words. "After, um..." I clear my throat. "After I left, I didn't go back to school. At least not right away. I went to a small college out in Texas. That's when I decided to switch majors. Well, I didn't exactly have a choice." The last sentence falls out of my mouth at nearly three times the usual speed at which I talk.

When Jude's eyes meet mine again, I know he understands what I mean. I didn't choose to switch majors because I simply changed my mind. I was forced to switch. My body was too damaged to ever consider dance a full-time career. At least not in the way I intended on making mine.

"Oh." He nods in slow understanding, pressing his mouth into a thin line. Sadness fills his eyes, and I watch as he looks away to focus on the group of men working behind me. He can't bring himself to look at me when he speaks again. "Seems like opening a bookstore turned out to be a good career choice, then."

"Yeah." I nod, chewing on the inside of my cheek. "I'm glad, though. It's nice to have something to call mine. I realize now that when I was out in Texas, I was basically on my own."

"I didn't know that's where you went when you left."

He's right, I never told him where I went. For weeks after I moved to Texas, I never answered Jude's unrelenting calls. I guess after a while, he'd given up. Resigned himself to believing I was the one who left him. The problem was, I felt like he'd given up on me long before the accident.

My chest squeezes with regret for the choices I made when I was in no position to be making choices.

"I stayed with Amy for a while before..." I allow my words to fade, not bringing myself to finish the sentence. Not that talking about Amy and Greg is heartbreaking. I can't bring myself to talk about them to Jude.

"Before what?" he asks, locking his eyes on me. "Before you moved back here?"

He's still standing close enough for me to touch. I swallow again, my thoughts growing as foggy as the dust clouds filling the bookstore.

"I guess you could say that. Let's just say I find it hard to trust the ones I love. History has a way of repeating itself."

I don't know what else to say. I've laid the truth out there, whether he wanted to hear it or not. A lump swells in my throat, and it's as if a brick has dropped through my stomach. It's the most honest I've been with Jude since we stepped back into each other's lives.

"Yeah." His voice hardens. "I guess it does."

His eyes darken, shadows swirling in his midnight blues. He doesn't flinch, but I can see my words have caught him off guard.

"Hey, man." One of the guys from Jude's crew walks over to him and places his hammer down on the opposite end of the sawhorse from where I am. He breaks Jude's attention away from me and our conversation. "We're headed out for our lunch break. You coming with us?" He hitches his thumb over his shoulder to the rest of the team who are already filing out the front door. I don't blame them, especially considering the work they've been putting in these past two weeks.

"Nah," Jude says, shaking his head. "I'll figure out lunch later. You guys go on ahead. I need to finish mudding these walls."

The man nods to Jude then me before he joins the rest of his crew.

Jude is still watching the men leave when I study the wall he's been working on. I nod my head, wanting to change the subject. Exposing my deepest, darkest thoughts to Jude is a road I'm not willing to explore right now. "So, that's what it's called? Mudding?"

Jude follows my gaze, looking over his shoulder before turning back to me.

I set my bag down by my feet and place my hands beside me, gripping the edge of the sawhorse. I lift myself up, readying to slide back to sit on it. The wood wobbles as I point my toe, lifting myself up. Before I get more than one foot off the floor, Jude's hand is suddenly gripping my thigh.

He presses down, preventing me from sliding up and onto the thin slab of wood.

His long fingers dig into my flesh. I decided to wear a dress today. The slit drives up my thigh, exposing my goosebump-riddled skin. It ignites under his touch. I'm busy processing how it feels to have him touch me again after four years that I don't immediately notice the flash of anger now embedded in his expression.

"Fuck, V," he barks.

There it is again. My nickname.

His hand presses on my leg, forcing my feet to touch the floor.

"What are you doing?" I ask, confused.

He points beside me with his other hand. "That's a sawhorse, not a bench."

I look down and to my left. The sawdust and dirt-covered surface is maybe about a foot wide and an inch thick. I'm uncertain about its reliability, but in the moment, I figured it made a good place to sit.

"I thought it could hold me." I'm quick to defend myself.

I'm fully aware his hand hasn't moved. His fingers are still pressed into my flesh, creating white halos in my skin around each of his fingertips. He catches me staring at his hand and he jerks it away.

"It's not meant for people to sit on," he repeats. "We use it when we need to measure or saw a piece of wood quickly."

"Fine." I hold my hands up in surrender. Jude backs away.

His face is still set into a scowl. His nostrils flare and his eyebrows pinch together. I haven't seen him this angry in a long time. Or worried. There's a hint of panic in his stare. It quickly flashes then disappears.

The fire that burned my skin with his touch has now turned cold. I grab my bag and sling it over my shoulder. I still have an entire paper to write on a social media platform that would benefit my future business, and I still haven't decided which one.

"Well," I sigh, unable to look Jude in the eye. My neck is warm, and my heart is racing. "I have a lot of work to catch up on."

I'm spinning on my heels when his fingers wrap around my wrist. I stop but don't turn around. My lungs squeeze as I hold my breath. I don't know why, but pressure builds behind my eyes.

"Victoria." My name falls softly from his mouth.

My eyes flutter. There he goes again, back to my full name. His voice slithers down my back, sending tingles down my spine.

I sigh and spin around, meeting his eyes.

They've softened now. The firm expression has fallen slack.

"I shouldn't have done that." I don't know if he's referring to his scolding or his hand touching my thigh. Maybe both. "I'm sorry."

"It's okay," I say, unconvincingly.

"Okay." He nods, letting his hand slip away from my wrist.

"I really do have to write this paper," I tell him. I have the entire weekend to write it, but I needed a quick excuse to get away. Being around Jude makes it hard to breathe.

"Yeah." He nods, scratching at his chin. "I need to finish mudding these walls, anyway."

I give him the smallest smile I can possibly give him before I turn around and walk toward the door leading up to my apartment.

My breath shudders, and it isn't until a tear slips down my

cheek that I realize no matter how hard I try to pretend it doesn't exist, our history is still alive and thriving.

"I FIGURE this is the perfect place for you to find stuff for your new store." Riley beams. "Or maybe even your apartment."

"The flea market?" I twist my mouth, staring at the sea of people milling around propped up tents and tables. Some tables are covered in trinkets and pieces of glassware. Others are surrounded by large pieces of furniture.

"It's not a flea market." Riley nudges me, wrapping her arm around mine. She pulls me, forcing me to take a step forward, and stops at the first table at the front to pick up a wooden plaque with a faded painting of evergreen trees. "Okay, maybe it is a flea market."

I laugh, scanning the table for anything that might catch my eye. I don't have a clue what I'm looking for, but I don't think Riley does, either.

After my interaction with Jude yesterday, I needed time away to think and process what happened between us. Not that I had the chance to run into him today, anyway. It's the start of the weekend. The two days Jude and the rest of his crew aren't required to show up.

Although Jude wasn't set to work on my shop today, my body begged for fresh air and time with Riley. It craved a moment where I didn't have to stare at the progress on my new bookstore without thinking of Jude in his white smudged, faded jeans. Riley asked if I wanted to take a trip with her outside of Boston. I jumped at the opportunity to get out of the city and as far away from the possibility of running into Jude on his day off. We seem to have a knack for serendipitous meetings.

"How is the store progressing?" Riley asks.

I place the glass pitcher I'd been inspecting for absolutely no reason back down on the table and look up at Riley. She sits in an old wooden chair, looking down and testing the sturdiness by wobbling back and forth.

"That's not for sale." The woman behind the counter points to her. "My husband just put that there so he can rest his feet between talking to customers."

"Oh." Riley shoots up, and I break out into laughter. "I'm sorry." She grabs onto my arm again and pulls me away.

Our laughter doesn't subside until we make it to the next tent where a vendor is selling handmade wood carved pens.

"Now, back to my question," she starts. "How's the store coming along?"

"Good." I nod. "I think."

"You think?"

"Yeah." I shrug one shoulder and run my fingers down a dark blue stained pen. "They have the whole place cleaned up now, and Jude started on the walls yesterday."

His sweat covered forehead. Toned arms. White smudged, faded jeans.

It's been difficult to get the image of him out of my head.

"That's great." Riley claps her hands together. Her grin stretches from ear to ear.

I press my lips together and give her a smile. A weak one that doesn't meet my eyes.

"Come on." She nods her head back. "There's a tent over here I want to check out."

I follow her down the row of vendors. The sun is hiding behind the clouds. The grass presses into the damp ground with each step I take. I have no idea what town we're in, but the city feels far away.

Riley walks beside me. "How's it working with Jude?" Her question is slow and tentative. She knows it hasn't been easy to navigate.

"It's..." I pause to consider what words to use. "It's going."

"That's it? Have you talked at all?"

"A little." I sigh. "I don't know. I think it's strange."

"What is?"

"How at one point in time you can love someone so deeply, you swear you couldn't breathe unless they were near you." I swallow, flashes of my memories with Jude playing in my mind. "And now it's as if I can't breathe when I'm around him."

"Huh." She nods. "I'm sure it's not easy being around each other. Especially with how it ended between you two."

"He's still angry with me for how I left," I mutter. "At least I think he is. He definitely treats me like he is."

"He hurt you, too. Don't forget. Jude Harding has never been an innocent man."

Riley has slipped from her friend role to the protective aunt role.

"No, he hasn't. Sometimes I forget he's the one who messaged me that night saying he wanted to end things. Then when I called him later, he begged me to pick him up so we could talk. That's why I ended up in the accident." I swallow back the flood of memories. "But something in him has changed. Don't you wonder why he's working for Cain? It's bizarre, considering how dedicated to his family's firm he used to be."

"People change, Victoria," she says, elbowing her way past a group of people. "Some do and some don't. But when you go through what the both of you went through, I'm sure you're bound to change in some capacity. Physical scars eventually disappear. Emotional scars can last a lifetime."

"I don't know." I blink, shaking my head. "Sometimes I think it's best for me to ignore him. Or at least I try to."

I'm thinking of Jude and how close he was to me yesterday. It's been years since he's been close enough for me to smell him. Close enough for him to touch me. The spot where he touched may have grown cold, but I still feel it just the same. I think Riley was right. Emotional scars can last a lifetime.

"Do you think you're ready to date again?" she asks, tucking her bottom lip under her teeth. She lifts her shoulders and slides her hands into the pockets of her shorts.

"I don't know. It's been a while since I broke it off with Greg. In hindsight I don't think I ever truly loved him, anyway. It isn't exactly hard to get over something you never had in the first place."

"Right." She nods once.

I'm thankful she doesn't ask me to elaborate because the next words out of my mouth would have likely involved Jude.

"Here," Riley says, tearing me from my thoughts. "This is the main reason I wanted to bring you here."

My eyes widen, and my jaw drops when I look at the tent Riley's dragged me to.

It's a tent filled with books. Tables and bookshelves and boxes, all filled with books.

"What do you think?" she asks.

"I think this is fucking amazing." I grin.

"Good." She plants her hands on her hips with a satisfied grin. "Let's get to sorting so we can start building that inventory."

I rub my hands together, thankful to dive into something that doesn't involve Jude.

CHAPTER TEN

Jude

History has a way of repeating itself.

Victoria's voice speaking those words has been running through my head on repeat ever since she uttered them last week. I'm rubbing the sand block over the same strip of cured mud, dissecting her words and the meaning behind them.

I know she directed her statement toward me, but knowing her dig was meant for me didn't make the dagger any blunter.

"Watch out, man," Craig, one of my crew members, says beside me. "You're sanding too hard. You're starting to see the screw."

He points to the spot I've over sanded. The black star-shaped head of the screw is visible through what's left of the wall mud.

"Fuck." I groan, threading my fingers through my hair and pushing it off my forehead. "I must have spaced out."

"Might be a good chance to take a break," he suggests. "I can take it from here."

"Thanks." I cave, giving in to his offer to take over. "I'll be back in a few." I hand him the sanding block and head to the bathroom to wash my hands. White powder covers my hands and arms.

I'm watching the water wash over my fingers and palms, thinking about Victoria again. I haven't seen her much since the day we had the conversation before she attempted to sit on the sawhorse. Our meetings since then have been cut short and slightly awkward. Her confession about where she escaped to after she left has been weighing on me heavily. She left me to go live with her stepsister. Instead of turning to me, she went to Amy.

The realization of how Victoria felt about me after the accident has been slowly gutting me over the past week. When someone is in love with you, you want to be the person they run to, not away from. The truth of how Victoria has felt about me these past four years has been staring me in the face. I'm the one who shattered her faith in those she loved.

I'm *that* guy.

When I finish drying my hands, I reach into my pocket and pull out my pack of weed gummies. My palms begin to sweat, and my mind is quickly slipping down the rabbit hole of every bad decision I've ever made in my life. I'm taking inventory, and when that usually happens, my urge to escape those thoughts escalates.

I clench my hand into a fist, resisting the impulse inside me, compelling me to leave and find the nearest pub. Years ago, it would have easily been my first choice—a decision made without hesitation. I close my eyes and inhale a steadying breath.

I pop two gummies in my mouth, close the pouch, and slip it into my back pocket. I look at myself in the mirror. My face is covered in sweat and dust. Scars that are invisible to others are painfully obvious in my reflection.

I need to not think about her.

I need to not think about the accident.

I need to not think about the twelve beers and three shots I'd had that night.

I need to not think about how I'd lost the only person I'd ever loved more than Victoria.

I need to forget.

I turn the faucet back on and cup my hands under the stream. After a few splashes to my face, I dry myself off and step back out into Victoria's building.

My phone buzzes in my pocket. I slide it out and read a text from Lennon, reminding me about the dinner he has set up for me three days from today. My dinner with Laurel. I quickly text him back, reassuring him that I haven't forgotten.

I'm heading back over to the wall I was sanding earlier when Victoria emerges through the door leading up to her apartment. Most of the other men don't notice her. For me, it's impossible not to. She's wearing a woven crop top and high-waisted jeans covered in tears ripping down her legs. They mold perfectly to her round ass.

A few of the crew wave or nod their heads in acknowledgement. She greets some of them as well. As for me, she simply gives me a small ghost of a smile.

She must be replaying the conversation from the other day in her mind, too.

History has a way of repeating itself.

I grab the sanding block from Craig before he has the chance to continue onto the next strip of dried wall mud.

"Hey." Her soft voice washes over me like a cascade of water. My spine tingles, unable to turn around and face her.

I imagine her standing behind me, her braid tied effortlessly and resting casually over her shoulder. Her flushed cheeks and pink lips.

Fuck.

"Jude." Her saying my name finally causes me to turn around.

"Yeah?" I ask her. She's standing inches in front of me with her hair twisted into a braid, with flushed cheeks and pink lips. She looks exactly how I imagined she would.

My dick twitches, remembering a time when I wouldn't have hesitated to wrap my arms around her and press my mouth to hers. My body reacts to her, craving her once again.

"Riley took me to a market the other day, and I found a ton of books to sell in the store when it's open," she explains. "The guy I bought them from should be here any minute to deliver the boxes, since they wouldn't fit in her car. I'd hate to have to carry them up the stairs to my apartment, so I was wondering if there was a good place I could store them that wouldn't get in the way of you and the crew."

"You went to a flea market?" I ask, amused.

"Yes." She rolls her eyes. "I doubt you've ever been to one. I'm surprised you even know what it is."

"Of course, I do." I laugh. "I might not have ever been to one, but I've seen those shows on the home improvement channels. You can find some interesting items there."

"I was hoping to find some pieces to decorate the store with, but there wasn't anything left in my budget after I bought the books. Luckily, the man included delivery as long as I bought his entire lot."

"Nice." I take a deep breath and look around the store, thinking of a place for her to store them. "We cleaned out the storage room the other day, so you should be able to put them in there."

She tucks a few loose strands of hair behind her ear. "Okay, thanks."

Her pink lips spread into a genuine smile. It pierces my torn heart, blanketing it in a warmth I haven't felt in a long time.

She starts to back away from me but stops when a man walks through the front door carrying a large, white box in his arms. He looks over the top, searching the room. He's wearing a backward Celtics hat and a button-down denim shirt. He smiles the second he finds the person he's looking for.

When Victoria sees him, she lifts her hand in a greeting and leaves me where I'm standing to meet him, offering him her wide grin.

"Right on time," Victoria says, fingering through the books laid on top of the pile stacked into the box the man is holding. She looks back up at him. "I hope you didn't have a hard time finding the place."

"No," he says. "It wasn't too bad. I'm originally from the city, so I know the streets like the back of my hand."

"Same here." Victoria giggles. She leads him farther into the store, stopping in the place she was standing in moments before this asshole showed up.

"This is Jude." She introduces me to him as if I were expecting her to. I wasn't. "He's in charge of the remodel and renovation."

Honestly, I find it odd she's introducing me to a man who is simply here to deliver a few boxes of books she purchased from a flea market.

"Hi." He grins, attempting a wave with the hand he's using to hold the box with. His greeting is awkward. "Nice to meet you. I'm Tyler."

"Hi." I nod in acknowledgement but don't speak another word.

I glance at Victoria, attempting to get a read on her thoughts. She narrows her eyes and shoots me a glare with her piercing green eyes. Between her morning class and her distance since our conversation last week, she hasn't said much. She's kept the space between us. It's been driving me fucking crazy. Spending years without Victoria made it easier to live the day to day without her. But now that she's back in my life, it's becoming increasingly difficult to stay away. We're like two magnets, drawn to one another when we're together. Lost when we aren't.

This is the longest she's faced me since, and this is how she chooses to act. Annoyed, allowing me to get under her skin.

Despite the pain I've felt from her reminder of how terrible and ugly our past is, I find her reaction amusing. The corner of my mouth lifts into a smirk.

The glare she's giving me tightens before she replaces her scowl with a friendly grin and she turns back to Tyler.

"Here," she says. "I'll show you where you can drop the boxes."

Tyler gives me a smile before he follows Victoria to the storage room. After he places the box in the back, he walks back out to his truck to grab the other two boxes Victoria ordered. She stands at the front door, holding it open for him.

When he's finished, he surprises me by not immediately leaving.

"Hey, um, Victoria." He nervously adjusts his Celtics hat and slides his hands into his pockets. She crosses her arms beneath her chest, stepping closer to him.

"Yeah?" she asks.

I've finished sanding the wall and am standing in front of the sawhorse, measuring a trim piece I'm intending on using as baseboard. I overhear their conversation even as I line my measuring tape to the wood.

"I was wondering if you'd like to go out some time." He nervously grabs the back of his neck, looking down at his feet. He looks back up at Victoria, his eyebrows arched across his forehead. Douchebag is waiting for an answer, hoping she says yes.

I don't know this man, and if he were asking any other woman out, I probably wouldn't give two flying fucks.

I'm in no position to care who Victoria decides to date or go out with. We haven't been together in four years, and I never claimed to be the poster boy for the perfect boyfriend—I was far from it—but I won't deny the way my stomach lurches watching it play out in front of me. It's as if I've been punched in the gut.

Victoria isn't quick to give him an answer. I'm still holding my pencil in one hand, the measuring tape in the other, staring up at her.

She twists her mouth and glances over her shoulder.

My eyes catch hers before I snap them back to my work, pretending as if I'm not listening to every single word of her conversation with Tyler.

"Sure," she eventually says, her voice light. Happy, even. "I'd love to."

My stomach lurches again. I need this fucking high to kick in. It hasn't had enough time to absorb into my system, but I'm hoping it won't take much longer.

"Great," Tyler says. "I'll text you and let you know when and where."

I grip the pencil in my hand a little too hard, snapping the end of the sharp lead tip. It breaks off, rolling across the piece of wood and onto the floor.

Tyler leaves, making sure to give me a wave before walking out the door. I give him a closed mouth grin for appearances. A skill I've mastered as a Harding.

After Tyler disappears, Victoria spins on her heels, and her eyes zero in on me. The smile she was wearing for Tyler fades.

Watching how her mood has shifted from the way she was looking at Tyler to the way she's looking at me is the final blow. I may be a Harding designed to pretend like our lives are picture fucking perfect, but inside I'm broken.

Every cell in my body begs to cross the room to touch her—to remember what it's like to feel alive inside. My body aches, and my hands twitch. I clench my fingers into a fist, unwilling to break eye contact from her. She's stunning and beautiful. She's kind and innocent. She's the only person who has ever been capable of destroying me.

She turns her back on me and walks up to her apartment in silence. I loosen my clenched fist and take a breath.

Every second of the past four years has been spent living in agony knowing the truth.

History can't repeat itself when it's always been the same.

I never stopped loving Victoria.

CHAPTER ELEVEN

VICTORIA

My life could have been different. My life used to have a different plan.

Graduate from Boston College with a dance degree. Move to Paris. Marry Jude. Get pregnant. Have children.

Fate has a way of rearranging your plans without notice. Sometimes it can be savage and erase them completely as if they had never existed in the first place.

The plans fate had savagely erased from my life are staring me directly in the face in the form of two midnight blue eyes.

Or at least I imagine them staring back at me through my reflection in the mirror. Between the black mini skirt I'm wearing and the cropped, dark blue, silk tank barely covering my breasts, I'm rethinking my decision to go out with Tyler. My shirt is cut low and tight. My shoulders are bare. The skirt stops above mid-thigh. It's an outfit Riley helped pick out for me yesterday when I told her Tyler planned to pick me up tonight at seven.

My mind has been consumed the past hour with a million possible excuses to back out.

The muscles in my leg are aching. I have a ten-page paper

due for my class. I've come down with the flu. I even considered coming up with the excuse that maybe I'm simply not ready to date. Anything to back out of my date with Tyler.

It's not that I don't find him attractive. He has soft, kind eyes, and his smile is the type that makes you feel safe. He's an avid book lover, too.

All admirable qualities.

I don't truly know him, but I knew the second he asked me out that the spark wasn't there. Something was missing.

Or it could have been the hole I felt burning in my back from Jude's stare. Two midnight eyes scorching me from across the room. To say Tyler asking me out in front of Jude was awkward would be an epic understatement.

My heart sank into my chest, and I wanted to disappear, but Tyler's hopeful expression made me think it might be for the best. Maybe I needed to get out, meet new people. Maybe it wouldn't hurt to move on. I could add it to my list of ways I was accomplishing my fresh start.

I check myself in the mirror one last time before heading downstairs, forcing the image of Jude out of my mind. I run my fingers through my beachy waves and apply another layer of lipstick.

Tyler is right on time. His truck is parked out front. He steps out and walks around to the passenger side, holding the door open for me while I lock the door to the store. I'm thankful he picked a time when Jude and his crew weren't working, forcing the men to watch me leave for a date.

I climb into Tyler's truck and wait as he climbs back into the driver's seat. The strong scent of cedar fills the cab. He's removed the Celtics hat he'd been wearing the other day when he delivered the books, replacing it with clean, slicked back hair. He's wearing a white button-down shirt with a red tie wrapped around his neck. His black slacks blend in with his black leather seat.

He's different. Shinier than he's been the two occasions I've seen him.

We make small talk on the way to whatever restaurant Tyler's picked. We talk about the basics. I'm relieved, and I avoid going deeper, keeping our conversation surface level. Tyler shares about his childhood and growing up in Boston. He confesses he's been to practically every single Celtics game since he was three.

I stick to the safe topics: books, favorite authors, favorite color, foods. Nothing involving dance, college, or Jude. Most importantly Jude.

I get so lost in our mundane conversation, I don't even notice where Tyler's taken us until we stop alongside the curb.

Panic sets in the moment I peer through my window, looking up at the building beside me. The valet standing at the end of the entrance opens my door, holding his hand out for me, but I don't immediately take it.

"Are you okay?" Tyler asks, still sitting in the driver's seat, his fingers wrapped around the steering wheel.

My cheeks are flaming red, and my throat is dry. Every cell in my body is immediately engulfed in flames. Anxiety. Panic. Uncertainty. It all slams into me at once.

"I'm fine," I lie, hoping saying it out loud will magically make it true.

Tyler's brows knit together, the softness in his eyes growing. "We can go somewhere else if you'd like. I wanted to take you here because Eclipse is one of the best places to eat in Boston."

I hold back my desire to tell him it is anything but the best place.

I've only ever eaten here once.

Until the day I found myself sitting across from the one man who wasn't afraid to share his true feelings about how he felt about me and the stain I'd become on his family, I'd never been here.

This place was off limits for someone like me. Someone unworthy of stepping into the coveted Harding public eye. Even if I was dating their prized son. Status, after all, is everything to the Hardings.

Part of me questions what status Tyler holds in the city. Only the elite of Boston ever come to this restaurant. One of their meals alone is worth more than some people's weekly salaries. Golden lights, crystal chandeliers, and red carpets are all indications the restaurant is out of over half the Boston population's price range.

Instinct is urging me to tell Tyler to find another restaurant. To go anywhere else in the city. But another part of me is telling me enough time has passed. Maybe the Hardings don't have the same influence over the restaurant that they did years ago. The probability of it being true is highly unlikely, but the resolve settling in my gut tells me I can't back out now. I shouldn't allow the lingering effects of my broken relationship with Jude four years ago to dictate the places I go and who I see in this city.

"No." I give Tyler a genuine smile. "We can eat here."

"Okay." He steps out of his truck and hands the valet his key, meeting me on the passenger side as I step out. He holds his hand out for me.

His grip is warm, but his hand doesn't fit easily into mine. I follow him along the red carpeted walkway, reading the restaurant logo printed in gold on the crystal glass doors. The last time I'd walked through these doors I was unknowingly walking into a den of vipers. I was cornered like innocent, unsuspecting prey.

When the doorman opens the door for us to walk in, I swear I see Jude's midnight eyes, just like they were back at my apartment in the reflection of my mirror. But it's just my mind playing tricks on me. I tuck my curled hair behind my ear and square my shoulders.

The soft piano playing in the background shoots straight to my chest like an arrow. The gentle sound slithers across my skin, sending chills down it. I adjust the bottom of my skirt and fiddle with the hem of my silk top.

Tyler drops my hand and greets the host waiting for us at the large podium. He lowers his voice and leans over the marble counter, bringing his face closer to hers. I barely make out what he says other than the words 'reservation' and 'patio'.

The hostess gives me a smile over his shoulder before she pulls away.

"Your table is this way," she says politely.

She holds her hand out, gesturing the direction for us to go. We follow her through the endless rows of white linen topped tables and booths wrapped in expensive red leather. Crystal drop chandeliers hang from the ceiling every ten feet. The place shimmers, blinding me with its image of perfection.

If I didn't already have a preconceived idea of this place from my past, I would have walked in here with awe. Now I find myself walking into it hoping my entire date will go well enough to distract me from where we're eating.

The hostess leads us to a table facing the back patio, over-looking the harbor. The water glistens in the moonlight, and I gasp. I never noticed this place was so close to the water—a beautiful part of the city often overshadowed by the ugliness inside this restaurant.

Tyler slides my chair out and allows me to sit down. He sits across from me, resting his arms on the edge of the table. He grins at the host and thanks her before she leaves us.

"This view is incredible." I lean forward, whispering to Tyler. I can't help it. The soft piano music makes me feel as if

I'm sitting in the middle of a library. One word spoken too loudly, and we'll be kicked out.

"This is my favorite view of the harbor," he says. "I was hoping we'd get a table on the patio, but I figured it might be a little too chilly tonight, especially since it's on the water."

"This is great. It's still a beautiful view," I say, removing the napkin laid out on the small white plate in front of me. I place it on my lap, and when our waiter comes to our table, my eyes fall to the people sitting three tables over. I'm looking past Tyler's shoulder, focused on the woman sitting in the red leather wrapped booth. Her arm is draped around the man beside her. He's wearing a crisp black suit with a white button-down shirt underneath. His tie is loose, one button at the top of his shirt undone, exposing his neck. A gold watch is wrapped around his wrist, the light from the crystal chandeliers above glinting off the shiny metal. He lifts his hand, pushing his hair away from his forehead. Pieces fall slack as he turns his head to look at the woman sitting beside him.

My spine tingles, and heat spreads across my cheeks. The woman throws her head back in laughter, placing her hand on the man's chest.

Jude's chest.

Jude is the man sitting in the red leather wrapped booth with a woman draped around him.

Jude in a suit.

Tyler orders us a bottle of wine, but I don't hear him say what kind. Every sound in the restaurant is muffled, drowned out by the woman's exaggerated laughter.

My pulse races—I shouldn't be surprised—but something about seeing Jude in this place catches me off guard. Maybe I was foolishly hoping he'd let go of this lifestyle. Maybe it was the reason he was working for Cain's renovation business. But the proof is staring directly at me in the form of two midnight blue eyes.

Jude's gaze is on me, staring me down. His eyebrows are set firm above his hardened glare. He's shocked to see me here. From the expression on his face, he's more shocked than I am to see him here.

Without flinching, he lifts his hand and rubs his fingers on his chin. Unsettled. The thoughts are clearly running through his mind. The woman beside him doesn't seem to notice. She still has her arm draped around the back of the booth, her fingers playing with the collar of his suit on his opposite shoulder. From the looks of it, she's his date.

My pulse quickens, and the blood drains from my face. I don't know why, but my chest squeezes at the sight of him with her. I shouldn't be angry. I shouldn't be jealous.

Eclipse. Jude in a suit. A woman practically dry humping him in public.

The realization of what I'm seeing balloons inside me. It swells, and I can't think straight. My mind is fuzzy, and I can't make out a coherent thought. I need to get a fucking grip.

Jude is still glaring at me from across the tables. There's no one in between us other than Tyler. I'm doomed to spend my entire date with Jude sending me daggers.

Tyler is studying his menu when I slide my chair back. "I need to use the restroom," I clip out. "I'll be right back."

"Okay." He smiles, looking up at me. "I'll wait to order until you're back."

He's too fucking kind.

I eye the restroom sign down the row of tables. Past Jude in a suit and his horny date.

I curl my hands into tight fists and will myself to keep walking. Maybe if I don't acknowledge him, the balloon inside my chest will disappear. I can go back to my date with Tyler and enjoy the view from our table.

My heels click across the marble floor as I quickly make it past Jude's table. I don't look in his direction, focusing on my next step instead. Then the next.

When I reach the bathroom, I shove the door open with force and beeline it to the sink, quickly turning the faucet on. The sound of water rushes in, filling the empty bathroom. It's a small restroom with only two stalls. It's white and shiny, with gold accents dotted around, accenting every surface. My chest contracts dramatically with every weighted breath. I rest my hands on the edge of the sink and stare up at myself in the reflection.

Those fucking eyes. Midnight blues stare back at me. Only this time it isn't my imagination, and they aren't staring at me from three tables down.

Jude is standing behind me. He allows the door to slowly close behind him. He spins around, locking it. The metal clicks loudly, drowning out the sound of the rushing water.

We stare at one another in silence, allowing our breaths to dance. I breathe in, he breathes out. The tension in the bathroom is heavy.

"This is the women's restroom, Jude," I point out. My strained voice echoes, vibrating off the walls. My pulse is still racing, but the rhythm of my heartbeat now vibrates down to the tips of my toes.

"Do you honestly think that matters to me?" His eyes darken.

"No, of course not." I press my mouth into a tight line. I know it doesn't. Jude has always thought he was invincible and never had to play by the rules. Especially in a setting where he knew his family had the upper hand. Especially in places such as Eclipse. A knot weaves at the center of my chest, and my shoulders stiffen. I rest my hands on the edge of the vanity, gripping the edge to use as an anchor. "But contrary to what you and your family believe, this restaurant doesn't belong to you. It doesn't mean you have the right to come in here."

"How's your date going?" he asks, ignoring my comment and still staring into my eyes through our reflections. "Looks like pretty boy over there has traded in his Celtics hat for that sad excuse for a tie."

"I'm free to date whoever I want," I choke out. "It's been four years, Jude."

"I'm very well aware of how long it's been, V."

His use of my nickname makes my thighs twitch.

I purse my lips, shooting him a hard glare. My skin is hot with frustration. Even when I try to escape Jude, I can't. He haunts me, following me. But I know deep down I don't want him to stop.

My internal confession knocks me in my hammering chest. I grip the faucet and turn the water off. The silence is immediate. I spin around, shooting him daggers with the iciest glare I can muster.

"Don't you think your date is missing you?" I ask him, popping an eyebrow and nodding toward the door. "Her body seemed effortlessly glued to that expensive suit of yours."

The colors in his eyes are a kaleidoscope of blue and black. The intense shade magnifies against his harsh black suit. I've forgotten how they change when he's dressed like this. Expensive.

He even smells expensive. The scent kicks up my racing heart.

I step forward, inching my way to the exit. Jude is blocking my path, but I don't care. I need to get out of here before I explode. Or float away. I can't make sense of where this conversation is headed or the point, but I know the longer I stand here in this room with Jude standing in front of me, the likelier it is that I won't be able to stop myself from slipping back into old habits. Being with Jude is like a drug. Once I've had a hit, I won't be able to stop.

"You shouldn't be here," he warns in an icy tone.

I stop in my tracks, staring up at him. "Why? Because someone like me has never belonged here? In your world?"

He doesn't answer me, just stares in wide-eyed silence.

My patience wears thin. I shake my head and step forward. "Thank you for solidifying that nothing has ever changed, and nothing ever will. You will always be a Harding. No amount of sawdust or time away from your office will ever change that."

I reach for the lock when Jude's hand catches mine. He firmly wraps his fingers around the back of my hand, urging me to lower it.

I hold my breath when he brings his mouth to the hollow of my ear. My thighs twitch again. But this time, the twitching doesn't stop.

"You're wrong," he growls.

"How am I wrong?" I ask him, this time in a whispering tone. "I don't think I'll ever believe a word that comes out of that mouth of yours, Jude."

I choke on the last few words, my confession suspended in time because we both know it's been the crux of our past.

Jude's endless lies. I never knew what to believe. I could never tell the difference between those and his truths. One minute he was promising protection and a forever. The next I'm battered, bruised, and broken. A hollow version of the woman I used to be.

And now that I'm finally resolved to get my life back together, here he is, standing in front of me in another suit with the same smug expression I'm all too familiar with. Cornering me like a viper ready to strike his prey. And I grow weak, fighting my willpower to stop him.

I reach for the lock again, attempting one last time.

"Do I need to prove it to you?" he asks, his voice sending shivers down my spine. My thighs grow hot, already wet for him.

"Prove what?"

"Prove to you that although it's been four years since I've tasted you, I haven't forgotten how you were made for this mouth you find so untrustworthy."

I slap my hand against the door, using it to steady myself the second Jude's hands are on me.

"I have to say," he grumbles in my ear. "I'm jealous pretty boy's eyes were the first to see you in this outfit instead of me. But there is one advantage I have over him."

He slides his hand across my stomach. At first, I think he's going to start inching south, but he surprises me by immediately cupping my breast. He finds my already peaked nipple and pinches it between the tips of his fingers.

I hiss at the sharp pain, leaning into the side of Jude's head. He's warm despite the icy tone in his voice.

He's jealous. He's jealous of Tyler.

"What advantage?" I ask as he rubs his fingers delicately over my nipple.

"He didn't get to touch you first," he confesses. "Your body was made for me."

My eyes flutter shut, and I tilt my head back, relishing in the way Jude's hands effortlessly explore every inch of my body.

I want him to stop. I try to think of the pain and hurt he's caused since the day I met him. I try to remember all the lies his family told. How they tore us apart, and how he chose them over me. He chose them over me and the future we were carving out on our own. But my thoughts struggle to make sense, caught in the haze of his touch.

He drags his nose along the back of my ear, bringing his lips to my skin, then he bites into my shoulder. Both his hands land on my hips, and he slides his large palms down the front of my skirt, lifting the hem and pulling it up to the tops of my thighs. He pulls the back high enough to expose the curve of my bare ass.

Jude wastes no time. His fingers are pressed firmly to the front of my thong, the lace acting as the only barrier. He drags them down my center, playing along my slit.

I gasp, tiny bursts of electricity exploding across my skin.

He moans and jerks his hips forward, his erection pressing into my bare ass as he rubs against me. I gasp again, pressing both my hands to the door for support.

"Tell me you haven't forgotten," he urges.

My wetness seeps through the fabric of my thong and onto his fingertips. He begins rubbing me, and I instinctively move against his hand, not wanting him to stop. Every move of his fingers is familiar.

"I haven't." I squeeze my eyes shut and tilt my head back. He shoves my thong aside, parting my wet lips. His fingers are slick, easily sliding between my folds, finding my swollen clit.

It's been months since I've been with a man, but when I think back on it, I haven't felt this since the last time I was with Jude. I push my hips back and into him. He groans, moving his wet fingers from the front of my thong to my mouth. He pries my lips apart, forcing me to suck on his fingers, tasting myself, then he pulls his fingers out and drags them down my chin and along my stretched neck. I press my back into him again. This time his whole body vibrates against me with a growl.

"Fuck," he grits out. "Keep grinding this beautiful ass

against me and I'll destroy this five thousand dollar-suit without regret."

The corner of my mouth lifts into a smirk. Good.

"Turn around," he demands.

I do as he says, pressing my back firmly to the door.

He surprises me by kneeling in front of me. Jude pries my legs apart, looking up at me with his hooded midnight eyes. My chest swells, the balloon inside inflating to an impossible size.

"I want to see if your sweet pussy remembers what it feels like to have my mouth against it." My entire body hums when he leans forward and shoves my thong aside, immediately bringing his mouth against me. He kisses my folds before he quickly slips his tongue between them. His tongue lands on my swollen clit, and I bite the tip of my tongue, relishing in the familiarity of it all. I didn't know it was possible to remember being with Jude in this way.

He sucks on me and breathes me in, groaning against me, his voice vibrating through my thighs. My legs are unsteady. My back stays flush against the door, and when I look down, he's staring up at me. There's an intensity in his eyes, as if he's seeing me for the first time. The fire and ice waging war are begging me to fall apart at the hands of his perfect mouth.

My body quivers, knowing it won't be long before I orgasm against his mouth. My nipples are peaked through the delicate silk of my top. Every nerve in my body is on alert.

He takes it one step further when he hooks two fingers inside me and rapidly pumps them in and out, curling them to land on the spot, working in tandem with my clit. I grasp the ends of his hair, burying them in his brown strands, anchoring myself to him. My knuckles turn white. My veins swell under my skin.

"Oh, God, Jude," I rasp.

He pulls his mouth away from me, continuing to pump his

fingers inside me. His lips are glistening from my arousal, and it turns me on even more.

"Does it remember?"

"Yes," I breathe.

"Do it for me, then, V. Come for me." He growls.

"I'm going to—" My heart races, and my body is nearing the edge when three knocks land on the door. They vibrate against my back, near the side of my head.

"Victoria?" Tyler's voice calls from the other side. He jiggles the handle. "Is everything okay in there?"

Jude hasn't moved his mouth or his hand. He continues working me, pretending as if Tyler isn't on the other side, and he isn't pumping two fingers inside me. He wraps his other hand around to my backside, gripping on to one of my bare ass cheeks. The sensation building inside me intensifies. I squeeze my eyes shut, not knowing what to do. I don't want Jude to stop, but now that Tyler is standing at the door, pounding his fist against it, I'm at odds.

Jude pulls his mouth away from me and lifts his free hand. He holds his finger against his mouth, silently begging me not to answer Tyler.

He winks, dragging the pad of his thumb across his bottom lip. He sucks on it before bringing his mouth back to my center. Fuck, I'm going to come just from that gesture alone. I'm on the edge once more when Tyler's fist lands on the door again.

"I'm fine," I choke out, resisting the urge to cry out from my impending orgasm.

"It's been a while since you went in there," Tyler calls. "I wasn't sure if you were sick or if something had happened."

"No..." I lean my head to the side, swallowing. "I'm fine, really."

"Jude," I hiss, looking down. All I see is the top of his head, moving against me. "We can't. You need to stop."

It takes everything in me not to regret the words I'm speaking right now, but I can't continue knowing Tyler is on the other side. The knot in my chest unraveled the second Jude touched me but now it's twisting again. I can't, knowing I'm on a date with someone else. Even if I only just met Tyler the other day, it feels wrong.

Jude pulls away from me. He groans and pulls himself to a stand. His hair is a mopped mess on top of his head, a contradiction to the way he appeared when he first walked in here.

His mouth is still glistening from my wetness, but his eyes have narrowed in anger.

"Fine." Jude groans, licking his lips.

"I'm on a date," I point out again. His eyes flicker in anger. "And so are you."

The corner of his mouth curls. I don't know why he finds our situation amusing but his expression shifts. He drags the pad of his thumb across his lips again before he presses it to my bottom lip. His eyes fall to my mouth, watching as he spreads the mixture of the both of us onto me. "But just remember... if you end up fucking pretty boy tonight, don't forget who tasted you first."

Anger bursts across my skin in flames. Jude has no right to be bitter for me stopping what we've done. He's on a date, just the same as I am. Only my date is pounding on the other side of the bathroom door, hoping I haven't ditched him.

Disappointment replaces the anger. I hold my breath as he reaches beside me and unlocks the door. I readjust my skirt and fix my hair while Jude slips behind the door, hiding in the corner. I eye him and grip the handle of the door. "I was right," I tell him. "You haven't changed in four years. You're still the same Jude Harding you've always been."

I leave Jude and open the door to find Tyler patiently waiting on the other side of it. I swipe my fingers across my mouth and sniff. I didn't bother looking in the mirror before walking out. I don't know if my lipstick is smeared, mixing with the concoction Jude left on my mouth. I don't know if my cheeks are still flaming red. My body aches, having never reached an orgasm.

I follow Tyler back to our table, passing Jude's date. She's still sitting in the booth, absently scrolling through her phone, waiting for him. And when Tyler holds my seat out for me again, I can't get the last words I said to Jude out of my head.

I spoke the truth when I said he hadn't changed in four years. I just don't know if I still meant how he'll always be a Harding, or if I meant how he was right...

My body was made for him to touch.

January 7th

Dear J,

I've never been more nervous than I was tonight. I spent hours changing my outfit. Nothing seemed to sit right on my body or make me look worthy enough to be in your family's presence. It wasn't just your father I was meeting. It was your older brother, Lennon. It was your youngest brother, Micah. It was everyone I knew would be at this dinner.

Everyone who mattered to you.

I was nervous walking into your father's house. We walked through the old Victorian, and I followed you into the dining room. I'd never seen so many staff for one single dinner. Servers and butlers. The endless shuffling in and out of a million rooms. Or so it seemed. I held my breath as you held out a chair for me. A seat at what I'm sure was one of many Harding tables. I sat beside you and patiently waited until your family asked me questions. You discreetly reached under the table and gripped my thigh. I savored your touch, clung onto it like a life raft, and placed my hand over yours.

Your father eyed me across the table, skepticism filling his dark stare. I knew he wasn't impressed the moment I told him my major. I knew he wasn't impressed when I told him my mother was a math teacher and my father was a landscaper. Lennon stared at me with polite interest. Micah asked most of the questions, eager to know the woman who'd somehow been able to light up his brother's face. He was the only one besides you who made me feel like I wasn't swimming alone in a pool of sharks.

The uncertainty I felt after dinner tonight has been weighing on me. If only because I know how much your family means to you. I just didn't realize I was doomed before I'd even stepped foot in that house. Because it didn't matter what type of dress I chose or how polite I was, I was never going to fit in. I would never be good enough.

Despite all of it, though, I know you love me.

I won't lie and say we're perfect. Some days I'm secure in what we have. I know you're falling in love with me, the same way I am with you. But then there are nights like tonight. The nights where you promise me you'll come to my dorm or meet me and my friends for dinner. Instead, you don't show until you're knocking on my door at three in the morning. Your eyes blood-shot, your speech slurred. Every time I ask you where you've been, you tell me you've been spending time with Kappa Sigma. Networking, you call it. I say it's bullshit. You tell me you drank too much, and you didn't want to drive home. You felt safe with me. You tell me it's only temporary. That once you're in their fraternity, you'll pull back. You'll be more reliable. You swear it's because you need to follow in your father's footsteps. Live up to the Harding legacy.

I have a hard time digesting those nights. Some nights I lie in bed and watch you sleep. Your small breaths push out from between your perfect mouth, and I think about what you told me about your mother and how she died. How you couldn't help her, and you feel like it was your fault. You've sworn to protect me, unlike you were able to for her. I don't know why you worry about that when I know my love for you is stronger than anything you could ever do to me.

I lie in bed and watch you, memorizing all the places on my body where your hands have touched. When the list becomes too long, I start over. I remember the way it felt to have your mouth between my legs and your tongue sliding across my wetness. I remember how it feels to have you buried in me so deep, it's as if we've become one person instead of two. I remember the way your fingers mold to the curves of my flesh, and the way you kiss me, whispering promises of how you will love me forever, even after this life.

I keep those memories bottled up on the nights you come to me with half your heart guarded. The other half spilling over with love for me.

CHAPTER TWELVE

Jude

THREE MINUTES AND TWO GUMMIES LATER, I SNEAK OUT OF the women's bathroom and head back to my table where Laurel is waiting for me.

My mouth is still warm and swollen from rubbing it all over Victoria. I can still taste the sweetness of her on my tongue, even though I've chewed two orange gummies. I fix my hair and tie before sliding back into the booth beside Laurel.

"About time," she says beside me. "I ordered another glass of champagne for myself. I hope you don't mind."

"Not at all." I shake my head and wrap my fingers around my glass of seltzer water. I bring it to my nose, smelling it just in case Laurel decided to slip something inside it or convinced the waiter to swap it out for something stronger.

Either scenario wouldn't be surprising.

When I'm satisfied that Laurel hasn't spiked my drink, I take a long sip while she downs her entire glass in one gulp.

I'm disappointed in myself. Everything I put in my mouth washes Victoria's taste away. It's been years since I've tasted her and felt her warm pussy on my mouth. Watching her reaction to me after all this time, knowing it hasn't changed, made my dick perk up, and my heart beat like a sledgehammer.

For years, I've felt hollow. I still haven't processed the reasoning why she left as abruptly as she did, and the pain of knowing I was the cause of it has left me broken. But being with Victoria those few minutes in the bathroom smoothed over the pieces of me that are fractured. It didn't matter that the fucking pretty boy she was on a date with interrupted us.

I peek over the rim of my glass, expecting to see Victoria and Tyler sitting at their table near the window. Two empty wine glasses sit on the top of the table, though, and now both seats are empty. They've gone.

I scoff and shake my head.

"So," Laurel says, leaning into me. I'd almost forgotten she was still sitting beside me.

She adjusts herself in the booth to face me and wraps her arm around the back of my neck. She keeps fucking doing that, even when I've shown her I'm not interested.

I should have known this dinner was going to turn out this way, and it was only made worse when Victoria showed up with her fucking date.

Lennon ditched me at the last minute, telling me he was stuck at the office scheduling meetings for a few accounts our firm has overseas. And there was no shot in hell Madison was going to show up without him on her arm. Which left only Laurel and me.

Deep down, I know Lennon did this on purpose. He knew I'd snag his bait when he threw his pathetic little pity party, begging me to meet Laurel.

We've been sitting here for over an hour, and she has yet to bring up what she's wanting from our family's firm. Lennon was right about one thing: I am the best negotiator out of the three of us Harding men. But it's impossible to negotiate when you aren't talking about anything that needs negotiating.

"Have you ever been to London?" Laurel hiccups. Her eyes are glossed over, and her cheeks are pinched pink. She's drunk. *Fucking great.*

"I have," I mutter, rolling my eyes.

"Well," she hiccups again, followed by a giggle. "My family has an office out there, and I try to go at least a few times a year. If you ever wanted to take a trip over together, we could." Laurel plays with the collar of my suit, rubbing her fingers across the smooth fabric. Her nails are perfectly manicured, each one painted in gold. She matches the accents of this restaurant. It makes my stomach sick and my skin crawl having her draped all over me.

But the faraway look in Laurel's eye tells me we're past the point of talking business. We're almost past the point of us being able to make any sort of coherent conversation. My high finally starts to kick in. *Thank God.*

"Oh." She pouts, lifting her glass to her face. "I'm empty."

I shove the glass away from her face and place it back down on the table, sliding my glass toward her. "Here, drink mine."

She lifts her hooded, hazy eyes to mine. Her brown hair is curled around her face, and her lipstick has faded. Guilt seeps into my bones. Knowing my father is simply using her for his benefit eats away at me. Laurel is collateral damage for a larger goal my father has to make as much money off Laurel's family as possible, and they're using me to get to it.

Laurel dramatically waves her hand at my glass, the corners of her mouth turning down into a frown. "Your drink is boring. I took a sip of it when you were gone for what felt like forever. That's why I ordered more champagne. I practically had to flag down the waiter to come back to our table just to bring it to me," she scoffs, turning away from me.

She's blaming me for being drunk. She's drunk because I couldn't help myself and followed Victoria into the bathroom. It's my fault.

She lifts her empty glass and tilts her head back, desperate for another drop of champagne. She sticks her tongue out, licking the inside. When she doesn't get much, she turns toward me with another frown. "Can we order another?"

"Maybe next time," I tell her, removing her hand from my lapel.

She sits back in the booth and tilts her head back, rolling it to the side and looking up at me with her champagne-soaked eyes.

"You're being nice to me considering we didn't get a chance to talk about work."

"It's okay." I nod, reassuring her.

She looks off into the distance and blows out a heavy breath. "Why is it okay, though?" The corner of her mouth lifts into a smile. "I probably cost you and your family a deal. At least not until we can meet up again. Maybe when I'm not as drunk."

I stare at Victoria and pretty boy's empty table. The wine glasses are gone, and the silverware has been replaced.

I look back at Laurel to find her eyes pinned to mine. They may appear to be far away, but her thoughts are as obvious to me as a neon sign. She feels trapped. A situation I'm all too familiar with.

"It's okay because I get it," I tell her. "I've been there myself."

"WHAT THE FUCK, JUDE?" Lennon yells. "You had one job, and you didn't even get it done."

"Are you fucking serious right now?" I yell back.

Lennon and I are standing in the middle of Victoria's store.

I'm thankful I'm the only one here. I told the crew to not show up until after lunch when we were ready to begin painting. The hardware store Cain ordered the paint from mixed the wrong color, setting us back half a day. We ran the situation by Victoria before she headed to her morning class, and she said it was fine since she had plans tonight, anyway. I wasn't entirely sure what her plans consisted of, but the sinking sensation in my stomach didn't go unnoticed. I imagined her going on another date with Tyler. Perhaps I'd ruined their date last night and that's why they left early. Or she enjoyed the rest of her date so much that she agreed to meet him again tonight.

I also could be overthinking it.

"Yes, I'm fucking serious!" Lennon yells, pulling me back to our conversation.

He's out of place in Victoria's store. He looks like one of those corporate assholes in the movies who show up to construction sites wearing those stupid ass hard hats. Where they stand around watching everyone else work but don't do the actual work themselves. Typical.

He hasn't moved more than a few feet into the store, staying close to the door. Granted, the floor is still covered in a dust of white powder from finishing the drywall sanding. I was in the process of vacuuming it up when Lennon suddenly showed up to the store unannounced. He stands in front of the door with one hand slid into the pocket of his slacks, using the other to massage his forehead.

"It's not that big of a deal, Lennon," I tell him, attempting to lower our voices. "It isn't my fault she decided to drink an entire bottle's worth of champagne."

"No," he says. "But what? You just sat back and watched her down it all without talking to her about a single product or term we offer?"

I bite down on the inside of my cheek. My mind wanders to

the reason why Laurel was practically wasted by the time I made it back to our table.

Black mini skirt hiked up over two full round cheeks.

A blue, silk tank barely covering Victoria's perked breasts.

The way my fingers pressed to her center, immediately soaked with her wetness.

The way her mouth fell open as I stared up at her, my tongue pressed against her warm clit. The familiar feelings I once had for Victoria sparked, coming back to life.

But then I remember the fiery glare she shot me before storming out of the room.

No matter how long it's been, I still hate myself for causing Victoria pain. All I've ever caused her is hurt and pain. We aren't even together, and I still manage to hurt her, one way or another.

I hold on to the best parts of last night, telling myself she doesn't hate me as much as she'd like me to believe.

"Laurel is a grown woman, Lennon," I continue, shoving my feelings for Victoria aside. "I made sure she made it home safely, and I can meet up with her another time."

"You're insane if you think Dad is just going to let this go."

"I didn't think he would. And let me guess, he sent you down here to lecture me on how I, once again, proved I'm a failure."

"Jesus, Jude." He slides his hand down the side of his face with a frustrated groan. "You aren't a failure. I admit, this doesn't help your case to Dad, though." He nods his head, gesturing to Victoria's store.

"It's *your* opinion that I'm not a failure. Not Dad's."

"You got me there," he admits with a laugh.

I don't find him amusing.

My dad might be the biggest cock sucking asshole of the century, but that doesn't mean I don't know there's still an inherent part of me that seeks his approval. A small, microscopic part, but it's there, nonetheless. Out of all my traits, I loathe that one the most.

"Thanks for the reassurance, asshole," I grumble to Lennon. "Makes me feel a shit ton better."

I walk over to one of the worktables and begin absentmindedly sorting a pile of nails. I separate them by size for absolutely no other reason than to make it appear like I'm busy. I'm hoping if I do, Lennon will take the hint and leave.

Not that I don't enjoy my brother's company. At least about ninety-nine percent of the time. The other one percent I spend wishing he resisted our father more. I wish he didn't sink into the lifestyle as easily as he does.

Minutes pass without Lennon speaking another word. For a second, I think he might have left, too angry with me to continue our conversation, but I'm surprised when I look up and see him still here standing by the front door.

With Victoria standing beside him.

I swallow, prickles making their way down the back of my neck.

"Victoria," I say quickly, dropping the few nails I was holding back onto the pile I still haven't sorted.

She ignores me, turning to my brother. Her cheeks have paled, and she fusses with a few strands of hair that have fallen in front of her face. "Hi, Lennon."

"Victoria," Lennon says, shifting his eyes to me, then back to Victoria. "I didn't know you were back in the city."

I cross the room, growing closer to the two of them. It's the closest I've been to Lennon since he walked in here, but my need to be closer grows since Victoria is standing beside him. At one point in time, I would have considered Lennon and Victoria friends, despite the strain her mere presence had on my family. Mine and Lennon's relationship has always been complicated and complex. At the same time that my brother begs me to play the same part he does in this family, he also understands the double life I've lived for as long as I can remember.

For a brief moment, I nearly forget all the ugliness that happened between Victoria and my family, naively believing this reunion with Lennon would be a happy one.

It isn't.

Victoria's breath hitches, her emerald green eyes on the verge of tears.

"Lennon," she breathes and fusses with her hair again, tucking the strands behind her ear. She sets her bag down on the table behind her and turns back to him. She folds her hands in front of her, nervously looking down before she lifts her eyes to mine.

I haven't seen her since last night. She left in anger and disappointment, but now she's looking at me for a way out, wanting me to rescue her. It's the same expression she gave me the night she met my family for the first time. The night my father wore a permanent scowl all while grilling her about her menial upbringing. His words, not mine, nor Lennon's.

"This is Victoria's shop," I quickly say.

"Really?" Lennon asks with a quirked brow.

"Yeah," she mutters. "Riley gifted it to me when I came back to the city about a month ago. She hired Cain's crew to help renovate it." She points to the ceiling. "I live upstairs."

I hold my breath; I'm not certain why. Lennon may question my choices, but he never says things to hurt me. He's always had my back, knowing our father never did.

"Wow." He smiles weakly. "Congratulations, then."

"Thank you. How have you been?" Kind. She's always been so fucking kind. Her eyes soften. She still seems in shock seeing my brother, but she seems calm enough now to speak cordially.

"Great." He nods. "Busy."

"That's good." She nods, too.

I watch as Lennon's gaze falls to the scar on Victoria's knee. She's wearing a pair of frayed shorts, and the scar runs from the top of her knee, disappearing underneath the loose threads. Lennon frowns.

Victoria follows his eyes and looks down. She drops her shoulders, quickly placing her hand over the front of her shorts. She isn't covering the scar, but Lennon's stare has definitely made her more self-conscious.

"Well," Lennon sighs, clapping his hands together. "I better go. I have a meeting in an hour across town." He looks at Victoria. "It's good to see you, Victoria. I'm glad you're doing well. You seem happy." Then he looks at me. "I'll text you later with a new time to meet up."

Victoria might not know what he means, but I certainly do. Another scheduled meeting with Laurel.

Lennon leaves. When the glass door closes, I turn to Victoria. She snatches her bag from the table, already heading in the direction of her apartment upstairs.

"Wait," I say, stepping forward.

She stops, tilting her head back. She has her back to me, her tan shoulders on display from her sleeveless top. It's a tank similar to the one she was wearing last night, but it isn't cut as deep down the center of her breasts, and her stomach is covered. The loose, white fabric sways as she spins around.

"I don't want to talk right now, Jude."

"I just want to make sure you're okay."

"Why?" she asks. "Because your brother was standing in my bookstore looking at me the same way he always has? With pity and disdain. Pity for what happened." She points to the exposed scar on her knee. "Disdain for, I don't know, existing in your world." She scoffs in disbelief and feigns a laugh of irony. Then she stares at me between tear-soaked lashes.

"We exist in the same world, Victoria." Flashbacks of arguments we've had in the past come flooding back. Arguments in Victoria's dorm. Arguments on the rooftop of the frat house.

"No." She blinks and inhales a deep, resolving breath. "We made a deal not to let our past affect you working here. Last night shouldn't have happened, and seeing your brother made me realize I don't want to make the same mistake twice."

She grips her bag in her hand and spins around again to head upstairs. But, being the idiot I am, I stop her.

I grab onto her wrist and place my hand firmly on her hip. I walk her back until she meets the wall. Her bag drops to the floor, and she gasps as another tear falls.

"You're lying," I growl, placing one hand above her head, caging her in. Calling her out on her lie was the first thought to pop into my head. There's too much history, pain, tragedy, ugliness, and love for her to not feel something. *Anything.*

I'm being selfish, I know. Selfish for still wanting to be near Victoria when I know being around her is a double-edged sword, piercing her heart over and over.

How is it that the person you love the most can hurt you the most?

Tipping her chin higher, she leans back against the wall. Her cheeks heat, and her glare turns ice cold. "I think we both know who the true liar is between the two of us."

"I may be a liar, but at least I'm being honest about last night." I growl, leaning into her. "You wanted me to touch you. You wanted me to press you against that wall and fuck you, even when Tyler was pounding his fist on the other side of it. Because you know when you're with me, your body feels more alive than it ever could with anyone else. It always has."

She smells like coconut, and my heart pounds, drawing my nose closer to her. The tip of it is almost touching hers. It wouldn't take much for me to close the inch space between us and kiss her. I resist the urge, waiting for Victoria to give me a sign.

"Now, why don't you be honest with me?" I ask.

"I am."

"Another lie. Try again."

I tilt my head and slide my hand along her hip, drawing her closer. Her stomach is pressed against me, and my growing erection pushes against the zipper of my jeans.

She lifts her mouth, and for a moment I think she might give in. I want her to give in.

I'm staring into Victoria's eyes, watching as the colors swirl, when she lifts her hand and slides it between us. She places her palm on her stomach, never once breaking eye contact. The back of her hand presses against me, and I'm suddenly aware of what she's doing. My heart bleeds, and my vision blurs. The world around me fades. All I feel is Victoria's hand pressed between us.

I allow my hand to fall away from her side, and I take a step back.

"Like I said," her voice quivers. "Last night was a mistake."

She pushes off the wall and grabs her bag off the floor to sling it over her shoulder before she opens the door and then slams it shut behind her.

I, being the idiot I am, don't move from the spot where I'm standing. Instead, I stare at her door until I can bring myself to go back to work.

CHAPTER THIRTEEN

VICTORIA

I HOLD MY BREATH AND WAIT.

I wait until I no longer hear Jude downstairs and I can sneak out before the rest of the crew return from their lunch.

They're working a late shift today since the paint order was screwed up. That's what Cain told me, anyway.

I quickly type out a text to Riley, hoping she's available for a night out. I originally didn't have plans for tonight, but I knew I couldn't be here to face Jude after what happened last night in the women's restroom of Eclipse. It's ridiculous, truly. Making up excuses not to face someone whose face was literally buried between your legs the night before. But I know I can't face Jude. If only for the fact that I haven't stopped thinking about him since.

The way his tongue effortlessly slid between my folds. The way my stomach ignited at his touch. From the way his hands melded to my body, you would think he'd spent the last four years forcing himself to remember. Maybe his hands retained muscle memory.

It's the only explanation I can come up with.

I'm wearing the same black mini skirt as last night but have paired it with the shirt I wore to class today. A white silk top. It isn't cut as low or short as the one from last night. I'm a little more comfortable in it than I was with the blue one.

I step onto the sidewalk when I get a reply from Riley saying she won't be able to make it as she had to take a quick trip to the Providence mall in Rhode Island to grab a few things for the studio. I'm not entirely sure what items she would find at the Providence mall that she couldn't find in Boston, but I leave our conversation there. I don't prod her for more details, determined to keep my night going.

Not one single part of me considers asking Tyler if he's busy. Not that our date last night was terrible, but I found it impossible to look at him without feeling immense guilt. I've never been the type of woman to go on a date and end up with my thighs clamped around someone else's head in a restaurant bathroom. I figure it's safe to say that Tyler and I won't be going on a second date.

I don't have to venture too far down the street. I keep close to the sidewalk and search for a pub that calls to me. Certain areas of Boston have streets lined with dozens of dive bars and pubs. I set my sights on heading in the direction of campus, hoping I can grab a few drinks there. Surely, there will be a sizeable crowd. I slide my phone back into my purse, knowing there isn't anyone else I would rather invite than Riley.

My mother used to worry I'd kept my social circle too small. *You can't live your life thinking you're the only one to exist in it,* she used to tell me.

I blink my mother's words away and step into the first pub I come across. The front of the restaurant is lined with curved picture windows, and the walls are painted a rich, bright, crimson red. Above the row of windows is a dark stained, wooden sign with the name *Lights Out* painted in gold letters. The warm scent of whiskey greets me when I step through the front door. I elbow my way through the thin crowd, finding a seat at the end of the bar.

"Hey there," the bartender is quick to greet me. He lays a coaster on the counter. "What can I get for you?"

I twist my mouth, unsure of what type of drink I'm in the mood for. Anything to erase Jude from my thoughts. "What do you have that's super strong?" I ask with a grin.

"That kind of night, huh?" He arches his eyebrows and laughs.

"Yes." I sigh, dropping my shoulders.

"Right on." He nods and tilts his head up as if he's sifting through a mental menu of cocktails. A few seconds later, he eyes me. "How do you feel about gin? It makes for a good vessel when you're aiming for the strong end of the scale."

"I love it." I grin.

I don't love gin. Actually, I don't know if I do or not. I've never been a big drinker, and if it weren't for the night that ruined mine and Jude's lives, I would probably drink more often. But I don't, so I figure it's about damn time I let loose.

Jude's choices four years ago don't have any effect on the ones I make for myself today. I'm an adult, and if I want to fucking drink at a bar, I can.

"Sounds good." The bartender grins. "I'll be right back."

"Thank you." I set my purse in my lap and drape my hands over it, looking around the bar.

The exposed brick is dotted with an array of framed photos of everything from scenery of Boston to celebrities and cars. None of it makes sense. I feel myself smiling, anyway, taking in the rest of the place. It's a college bar for sure, with Boston College banners draped above the doors and hallways. The groups surrounding the small space are all decked out in campus gear. Shirts, hoodies, and hats.

The bartender returns with my drink, setting it in front of me.

"Name's Brandon, by the way." He nods once. "I'll set a tab up for you. Let me know when you're ready for another."

"Thank you, Brandon."

He raps his knuckles on the end of the countertop with a smile before heading back toward the front of the bar.

I eye the concoction in front of me and wrap my fingers around it to lift it to my nose. It smells great despite Brandon suggesting it as a strong sort of drink.

I take a sip, the alcohol dry and bitter on my tongue as I swallow it back. The more I drink, the warmer my chest and belly grow. I start to feel the effects when I've downed my first drink and asked Brandon to make me another.

My vision wobbles slightly. I should have grabbed something to eat before I left, but I was desperate to get out of my building. I knew Jude was no longer downstairs working, but the four walls surrounding me were suffocating.

Seeing and talking to Lennon on top of what happened with Jude last night is enough emotional baggage to last me a lifetime.

Dance used to make for a great escape when my thoughts overwhelmed me. Then when I lost dance, I tried to turn to reading. But when I was caught up in my own thoughts, I found myself reading the same sentence over and over.

I'm halfway through my second drink when I feel someone slide onto the stool beside me.

"You used to be in one of my classes, didn't you?" The heavy voice beside me pulls me out of my drowning thoughts.

"I'm sorry?" I spin on my stool and face the man sitting next to me. His sandy blond hair is tousled on top of his head, and his white teeth shine under the gold lights of the bar.

"Economics? With Professor Stevens?" He quirks an eyebrow

and leans back in his seat. "Two years ago." He's facing me now with his fingers resting on his chin. He keeps one arm outstretched; his hand wrapped around his beer bottle sitting on the counter.

I narrow my eyes and smirk. "No, I don't think so." I giggle, and my cheeks heat. "I'm sorry, I think you have the wrong girl."

It's impossible he would be talking about me. I was in Texas two years ago.

"Huh." The corners of his mouth curl into a devious grin. "I could have sworn I've seen you around campus at least."

"Maybe." I shrug my shoulder and take another sip of my drink. Brandon has already placed a fresh one next to the one I'm working on. I can't remember if I flagged him down for another one or if he knew I would end up asking for a refill, anyway. Either way, I'm thankful when I slurp up the rest and start on the next.

Yep, this is definitely edging on helping me forget about Jude and his brother.

"So, you do go here, though?" the man beside me asks.

"I do." I nod, grinning against the straw. I pull it into my mouth and take a long sip. The more I drink, the easier the liquid slides down into my belly.

The man stares at me, expecting me to expand on my answer, but I don't. My body feels lighter. The alcohol warms my blood and clouds my thoughts. I'm staring at the man in front of me, but all I see is Jude. Jude and his fucking five thousand dollar-suit. Midnight eyes. His mouth on me.

"Name's Reese!" the man yells over the music.

"What?" I ask, unsure I heard him correctly.

"My name is *Reese*."

"Victoria!" I yell back, pointing to my chest.

Reese continues the conversation, but it's difficult to make out what he's saying. His voice is drowned out by the music blasting through the bar. My phone vibrates in my purse. I pull it out, ignoring him. Maybe Riley got back from Providence early and decided she was able to carve out a little time to meet me after all. Maybe it's my mother sending over another hundred photos of her villa in the Mediterranean.

But the text open on my screen isn't from Riley or my mom. It's from Jude.

I narrow my eyes, hoping it will bring my vision into focus. Perhaps gin makes you hallucinate. I'm tempted to ask Brandon, but I'm too interested in the possibility the text truly is from Jude.

> Jude: Where are you?

I swallow the dryness coating my tongue, staring at the words on my screen. Reading Jude's name at the top of my messages is surreal. I could have sworn I'd deleted his number after he'd made several attempts to call me once I moved to Texas. I must have convinced myself I had and forgotten about it.

My heart pumps faster, already accelerated by the alcohol-soaked blood in my veins. I quickly glance at Reese beside me and nod as if I'm listening to the story he's telling. After a few seconds, I snatch up my phone and respond to Jude.

> Me: Jude? You still have my number?

His response is quick.

> Jude: Of course, I do. And apparently you still have mine. I asked you where you were.

> Me: I don't have to tell you where I am. I don't belong to you anymore.

My fingers fly across the screen, despite my double vision. I drop my phone in my lap and look at the man sitting next to me. He still hasn't moved, determined to finish his explanation of the classes he's taking. I blink away the fog clouding my brain. Am I truly so tipsy that I'm unable to keep up with casual conversation?

But then again, even if it weren't for the fact that Jude was texting me in the middle of my drunken adventure, I wouldn't be able to focus on the conversation Reese is attempting to have.

My phone vibrates with another text.

> Jude: I need to talk to you.

> Me: No. I'm busy.

> Jude: Are you with Tyler?

I don't immediately answer Jude. My eyes find their way to the back of the bar. I didn't notice when I'd walked in here, but there's a small dance floor set off in the back corner. A man sits at a small table with a laptop in front of him, his face lit in blue and white. His headphones are placed cockeyed on his head, only one side covering his ear. He bobs his head, watching the music he's playing move through the crowd.

> Me: Yes, we're on our seconddd date.

> Jude: Where?

I don't give my next text a second thought.

> Me: I'm at the bare nearrr campus. Lisdhts out.

I grin, satisfied with my response to Jude. The room spins, and my arms and legs go numb despite the warmth radiating across it. I stick the straw of my drink in my mouth and draw out what's left of the liquid. It gurgles and bubbles against the cubes of ice sitting at the bottom. When I run out of alcohol, I frown and set the glass down on the bar.

"Here," Brandon says. "Drink a bit of this water and then we'll see if you want another."

I nod, unable to look him in the eye. I feel ridiculous for getting drunk off three small drinks, but I guess it truly doesn't take much when your body isn't accustomed to alcohol.

I mutter a thanks in appreciation, and my phone vibrates again.

> Jude: Are you drunk?
>
> Me: Maybe. Maybee not.

I wait but don't get a response, so I smile to myself and stuff my phone back into my purse, then wrap it around my shoulder and slide out of my seat. I make note to hold onto the counter to steady myself. My feet land on the floor clumsily. It feels as if I'm stepping on one of those wobbly, worn-down bridges.

"Woah," Reese chuckles, holding onto my free hand. I look up and catch his kind eyes. "Are you okay?"

"Yeah." I nod. "I think so. It's been a while since I've had a drink, so I think it's hitting me harder than expected."

"It always does." He laughs and leans forward, bringing his mouth to my ear. "Do you want to dance?"

My throat runs dry, and I tuck a few loose strands of hair behind my ear. I ditched the braid this time, opting for long waves.

I close my eyes and shake my head. "I don't dance anymore."

"Come on. Just one dance."

"I don't know." I chew on the inside of my cheek and stare nervously at the dance floor. Everyone seems to be having fun. The expressions on their faces look like the ones I used to wear.

I'm still standing in between my seat and Reese. He has his hand wrapped around mine, drawing circles on my palm. If I wasn't watching it, I wouldn't have known his hand was on mine. I feel nothing. I'm numb. I inhale a deep breath and nod. My legs are numb, anyway, so maybe it won't hurt as bad to dance. That's what I tell myself, at least. I might feel the consequences of it tomorrow, but Jude's texts have lit a fire inside me.

Reese tugs on my hand, and I follow him to the edge of the crowd. He pushes our way through to the middle, the couples around us not caring that we're searching for our own spot. But I'm thankful when his hands land on my hips, guiding me.

It feels like it's been forever since my body has moved to a steady rhythm. I sway my hips and lift my arms over my head. It doesn't take long for my body to move the way it used to. It's as if I'm riding a bike for the first time after four years.

Reese moves behind me and grabs onto my hips, pulling me flush against his chest. I tilt my head back and rest it on his shoulder. Flecks of gold spin above me. They spin like the kaleidoscope of blue and black burned into my memory. My chest swells as Reese moves us faster. Sweat drips down my neck, and the song we're dancing to bleeds into the next. I don't know how many songs we've danced to, but suddenly my body feels heavy.

When I open my eyes again, I see my hands pressed flat to the floor. Dozens of feet move around me. My dark blue nail polish blends in with the hard tiles beneath me. My eyes water, and my breathing becomes shallow. I try to pull myself to a stand, but I can't. I'm frozen, my legs refusing to move and lift me up. The people around me don't care. Their feet don't stop. A tear slides down my cheek, then another. My entire body is numb aside from my cheeks. Warm liquid slides effortlessly, soaking into my skin.

I look up, hoping Reese is still above me. I search for his hand but instead, I see Jude. At least I think I do. He's wearing a suit like the one he was wearing last night. He's out of place here, surrounded by college students in their maroon and gray Boston college gear.

The people around us have parted slightly, but only for the interaction I see unfolding above me.

White light flashes across Jude and Reese. Their shouting is mixed with the heavy, pulsating beat vibrating through the floor to my palms.

"Get away from her!" Jude yells.

Why is he here? How did he get here? Nothing makes sense. All I focus on is the fact that I'm suddenly on the floor, and I can't move.

Reese yells back, but I can't hear what he says. His mouth is open wide, and his eyebrows are knitted in anger.

Jude leans down and attempts to wrap his hand around my arm. I try to reach for him, but he's pulled away.

"Stay away from her," Reese bellows.

"Fuck you, man," Jude seethes, pointing a finger in Reese's face. "Don't fucking touch her."

"Jude!" I try to yell. "Stop."

No one hears me, and I'm still on the floor. I grunt, trying to muster enough strength to lift myself up. Suddenly, as if my body has decided to wake up, a sharp pain shoots down the back of my leg. I cry out, releasing another sob. I'm so fucking stupid. I'm so fucking drunk.

I look up at Jude again. His suit is unbuttoned, and he's ditched his tie. Anger is etched into every angle of his gorgeous face. Even when he's angry, I still find the beauty in him.

"She's the one who wanted to dance." Reese gestures toward me. "How was I supposed to know she was too wasted to stand on her own?"

"I swear to God," Jude spits, his voice sounding more

strained. He moves a step over, shielding half my body with his. "Try to touch her again and you're fucking dead."

"Fine. She's your wh—" Reese retorts with a sneer, but the next words out of his mouth are lost on me. I can't make them out. They get lost in the events that happen next. It all happens so fast. Jude's arm flies out, and his fist connects with Reese's jaw.

Jude only punches him once. Reese stumbles back, falling into a few people dancing behind him. They catch him and help him stand back up. Blood drips from his mouth.

Reese gently taps his finger to his mouth and gives the both of us a sneer.

My stomach wobbles, and my throat swells. I think I might throw up.

I'm still sobbing when two arms wrap around me and I'm lifted from the floor. A searing pain shoots down the back of my leg, but I'm thankful to at least not be on my hands and knees anymore. I crack my eyes open, watching as we make our way through the crowd. Lights flash across Jude's crisp, white shirt. His chest is warm and safe.

We've made it halfway through the bar when Jude gently sets me down on a nearby stool. It's not the same one I was sitting at before, but I recognize the face on the other side of the bar. I hiss and grit my teeth, attempting to adjust myself on the seat. Why can't I go back to a few minutes ago when my body was numb? Now it's as if every nerve is exploding like a show of fireworks.

Jude places his hand on my cheek, bringing his face to mine. The closer he leans in, the more focused he becomes. "Are you okay?"

I squeeze my eyes shut. I can't tell if I'm nauseous from the drinks or from the pain. I shake my head, pressing my lips together.

"Okay," he reassures me. "You'll be okay."

"You were supposed to be painting." I struggle to make the words out, the glint of his gold cufflinks catching my attention. "Suits aren't exactly the best clothes to wear for that sort of job."

"I couldn't stay long. I had a meeting afterward." He clips followed by a heavy sigh.

I open my mouth again but stop when he cuts our conversation short. He digs in his pocket and slaps his hand on the counter.

Here," he tells Brandon behind the bar. "This should cover whatever drinks you gave her and your tips for the rest of the night."

"I can pay my own tab," I mumble.

Jude ignores me.

Brandon grabs the money and looks between Jude and me, stunned. I don't know how much Jude's given him. It's probably ten times more than my tab. Knowing him, he doesn't care.

He scoops me up again. I land the same way, with my legs over one of his arms while his other is wrapped around my back. Even in my drunken state, I'm aware of Jude's body against mine. My stomach aches, and the tears are still fresh on my cheeks. By the time he pushes us through the front door and begins carrying me home, I've rested my head upon his chest.

Everything after that moment fades to black.

CHAPTER FOURTEEN

Jude

THE MOONLIGHT POURS THROUGH THE TWO WINDOWS above Victoria's bed. I've been watching her sleep all night. She barely moved for the first four hours. At hour five, her lips parted. At hour six, she shifted positions, turning on her side. At hour seven, she whispered my name.

I'm still dressed in the same black pants and collared shirt as I was yesterday. The crisp fabric is now wrinkled, and black streaks run down the left side of my chest.

I recline in Victoria's wicker chair positioned in the corner of her small room, resting my elbow on the arm, and propping my chin up with my hand. Little pieces of broken wood dig into my back, but I don't care. I can't take my eyes away from her. I study her. Concentrate on her breathing. The way her ribs contract, shifting the sheets draped across her body.

I swallow the emotion thick in my throat. Seeing her drunk and sobbing on the dance floor will live forever in my brain after last night. Pain and torment ripped through me. The echoes still rattle inside me now.

My phone pings in my pocket, alerting me that the two

coffees and donuts I ordered from the twenty-four-hour café down the street have arrived. I'm not very hungry, but I could use the caffeine. At this point, I've been up for over eighteen hours. My mind weighs on me, begging my eyelids to take a rest, but I refuse. I sneak out of her room and tiptoe down the stairs leading to the bookstore, navigating my way around the industrial size buckets of paint and the pallet of flooring we have yet to install. I quickly grab the brown bag and drink tray sitting on the ground outside the front door, then bound back up the stairs as quietly as possible. Wearing these shoes compared to my usual boots helps. When I return to Victoria's room, I sigh with relief to see she's still asleep.

She's laying on her stomach with her arms raised above her head, tucked under her pillow. Her near bare back is exposed, though she's wearing the same shirt she wore yesterday when she went to class. The same shirt she was wearing when she saw Lennon standing in her bookstore. I didn't help her out of her clothes, only bothering to remove her shoes before sliding her under the covers and the safety of her bed. Scattered across her nightstand are dozens of sheets of paper scribbled with her handwriting. I can tell they're journal entries. Buried underneath the stack is a small, brown, leather-bound notebook, with a long, leather string wrapped around it.

With a sigh, I sit back down in the torture chair and resume watching Victoria. The white glow from the moon shines across her body. She's a bright light against the darkness, even in her sleep.

I grab one of the coffees from the tray and take a sip. The caffeine is a jolt of energy shooting straight to my bloodstream. I sit in silence for I don't know how long when Victoria finally starts to move.

Sliding her hand out from under her pillow, she groans and

rubs the heel of her hand on her tired eyes. She checks her phone from her nightstand and drops it, releasing yet another groan.

She doesn't notice I'm here until she curls her body inward, bringing her focus to the end of her bed.

At first, she doesn't speak. She simply stares at me.

I want to open my mouth to say something—anything. Even a *good morning* would suffice. But the words get lodged in my throat, refusing to leave. It's been forever since I've seen Victoria's face when she's just woken up. It's a sight I didn't realize I missed.

A full thirty seconds pass by before she breaks our silence.

"You're still here?" she croaks. There's an edge to her voice. Her lack of welcome isn't surprising, but I won't deny the slight prick of frustration tugging at me.

I take a heavy breath and sit up from the torture chair to grab the second coffee and walk it over to her bed. I place it on her nightstand.

"Brown sugar café latte. Extra shot of espresso," I tell her. "Looks like you could use it."

She shoots me a glare before sitting up, clutching the sheets to her chest as if she's naked. As if she doesn't want me to see her.

"Thanks," she mutters. "I'm surprised you remember what I like."

I allow her comment to slide off my back and sit back in the torture chair. "You really should get a different chair. I'm going to need to get stitches after I leave here from all the cuts I've been getting on my back."

Victoria swallows her first sip of her coffee. "Riley left that here. Or maybe it was the last owners. I'm not sure." She takes another sip of her coffee, but when she lowers her cup, she stares at me as if she's remembering the state of our relationship right now. She's supposed to be angry with me. Apparently.

She wraps her hands around the white paper cup and tilts her head to the side. "Why are you here?"

"I carried you home," I tell her, my voice cool and even. I'm screaming on the inside. My stomach aches with the image of her passed out in my arms.

"I could have walked back home. The bar was only a few blocks away."

"You passed out, Victoria. There's no way you could have walked home safely."

"I'm an adult, Jude." Her eyes cut me another glare. "I would have figured it out."

I curl my fingers into a fist and grind my jaw. The pressure of my clenched teeth vibrates up to my temples. The bruises from punching that asshole at the bar are varying shades of red and purple. I flex my fingers, willing the ache to dissolve. I don't give a shit about the pain. This time my patience wears thin. I stand from the chair, the broken pieces of wicker grating my back.

"Yeah, maybe, but you could have also gotten hurt." I clear my throat. "Or been taken advantage of by that fucking asshole you were dancing with."

Tears immediately fill Victoria's eyes.

I open my mouth to soothe her like I did yesterday when she saw Lennon. The memory of my brother and the tiniest bit of solace she found in his friendship four years ago had clearly affected her. My family was far from accepting of my relationship with Victoria. Lennon wasn't exactly rooting for our success, but he wasn't hindering it, either. He knew Victoria was a good person to her core and that I was in love with her. Despite the stain my relationship with her put on my family, Lennon didn't care.

But this time, I know no amount of words I say will comfort Victoria. The pain is buried too deeply for me to fix.

She tosses her blankets aside and stands. I don't miss the way she lets out a small hiss, or the way the corners of her eyes crease with a wince. I open my mouth to ask her if she's okay, but I'm stopped when she pushes my chest. She slaps both her hands against me, shoving me toward the door.

"Get out," she seethes. Her eyes are rimmed red, with streaks of old mascara running down her cheeks. They're the same pattern as the ones on my chest.

"Victoria." I try to grab her wrists to stop her but step back when she pushes me again.

"No, Jude." She shoves me harder. "I want you to leave."

"Why?" I ask, desperate to get an answer. She's angry, fury building behind her small frame. She's stopped pushing me toward the door now, and I'm standing with my back to it, watching as her eyes continue to well with tears.

"Because I don't want you here. I need you to leave." She quickly reaches around me for the doorknob. I move out of the way as she pulls it open.

She surprises me when she storms down the stairs. Her bare feet land on each step heavily, and the blood immediately drains from my face.

I run down the stairs after her, pulling her to a stop when she's made it halfway to the front door.

"Stop, V." I grab her wrist.

The store is darkened by the night. A small night light plugged into the far wall is the only illumination aside from the little glow coming from the street.

Her shoulders tremble, and she spins around. I used her nickname again. The one I gave her after the one she gave me. Her hands form fists at her sides.

"Why?" she yells. Her tears have finally shed. Pain rips through her. But this time I don't think it's from her leg. It's from me. But the pain I cause Victoria isn't unfamiliar territory. It's unfortunately a side effect of what happens when we're together.

She tries to pull my hand away from her wrist, but she's unsuccessful. I pull her to me, and her body slams against my chest. She's looking up at me through her exhausted, tear-soaked eyes.

"There are screws and nails scattered all over this place," I tell her. "You can't walk down here barefoot. Especially in the dark. It's dangerous."

Our breaths are heavy and weighted, beating in tandem. She looks how I feel on the inside. Torn apart. The memory of the past haunts me, the ghosts reappearing at full force when we're together. I can't escape the past just as much as she can't.

"It's not your job to protect me." Her bottom lip quivers.

My pulse quickens.

"It's always been my job to fucking protect you, V." I growl. As if it has a mind of its own, my hand finds a way to her hip, jerking her body against mine. I still have my other hand gripped onto her wrist, holding it between our pressed bodies.

"You can't protect me from everything, Jude." She tips her chin impossibly higher. She's standing on her toes, bringing her face closer to mine. "Didn't you learn your lesson before? You shouldn't make promises you can't possibly keep."

She yanks her wrist from my grip and steps back, her voice laced with venom intended to poison me.

My other hand is still gripping her hip, still holding onto her. I press my fingers into her flesh and tug her back. She gasps when I spin her around and walk her back until she lands against the wall. I press her against it, digging my hips into hers, then I bend at the knees, dragging my nose along the curve of her neck. She writhes beneath me. Bringing my face in line with hers, I stare into her eyes as another tear falls.

"Don't you get it?" I grind out. "It doesn't matter how many years it's been. It could be ten years from now. It could be fifty. I will always fucking protect you. Time doesn't exist when it comes to me caring about your well-being. Especially when you're fucking drunk."

Victoria opens her mouth. Her bottom lip trembles, and another tear spills over her red-rimmed eye. "I hate you."

Her confession cuts me, wounding me in the darkest parts of my soul. The parts I've kept hidden from the rest of the world. The only person I've ever allowed that deep is standing in front of me, admitting she hates me. I'd disagree with her, but it's hard to when I feel the same way about myself. I'd hate myself, too, if I were her.

But I'm not entirely convinced she's telling the truth. There's no conviction behind her words.

"I'll make this easy for you." I let my mouth drift closer to hers. "Tell me you hate me one more time and I'll go. I'll leave. But this time, say it like you fucking mean it."

Her body vibrates with electricity against mine. She rests her head back on the wall and stares up at me. "I..." She closes her mouth, then opens it again. "I..."

"That's what I thought." I wrap my hand around the back of her neck, weaving my fingers into her loose, tangled hair, and pull her to me, slamming my mouth to hers. And then, as if we've connected, the electricity from her body passes through to me. My heart hammers inside my chest, relishing in the sensation it gives me.

Victoria places both her hands at my sides, gripping onto my wrinkled, mascara-stained shirt. She holds me against her, as if she's silently begging me not to disappear. The tension in her body releases with every second I keep my mouth against hers.

She parts her lips during our kiss, gasping for air. A sob escapes her mouth before she presses it to mine again, pulling me in for more. She tastes sweet, like the brown sugar from her drink.

Keeping my fingers weaved in her chocolate strands, I grip onto her hip again. She opens her mouth, allowing me to slide my tongue against hers. I don't know where I'm leading her. I just need to feel her.

My dick immediately perks at her familiar taste.

Victoria is already tugging on my shirt, untucking it from my black dress pants. Once she's loosened it, she's unbuckling my pants. My dick strains against my zipper, begging to be freed, but I don't allow her to fully undress me just yet. I don't realize how far we've moved, until she stops. I break away from her mouth long enough to see where we are. She's standing in front of the sawhorse. I'd moved it toward the back of the store earlier to make room for the pallet of flooring and the buckets of paint.

I grin at the irony of this moment. Without wasting another second, I tuck a few strands of loose hair behind Victoria's ear. "Lift your arms," I order her quietly.

She does as instructed. The pain and sadness are still swirling in her eyes, but her eagerness for relief is evident. She lifts her arms. I grab the hem of her shirt and remove it, tossing it over my shoulder. To my surprise, she isn't wearing a bra. I lift my hand and cup one of her breasts, brushing the pad of my thumb across her perked nipple. Her back arches at my touch, and she moans and tilts her head.

It's the most beautiful sound. A sound I hadn't heard in four years until the other night.

My mouth waters, remembering the way she tasted against my tongue.

I rub my thumb over her nipple again and bend down, pulling it into my mouth. Circling my tongue around her pebbled nipple makes her grip the back of my head, keeping me held against her chest. I bite down, and she hisses.

My cock twitches. The hurt and exhaustion in Victoria's eyes when I pull away urges me to not take my time. I don't want this to be slow. I want to bury myself in her as quickly as possible. Not because I know she needs it. Not because I know the second she feels me inside her she'll sigh with relief, but because I will do the same. I'm broken, and I need her. I need to feel Victoria. I need her to heal me as much as she needs me to heal her.

Because being with her is the only time I ever feel whole— or the closest I've ever come to it. She's the cure to my wounded soul.

She lifts her skirt, not wasting any time by removing it. The black leather bunches around her waist. I slide my hand down her front, slipping my fingers into her slick center. She isn't wearing any underwear, either. There's no thong this time. No barrier between us.

I chuckle, giving her a devilish grin. "What a naughty girl you've become, V."

She stares up at me, doe eyed and panting. It's driving me fucking wild. I'm ravenous for her, ready to devour her. It's as if the last four years of our separation has driven me to a new level of sanity. I don't have any when it comes to her.

"I've never been innocent. It was simply easier to hide behind the dancer lifestyle. Everyone assumes we're innocent, but we're far from it." Her fingers grate against the back of my head. She's restless and impatient. So am I.

I slide both my fingers inside her. She groans when I hook them, finding the spot I know all too well. I press my thumb to her swollen clit and circle it over her slick center.

"Let's see how innocent you are now," I tell her.

She doesn't answer me verbally. Instead, she bites down on her bottom lip, throwing her head as far back as she possibly can. She moans, nodding her head and clamping her eyes shut as she stares up at the ceiling.

I remove my hand from inside her and grab her hips with both hands. She inhales a sharp breath at my absence, then gasps again when I lift her up and place her on the sawhorse.

Her mouth falls open, and she stares at me wide-eyed. Her breasts are on full display, and her skin is kissed by the moonlight.

She unbuttons my pants, slides the zipper down, and grips onto the waist of my boxer briefs before sliding them down. My dick springs to life, thankful for the freedom Victoria has given it. Wrapping both hands around me, she leans forward with her legs dangling from the edge of the sawhorse.

"I thought you said this wasn't meant to be a bench." Her hands stroke me, and she makes sure to cover every inch, sliding her fingers along my tip, down to my base.

"I did," I groan. "And it isn't."

"Well..." She removes her hands from my cock and sits up straight. She spreads her legs, placing both feet on the backs of my thighs, pulling me toward her. "What do you plan on doing with me on it?"

"I plan on figuring out how far your non-existent innocence goes." I shuffle the rest of the way out of my pants and kick them aside, wrapping my arm around Victoria, just in case. I told her it wasn't a bench when she attempted to climb up and sit on it the first day, and I meant it, but I can't help seeing her sitting on the bench now. It's as if her rebelliousness lights a fire inside me, igniting all the parts that were once left in a pile of ash.

I wrap my hand around my cock and position myself in front of Victoria's center. She places her hand over mine and guides me in, exhaling a heavy breath as I slide into her. She's warm, and the feel of her around me is almost too much for me to bear. My heart feels like it's going to combust from the amount of heat swelling inside my once hollow chest.

"Fuck," she moans. "You feel so good."

I slide out before sliding back in, careful not to push too hard. I don't want the sawhorse to break and Victoria to go down with it.

I keep one hand wrapped around her back. She moves in tandem with me, rolling her hips. Our breaths mingle, mixing with the hot air of the store.

I place my hand on her cheek and press my lips to hers. She lifts her hands and wraps them around the back of my neck, wrapping her legs around me, too.

"Fuck me," she begs against my lips. "Fuck me like you don't care if this sawhorse breaks. Fuck me the same way you've imagined fucking me ever since I left. Tell me you've missed this. Tell me you've missed me."

"I've missed this," I grit.

"You've missed *me*," she urges.

"*Fuck*. I've missed you and this sweet pussy of yours."

I bite down on her lip, driving myself into her harder and deeper. Her dirty talking mouth spurs something inside me. I pull away from her, tugging her lip between my teeth along the way. Her lip pops back when I let go, swollen and red, my teeth marks etched into her flesh.

My stomach warms, every nerve ending buzzing as I push in and out of Victoria. Her skin is hot against mine, and I can't break away from her. I'm afraid if I do that all this will be a dream. A nightmare playing the cruelest joke.

I don't know if Victoria means what she's saying. Does she truly believe I've imagined fucking her since she left?

If there's one truth in all the lies I've ever told, imagining this moment with Victoria would be it. She's right. I have.

The sawhorse rocks, and the wood creaks with every thrust. She wraps her legs around my waist again, pulling me impossibly closer.

The blood drains from my body, tingles prickling their way up my neck and across my cheeks. I can feel my orgasm coming but don't want to end this before giving Victoria her sought out satisfaction.

Clamping her legs tighter around me, she wraps her arm around my shoulder, clinging to me. I lift her up off the sawhorse, twisting my fingers in her hair before I tug on the ends.

"*Jude*," she cries out, tilting her head back on a gasp. "I'm coming."

"Come for me," I beg. Her pussy tightens around my cock, and I feel my own orgasm coming on. "I need to hear my name fall from that pretty fucking mouth of yours."

"Oh, Jude..." she gasps. "Fuck!"

Her legs flex around my waist, and her movements slow. Her body rocks against me, and her head tilts back. The light coming from the front of the store is barely peeking through the few picture windows, illuminating her face that is draped in light and shadows. Her pink lips part, my name spilling from the tip of her tongue is enough to pull me over the edge. I thrust inside her, pushing myself as deep as I can possibly go.

"Shit, Victoria," I groan. "You feel..." I can't finish my thoughts. The world around me becomes hazy. My cock pulsates inside her as I come. I grip the back of her head and pull her to me, placing my lips to hers. Our pants and heavy breaths blend together.

Rocking my hips, I ride out the rest of my orgasm. My lips

are still on hers when she moans against me. My cock is still buried inside her when she loosens her legs around me. I let her feet fall to the floor, and I slide myself out of her. We haven't broken our kiss, but my rapid beating heart suddenly comes to a screeching halt. A tear slips from Victoria's eye, soaking into my cheek. A reminder that this isn't a joke, and this isn't a nightmare.

Being with Victoria is a reality of my own making. One I've learned isn't permanent.

CHAPTER FIFTEEN

VICTORIA

When I moved to Texas, I used to find myself sitting on the balcony outside Amy's apartment, reliving all the mistakes that had brought me to the situation I'd found myself in. It's easy to believe my first mistake was falling for Jude. And every moment afterward was another mistake. Falling in love. Meeting the Harding family. Then it all came to a head the night of the accident.

The guilt and sorrow on Jude's face as I watched him talking to the doctor. He didn't know I was awake then. He was standing on the other side of the curtain, I was pretending to be asleep. I heard the crack in his voice when the doctor explained what happened to me.

She's shattered her leg in twelve places.

No longer able to dance. At least not anytime in the foreseeable future.

I'm sorry for your loss. Nothing we could have done.

With my heart and body too broken to cry any more tears, I laid there knowing the only reason Jude was able to talk to the doctor was due to his status in the city. The Hardings had their hands dipped into every major corporation and company. Even the hospitals.

My stomach immediately soured at the thought.

My parents were out of town, exploring Europe. Riley was down in Florida visiting a college friend.

Jude was all I had. But the longer I heard him talking to the doctor, the more their words started to blend together. Muffled and garbled, I couldn't discern one voice from the other, like being submerged under water, caught under the waves. I was forced to lay there, listening to them talking about me as if I were a stranger. Someone they'd found on the street, injured and broken.

I wanted to stay where I was, in the metaphorical depths of the ocean. It was safer to stay in the dark alone. No one could touch me. No one could find me. I wanted the darkness to swallow me. I wanted to disappear as if I never existed. Was the price of love truly at the cost of experiencing the greatest pain imaginable?

I snap my eyes open to the sound of sirens wailing in the distance outside. My throat seizes, and I'm left gasping for air. I sit up, clutching my sheets to my damp skin. I'm panting, the images in my dream still fresh in my mind.

Me in the hospital bed covered in blood.

The doctor's sad, timid voice.

The look on Jude's drunken face as he frowned, a tear slipping from his alcohol-soaked eyes. The sound of his father ensuring their name wouldn't be tarnished by their connection to the accident and his relationship with me.

My stomach clenches, twisting into a thousand knots. I'm no stranger to the sensation, but the pain it causes can't be ignored. I place my hand against my chest and focus on my breathing.

A large hand lands on my back. Calloused fingers glide

effortlessly across my skin, causing goosebumps to scatter down the length of my arms. I turn my head to see Jude sitting beside me. He's completely naked, the moonlight reflecting in his midnight eyes.

He gives me a weak smile, but his eyebrows are knitted in concern. "Bad dream?"

"Yeah." I sigh, wiping my fingers under my eye and across my cheek as if I've already shed a tear. I haven't, but dreams such as the one I had moments ago usually lead to me waking up with them falling. I brush away the shiver crawling down my spine at the memory. Or it could be from Jude's touch.

I want to lie back down and curl my body into his. I want him to wrap his arms around me and promise that he won't hurt me again. That he won't lie. But the memory of that night that has a permanent place in my dreams refuses to allow me any sort of ease.

I turn my head and rest it on my raised, bent knees, looking at him through tired eyes.

Seeing and feeling Jude throughout the night is something I never thought I would experience ever again. I never believed my heart would get to a place where I could. But I couldn't deny the pull I've had to him. Jude is like a drug I can't stay away from. I convince myself one hit is all I'll need, but I know I won't stop here. It's what got me in trouble with him in the first place.

I wanted to push him away. I didn't ask for him to show up at the bar and rescue me. I didn't know it at the time, but I needed him, and the second I woke up and saw him sitting on the wicker chair was the second I remembered the truth of what it means to have Jude in my life.

A protector. A liar.

A lover. A liar.

He was sneaking his way back into my life, pulling me in.

My mind and heart always wage war with one another when I'm in his presence. I guess when he followed me downstairs, stopping me from kicking him out, my heart won that battle.

Jude shoves the hair away from his forehead and tilts his head. He rests his elbow on his knee and his head in his hand. With his other hand, he traces a finger down the center of my knee. It brings a shiver down my back, and a flutter to my stomach. The wetness returns to my center, remembering the way it felt to have Jude inside me for the first time in four years. It all felt the same yet different, riddled with pain and loss.

He traces an invisible line from the bottom of my knee down my bare thigh. My skin prickles at his touch. "Is your leg feeling okay?" He treads his question lightly, figuring it's a triggering topic. Fear fills his gaze, worried I might suddenly run away simply because he brought up my injury.

"It is now," I say, swallowing down the echo of what I'd foolishly done on the dance floor of *Lights Out*.

I was thoughtless and stupid. I allowed my body to carry me, the veil of false comfort blanketing me caused by the effects of the four drinks I'd consumed.

Then there was Jude. Showing up like a knight in shiny fucking armor. But instead of armor, he was dressed in another expensive suit. The dynamic he has between working for me and his situation with his family is still unclear.

I tilt my head to the side, mimicking his pose. "The doctors told me I could dance again after I healed from the accident, but I never did. I tried, but I knew it wasn't the same."

"Everyone heals at different paces."

"No." I sniff, shaking my head. "I soon realized it didn't matter if my body moved like it did before. My heart didn't beat for it the same way."

"Huh." He slides his hand out from under his head, rubbing

his fingers on his chin and over his mouth. "I guess the same could be said for me."

His blue eyes shine in the early morning light. Flecks of gray peek through the darkness. I study him, wondering where his life stands now. It's impossible not to look at him and wonder what's happened in the four years we've been apart.

"Does this have to do with why half the time you're in a suit and the other half covered in sawdust?" I laugh lightly. "When I think about it, you have this sort of Batman-Bruce Wayne vibe going on."

"Shit," he says. "I wish I was as badass as Batman." He shakes his head, and his smile fades.

"So, what? You still work for your father's firm when you aren't here? I can't imagine James Harding loving the idea of you moonlighting as a construction worker. Or do you not work for him anymore? Maybe you started your own firm."

I'm grasping at straws, trying to understand the dynamic Jude has with his family.

The grin on his face returns. His blue eyes spark, and he leans forward, pushing me back on the bed. The sheet falls away from my chest, exposing my bare breasts. Cool air brushes against my peaked nipples, and goosebumps break out across my skin.

He hovers over me with his arms locked, caging me in on both sides. "You're asking quite a few questions this early in the morning."

My eyes flutter half closed as I tip my chin, looking up at his face. He's close. The tip of his nose brushes against mine. I open my legs, allowing him to go between them. His cock is already hard. He pushes his hips forward and presses it against my bare center. I'm already wet, my thighs tingling, begging to feel him again. I gasp, skipping a beat to catch my breath.

His avoidance and expert dodging leaves me more curious.

"You're avoiding my question." My train of thought will most likely derail if he stays above me like this.

"I try to focus on the future I want to make for myself." It's vague and cryptic, much like Jude has always been. "Haven't you wanted to focus on the future? Considering..."

I swallow the lump in my throat. The word 'future' falls from Jude's mouth as effortlessly as water pouring from a fountain, but the weight it bears on my chest nearly drowns me. I've envisioned a million different futures since I was a little girl.

My eyes mist, the past cropping up in my mind.

"I never had much time to think about my future," I say. "I've been too busy trying to clean up the mistakes of the past."

My confession is a slap to Jude. His facial expression falls, and his eyes darken. The flashes of excitement have dimmed, like shutting off the only lightbulb in a pitch-black room. I've spoiled the mood, now unable to take the words back. If I could, I'd swallow them back and bury them in the place I've harbored them for four years.

Jude frowns as his eyes search my face. He's clearly conflicted. Part of him looks at me as if I'm wounded. The guilt behind his stare is evident. The other part of him tells me *I'm* the one who wounded *him.*

I wouldn't be the first person to hurt Jude. I'm all too aware of the demons he has kept inside, as well as the secrets he holds close to his chest, guarded by a life run by veiled appearances. *Maintain the status quo,* as his father would say.

It's been four years since Jude and I have been together. I should let it go. None of what is in the past should matter anymore. After all, they say you can't move forward unless you put the past behind you.

I can't be with Jude and not think about what could have been. I can't kiss Jude without thinking about all the constant lies he told me. I can't feel his touch and not think about the power they held.

I hold my breath when he surprises me by lifting his hand to my face and drawing an invisible line down the side of my cheek, tracing my jaw. He drags it along my skin to my mouth. I open my mouth as his finger ghosts my lips. He doesn't utter a word, but he doesn't need to. Tears bite behind my eyes, threatening to spill. As if I've suddenly woken to the gravity of the situation I've found myself in with Jude, my chest swells and cracks all in the same breath.

He pulls away from me, and I immediately feel his absence. The hollow ache radiates down from my throat to my legs. I sit up and slide out from the bed to sit on the edge and look over my shoulder at Jude. He's climbing out from the other side, stepping into his pants. The sound of his belt clanking in the silence is deafening. I read the clock hanging on the wall above my bed and sigh, then I look over my shoulder again.

He's now slipping his arms into the sleeves of his button down.

"Jude," I whisper.

He doesn't look up as he works his way up, fixing each button.

"Jude," I repeat, this time above a whisper.

He stops, and the pain in his eyes is enough to widen the cracks in my already fragile heart.

It's difficult to reconcile my feelings. On the one hand, sleeping with Jude feels like a mistake. On the other, it felt right. My feelings for Jude are alive and well. The ashes of what we once were have somehow come back. The embers smolder and spark into a raging fire.

He shoves his hair off his forehead and allows his arms to fall slack by his sides. He doesn't move his wounded gaze away from mine.

"I'm sorry," I whisper, holding myself together the best I can. "I have to get ready for class."

"Yeah." He clears his throat. "Don't worry about it. I need to get back home, anyway."

The venom in his tone stings, but I don't argue. We can't seem to let go of our past, but it's hard to push past it when it's destroyed the person you used to be. Jude included.

CHAPTER SIXTEEN

VICTORIA

I COULD HARDLY THINK OF ANYTHING ELSE OTHER THAN Jude for the duration of my class. My professor asked me to write a paper on what matters most to us in life. A vague topic. I grumbled and began listing all the things that have ever mattered to me in life.

Books. Dancing. Coffee. Writing.

All general subjects that hold no weight. Until I scribbled the last word on my list.

Writing.

Up until this class a few weeks ago, I'd forgotten my passion for writing. Journal entries and letters were what used to keep me focused. On the days where I felt lonely or hopeless, writing my deepest, darkest secrets was an outlet. A way to express the feelings I couldn't speak out loud.

It's been years since I've written, though, and the thought of doing it now brings on more bad memories than good. I don't think I'm ready to write them down on paper because once I do, every thought I've kept bottled inside is no longer mine to keep. It's out in the world, exposed and vulnerable.

I hold onto my deepest thoughts and stand from my seat

once class is over. I begin heading up the steps toward the exit when I spot Riley leaning against the wall. Two coffees are perched in her hands. I sigh with relief the second I meet her.

I wasn't expecting her to respond to my text this morning when I was on my out the door after Jude left. Riley isn't exactly a morning person, but I needed someone to talk to about Jude and the mess I've found myself in. I still haven't shared mine and Jude's loss caused by the accident, yet she's still the one person I can confide in the most.

Trusting her over Amy or anyone else in my life is a given.

Riley holds out one of the coffee cups for me to grab. I follow her up the rest of the stairs and out of the classroom. We step out into the hallway and exit the literature building in silence.

The sun shines against my face the second our feet meet the pathway.

"I'm surprised you're here." I adjust my bag on my shoulder and bring the warm cup of coffee to my mouth. "Thanks for the jolt of caffeine by the way."

"I know I'm not the happiest person when it comes to the mornings." She gives me a sidelong glance, a grin lifting her soft, kind lips. "So, when I know I have a text from you at eight a.m. saying you need to talk, I take it seriously. Coffee is a must."

"Thanks." I give her a weak smile from behind my cup and take another sip. We take a few steps in silence again, heading toward the campus exit. I need to check in with Cain when we get to the store. Something about building the feature wall I had planned for the blind book section. Since Jude is my project manager, I can only assume he'll be there as well.

"What's going on?" Riley asks, concerned.

I wince and look up at the trees as we make our way down the sidewalk. The branches sway in the mid-morning breeze, playing a quiet melody I wish was louder. At least loud enough to drown out the sound of Boston traffic.

I haven't told Riley about getting drunk the other night at *Lights Out*. I haven't told her about how I'd collapsed in the middle of the dance floor, and I definitely haven't told her about sleeping with Jude.

I can still feel the ghost of his kiss on my mouth and the bite from his teeth as they clamped around my nipple. The way his cock slid into me and filled me easily. My body radiates with the memory of him. I fidget with the end of my ponytail, twisting my fingers around the end and nervously biting down on my lip.

"How much of that coffee have you drank?" I ask her.

"Almost half." She shrugs, eyeing her cup as if she can see right through it. "I didn't spike it if that's what you're wondering."

"No." I shake my head. "I didn't think that. I just figure this conversation might be too deep for someone who hasn't had enough caffeine in their system."

"Not going to lie." She stops in her tracks. "You're worrying me."

Her long blonde hair is twisted at the sides into two low buns. Her part is split perfectly down the middle. A side effect of the dancing lifestyle. Riley's winged eyeliner curves down as she looks at me with worry.

"You don't have to worry about me." I take her hand. "I just need to talk through the mess of thoughts going on in my head. I could use my best friend."

She nods once and tilts her head to the side, dropping her aunt role and swapping it for the best friend. I can see it in the way her softened eyes transition to ones of intrigue. I love Riley, and I love our meetings where we get to share the details of our lives. Situations such as these five years ago would have had me sitting cross-legged on the bed with Kate, but I haven't spoken to her since months before the accident. Our lives simply took different directions, though there are times when I still think about her. I'm thankful I at least have Riley to confide in now.

I inhale a deep breath. "Do you ever wish you could fix the mistakes in your past?" The words fall from my mouth before I've realized the weight of them.

"No," she's quick to answer.

"Really? You took no time to answer that question." I let out a humorless laugh.

"Victoria..." She exhales. "What's the use in spending your time nit-picking your past? How can you possibly go through each monumental decision you've ever made for yourself and decide to put it into one column or the other? Nothing is black and white."

"I guess you're right." She's already given me the answer I expected to hear. I just hate spending my time wondering what different outcomes I could have had if I'd made different decisions. I wince, giving her a sidelong glance. "Remember you dropped your aunt role and have slipped into best friend, right?"

"Yes." She nods, the corners of her mouth curling into a nervous smile.

I bring my coffee cup up to my mouth and peek over the lid as I prepare to take a sip. "Lennon stopped by my store yesterday when I got out of class."

"Lennon?" Riley asks, her eyes widening. "As in Lennon Harding, Jude's brother?"

I roll my eyes. "Yes, Riley. How many Lennons do you know?"

"None." She tilts her head back and laughs.

"Exactly."

"I only met Lennon once. Kind of mysterious, no?"

"Sort of," I admit. "He's always been good at playing both sides of the coin. We always got along, but I knew James still had one hand on Lennon. I imagine he feels stuck, considering he's the eldest Harding son."

"Maybe. But what does seeing Lennon have to do with you?"

"I don't know." I sigh, thinking back to the thoughts I couldn't let go of yesterday. "Seeing Lennon triggered something inside me. Memories of being with Jude and how I tried so desperately to fit into their family."

"Bullshit, if you ask me," Riley mutters.

"I know." I chew on my bottom lip, preparing myself for what I'm about to say next. I'm desperate to tell someone. I can't bottle it up any longer, and I need an outside perspective that I can trust. "There's more."

"Oh?" She sips the rest of her coffee.

"After I saw Lennon, I couldn't stop thinking about everything. Working with Jude hasn't been awful, and it's impossible not to feel at least *something* when we're around each other. I'd blame it on the past, but Jude and I are so much more than a past relationship."

"Are you telling me you still love him?" she asks, cocking an eyebrow.

I internally sigh with relief, thankful she's remained in her best friend role.

"I don't know," I admit. I inhale a deep breath and blow it out. "We, um... we slept together."

"Wait, what?" she sputters, practically spitting out her coffee. She wipes her chin, staring at me with two wide eyes.

"Please, no judgment." I squeeze my eyes shut, then pry one eye open to gauge her reaction.

"I'm not." She holds up her free hand. "I just want to hear all the details. How? Why? *When?*"

"Last night." I sigh, dropping my now empty coffee cup into

the trash. Riley follows and catches up to me, letting me continue.

I tell her everything that happened between us. Him texting me at the bar. Showing up and picking me up off the floor. I quickly run her through my misjudged decision to dance, causing me to collapse. She scolds me but sighs with relief when I tell her that Jude was there to pick me up and carry me home safely, preventing me from further injury. I even tell her about how he stayed all night in what he called Riley's wicker chair of torture.

She lets out a small laugh at that.

I tell her how he followed me downstairs, insisting he'd protect me. How he'd always protect me. How I struggle believing the words he was telling me. But the nagging sensation in my gut that brought me to bring this up to Riley in the first place rises to the surface.

"It's nearly impossible to regret sleeping with Jude," I confess when I'm finished filling her in on all the important details. "But I can't ignore the familiar feeling I would get when I was with him before."

"What feeling?"

"Back when we were together, I knew Jude loved me. I never doubted his feelings for me." I wipe away a tear threatening to spill. The memory of his mouth on mine coating my quivering lips takes hold of me. "But his love for me couldn't hold a candle to the influence of his father. If there's one relationship Jude valued above all else, it was the one he had with James."

I bite the tip of my tongue, refraining from telling Riley every single detail. She still doesn't know about the loss Jude and I truly felt the night I was struck by a drunk driver on the way to pick up a drunken Jude.

The endless alcohol laden frat parties caught up with him, and it cost us everything.

My heart cracks. I'm immediately sucked back into the same frame of mind I was in the other day when I saw Lennon. It's a rabbit hole I refuse to get lost in again.

"I'm still in best friend mode, correct?" Riley tentatively asks.

I nod. "Yep."

"Okay." She inhales a deep breath. "Did you ever find out why he's working for Cain?"

"No." I shake my head. "I tried asking but haven't been able to figure it out yet."

"I'll repeat what I told you the day we went to the flea market: people change, Victoria. That might mean Jude doesn't love you the same, but I imagine you don't love him the same, either. That's the beauty about love. It shifts and changes over time. Regardless of whether the two people involved in the relationship are together or not."

"This sounds like more of an aunt speech than a best friend one." I sniff.

"Oh, right." She snorts. "It's easy to confuse the two." She straightens her back and clears her throat, and I smile. "Honestly, I didn't think you'd be able to keep your work and personal life separate."

My jaw drops. I'm shocked at her blunt confession.

"Thanks for the vote of confidence," I mumble.

"You asked me my opinion." She shrugs. When I don't give her a smile in return, she lifts one shoulder. "I don't blame you for sleeping with Jude." She wraps her arm around me. "Just be careful. Keep that fragile heart of yours guarded, but make sure you don't completely shut him out."

I press my fingers to my lips, walking alongside Riley in silence. I think about Jude's mouth on mine. I think about the sounds he makes as his tongue glides across my skin, tasting me. I think about his hands and how they press into my flesh with more conviction than anything else he's ever touched.

"One more thing," Riley says, placing her hand on my arm and pulling us to a stop. "You both agreed to work with each other without letting your past get in the way. Don't you think it's about time you held up to your end of the deal? You're the only one standing in the way of allowing yourself to move on. You're the one with the power to not let it get in the way." She smiles, lifting her hand to tuck a stray strand of hair behind my ear. "I'll go back to answering your original question about making mistakes. Do you truly believe if you had a chance to do it all over that you would choose a different path? Even if it meant you might have never met and fallen in love with Jude?" She pauses, staring into my eyes. "Something tells me you wouldn't."

CHAPTER SEVENTEEN

VICTORIA

After I update Riley on the progress of my bookstore, I shove all my dirty clothes in my laundry basket and scrounge up as much change as I can possibly find. I wedge my fingers between the cushions of my small loveseat. I even check under the cushion of the torturous wicker chair. Once I find enough to pay for a load to wash and dry, I carry the bag down the stairs and lock the front door to the store behind me.

My apartment is a near exact replica of Riley's, even down to the lack of washer and dryer, but I don't mind the extra effort it takes for me to head to the laundromat. Especially since I go to the same one I went to the night Riley sent me. The one where I met Jude. Going the extra distance has helped distract me from my thoughts. It gives me a chance to connect with the city I left behind years ago. Not much is different because if there's one thing about Boston, it's that the heart of it never changes.

When I get to the laundromat, I drop my clothes into the washer and slide the quarters into the slots. Ever since the night I'd jammed my quarters into the mechanism and Jude showed up to my rescue, I've avoided going back to that machine. Every time I use the one next to it, I stare at it, recalling the way my heart skipped a beat and ached at the sight of familiar midnight blue eyes staring at me. I don't know if the owner finally fixed the mechanism, but I figure it's best to avoid it altogether, anyway.

I lean back on the washer and cross my legs at the ankle. I slide my phone out of the back pocket of my shorts and open to my thread of texts to Jude. The last message I sent him was the night at *Lights Out* when I was too drunk to spell correctly.

My heart hammers inside my chest like a pinball endlessly bouncing off the swinging paddles. It leaps from wall to wall, never stopping for even a moment. Fire radiates across my body, concentrating on the center of my stomach, bringing the heat between my legs.

It's late. The sky outside is black with a few ghostly clouds passing between the rooftops of the buildings surrounding us. The laundromat is deserted.

I tap my phone, bring up my keyboard, and type.

> Me: Hey, I was wondering if we could talk.

His response is quick.

> Jude: Yeah, I just need to finish up here. I can head over in five.

A small smile tugs on my mouth. It's temporary, fading quickly, and I'm reminded of why I'm asking Jude to meet me.

> Me: I'm not at my apartment. Laundry night.

He doesn't respond to my text. I spend the next twenty minutes moving from standing in front of the washing machine to sitting on the slippery plastic chair set along the wall. I tug my book out of my bag and try picking up where I left off. I reread the same sentence over and over, thinking about my situation with Jude. I think about my store. I think about where my life is now compared to months ago. A year ago, I convinced myself that life with Greg was where I should have been. Now I know I was wrong.

The laundromat is still deserted when I spot Jude through one of the small windows dotted along the front of the building. He's walking along the sidewalk with his hands shoved into the pockets of his slacks. This time he's dressed in a dark blue suit instead of his usual black. His gold watch glimmers in the street-lights and neon signs hanging above each storefront.

His eyes find mine staring back at him as he pulls the door open, stepping inside. No music is playing through the speakers. There never is. Instead, we're left to listen to the rhythm and melody of the washing machine.

"Let me guess..." He smirks, eyeing the machine next to mine. "You got your money jammed again thinking the owner fixed it."

"He should really put a sign on it so customers stop losing their quarters," I say, crossing my arms beneath my chest. We're facing each other but still standing beside the other. The scent of whatever cologne Jude is wearing surrounds me. My mouth waters. I swallow, forcing myself to temper my emotions.

We're merely engaging in small talk. We haven't even gotten to the grit of conversation yet, but I can feel it coming like being tied to a track, watching the train barreling toward you.

"I think he likes it that way." Jude sighs, his grin fading.

"Why? So he can steal people's money?"

"No." He shakes his head. "I think he just gets enjoyment out of watching others struggle with it before giving up."

"Luckily for me, I learned my lesson the first time." I let out a small laugh and nod toward the office door I've never seen open. It is always shut with a 'Be back later' sign nailed to the brown wood. "Do you know the owner?"

"No." Jude sighs, running his fingers through his hair. He shoves it off his forehead, allowing the watch on his wrist to glint in the light again. Gold cufflinks are pinned to the cuffs of his white shirt. He's polished and clean. Entirely too clean.

No matter how many times I've seen him like this, I can't get over the difference from when he's working on my store. It's like talking to two different Judes.

His eyes find mine. "I only know of him through Cain. When Cain opened his construction and renovation business, he started by doing a few odd fixer upper jobs around the city. Sort of like a maintenance technician, but he never stuck to one company permanently. He didn't charge as much as someone else in a permanent position would, either."

"Wow. That's nice of him." I bite down on my bottom lip, deciding whether I should keep the conversation going. For once, it feels as if Jude is divulging a part of his life he hasn't been willing to share with me up until now.

"He's a good guy," he says.

"How did you end up working for him?"

"I met Cain through Kappa Sigma." His mention of the fraternity turns my stomach sour.

"Oh." I nod, looking down at my feet.

"When he started telling me about his plan to open the business, I offered to work a job here and there. Especially when he couldn't make it out to the job sites due to his internship."

"Internship?" I ask, arching a brow. "What was his major?"

Jude leans forward, bringing his face close to mine as if he were whispering a secret. "Pre-med."

"You're kidding." I laugh. "I would have never guessed."

"No one does. But like I said, he's a good guy."

"So…" I start. "Is that why you're still working for him? To help him out while he's in class?"

"No." Jude sighs. "Cain quit medical school to expand his business. He does renovations full time. I help him because it brings me back down to earth."

"Down to earth?"

"Sometimes working at Harding Holdings can be stifling." There's no emotion behind his words. If I didn't already know from his appearance, I would guess he attempts to distance himself as much as possible. But by the suits I've seen him wear and the woman draped over his lap that night at Eclipse, I know that isn't the case.

"So, you made it happen?"

Sadness and regret fill his eyes with a blue haze. "Yes." The way the three-letter word falls from his mouth tells me he won't be expanding. He doesn't need to. I already know.

Jude did exactly what he set out to do from the moment he was born. Go to Boston college, get into the Kappa Sigma fraternity, graduate with a business degree, and work at the family firm. No matter the cost. No matter the obstacles that stood in his way.

I bite back the tears building behind my eyes and take a deep breath. I rest both my hands behind me and pull myself up onto the washing machine. It's still in the middle of its cycle. It vibrates and shakes beneath me. Jude shifts to the side, filling the now empty space. He stands in front of me with his face in line with mine, placing both his hands on my knees. I gasp as if he's stolen the oxygen directly from my lungs.

I flutter my eyes closed, then open them again. My confession sits on the tip of my tongue, ready to spill. I've kept my past well-guarded from Jude, unwilling to open myself to the man who single handedly brought me heartache, but I know it's the only way we can move on.

"When I decided to leave Boston, I wanted to escape. My whole world had gone dark. I felt cold and alone." I swallow back the tears, forcing myself to continue. "The only support I thought I had was with Amy in Texas. She said she had space for me, so that's where I went. Without hesitation. I never told Amy about what happened or why. She never asked. But now, when I think back on it, it isn't because she wanted to give me space. She simply didn't care enough to ask. She never wanted to know."

"What do you mean?" Jude whispers. His fingers massage my thighs, slowly and carefully inching their way up my legs. It's distracting, but not enough to stop me from wanting to continue. Jude's touch is simply comforting me for now.

"It took me a few years to start over and break out of the shell I'd built around myself. I eventually began dating Greg, who then became my fiancé." I clear my throat. "Looking back on it now, I realize we didn't truly love each other, but I think at that point I was desperate to feel again. I got caught up in the vicious cycle of chasing a feeling I was afraid I'd never experience again."

Jude's hands suddenly stop, but his attention on me doesn't waver.

"So," I continue. "On the morning Greg and I were supposed to be married, he sent me a text, but I quickly realized the text wasn't intended for me. It was meant for Amy."

"Wait," Jude scoffs, his eyebrows slanted in anger. "Greg and Amy were having an affair?"

"Yeah." I nod. Tears are still building behind my exhausted eyes, but I know they aren't for Greg and Amy's betrayal. Now, almost a year after leaving them in the courthouse, I'm more certain than ever that I never truly loved Greg. "It had been going on for quite some time." I twist my mouth in thought, tipping my chin higher. "Now that I think back on it, it was a blessing in disguise. I never wanted to marry Greg—not really. Afterward, I knew my place wasn't there. I was never meant to be there."

"I'm probably the last person who has any right to say this," Jude whispers, lifting his hand to my face to rub the pad of his thumb across the bottom of my cheek, above my jawline. "But I won't lie when I say you telling me this makes me want to fly down to Texas and beat the living shit out of Greg."

"It's okay." I shake my head, dismissing his comment.

"No." He pulls me back, grabbing onto my chin. "It's not."

I stare into Jude's eyes, speaking around the lump in my throat. "I never loved him."

"It doesn't matter if you loved him or not. You don't deserve it. You've never deserved the kind of hurt and betrayal you've received in the past." He continues to drag his thumb across the line of my jaw. He slides his hand farther down my neck, pressing the heel of his calloused hand to my throat.

The heat from his touch devours me.

"Why are you telling me this?" he asks in a grated whisper as he steps closer to me, parting my legs with his body. I allow him to slide between my thighs. His cock perks up for me, pressing against my soft, cotton shorts.

"This morning, I brought up the mistakes of my past. I shouldn't have said that."

"You were only speaking the truth." He smirks. "Your honesty betrays you, Victoria. You speak the truth before your mind can conjure up a lie."

I chuckle, and my heart swells.

"I told you I wanted to keep our past out of our arrangement with the bookstore." I place my hand flat against his chest. "This is me following through on my word."

"Okay." He places his hand over mine. "But I need to ask you a question now that I'm here."

"What?" I wrap my legs around his waist, pulling him closer. His hips jerk forward, his erection slamming against me. He's already hard as stone. I swipe my tongue across my lips, craving more.

"Is this too much for you?" he asks, ghosting the back of his fingers along the curve of my breast to my stomach, stopping at the waist of my shorts. He hooks his fingers into the elastic band and tugs on them. I gasp, heat radiating further along my body.

"Um..." My mind grows hazy. I close my eyes, attempting to clear my thoughts to give him an answer. If I'm honest, it's all too much. It's difficult to reconcile my feelings when Jude's hands are exploring my body.

"Does me touching you here bring pain?" he asks, sliding his fingers farther underneath the lace of my underwear. My skin prickles with goosebumps. I rock my hips on the washer. The vibration of the machine intensifies the sensation Jude's hands are giving me.

I grip onto the lapels of his suit, pulling him closer. He slides his hand out from my shorts and moves them to the inside of my thigh.

"Answer me." He groans, pressing his cock against me.

"No," I confess on a whisper. "It doesn't hurt."

It's the truth. When Jude touches me, my entire world fades into the distance. Every problem and every heartache disappear. It's a temporary high. One I know will only last until he pulls away from me.

"Good," he breathes. "Do you want me to stop?" He trails his fingers along the inside of my thigh. I squirm, the sensation making me wet already. His fingers disappear under the leg of my shorts, and he presses them to the front of my underwear.

I gasp and shake my head. "No."

He presses harder. I push against him, silently begging him to keep going.

"I knew you'd be soaking wet for me before I even truly touched you." He growls, leaning into my ear.

I tilt my head to the side and lean into the side of his face. I shift my eyes to the front of the store. The street is deserted, save for the occasional passing car. The lights inside the laundromat are dim. We're still the only ones here. If anyone were to walk by, they would assume we were simply hugging, or at worst, making out. Jude's hand between my legs can't be seen from the front of the laundromat.

I keep one hand wrapped around the lapel of his suit and use the other to run my fingers through the length of his hair. I tug on the ends, pulling myself into a steady rhythm of rocking my hips against him on the vibrating machine.

"I want you to show me," I tell him, bringing my mouth to the hollow of his ear.

His breath dances across my skin, and it nearly does me in. I'm a stick of dynamite, ready to explode, prepared to combust and shatter into a million tiny pieces.

"What do you want me to show you?" He digs his teeth into my neck, pulling and tugging on my skin. I hiss, begging for him to be inside me.

"I want you to show me how wet I can get." My cheeks blush with my confession.

He pulls away and looks into my eyes. His hands are on his belt, quickly unbuckling it, and his gaze never wavers. Once he has his belt undone, he wastes no time unzipping his pants and freeing his erection. It stands perfectly straight and ready for me.

I keep my eyes on him and scoot closer to the edge of the machine. It must be near the end of the cycle because the speed picks up. It vibrates beneath me when I grab onto Jude's cock. I brush my finger over the tip and grip onto his length, sliding my hand down from the tip to the base. His eyes flutter with a groan, then a hiss escapes his perfect mouth.

I lean forward, bringing my mouth to his. "Show me, Jude."

"Are you sure?" he whispers back.

I know exactly what he means. He isn't asking if I'm sure I want him. He's asking if I'm sure I'm willing to let the past go to feel this. Whatever this is between us.

I thought when I left Boston years ago, I could forget. I could forget the life I once had and all that lived within it. But it doesn't matter where you go. You can't escape your past. It latches onto you and becomes a part of who you are, like a shadow following you wherever you go. All you can do is hope to learn and grow from it. Hope to move forward.

Jude is hoping this means I'm willing to move on from our demons.

I know I will never fit into his life now. Even if he's working part time for Cain and part time with his father, Jude Harding is still the same man he was years ago. Only this time his jaw is a bit more sculpted, and his midnight eyes have darkened.

My chest swells, knowing this is it. This is all we'll ever be. Two people starving to move on, unwilling to let go of the only spark to ever make us feel alive.

Alive. It's the only word I can use to describe the way I'm feeling in this moment. In a twisted way, there's pleasure in the pain. There's pleasure in the way his hands gloss over me as if he's tapping into every single memory embedded in my skin.

I twist my fingers around Jude's black tie and pull him toward me. "I'm sure."

With my hand still wrapped around his erection, he slides his hand between us, hooking two fingers into my underwear. I don't have time to register what's happening before he shoves the fabric aside and slides into me.

I pull my hand away from between us and wrap it around

the top of his shoulders, keeping my fingers of my other hand tangled in his tie as I press my lips to his.

The stifling air. The sound of the vibrating machine. Jude's mouth on mine and his cock pulsating inside me. Everything surrounds me. Consumes me.

This time he doesn't take it slow. Jude pulls out and quickly pushes in. I rock my hips against him, keeping him pressed to me. No separation. No distance. From the outside, others would think we were still hugging or simply kissing.

Jude doesn't break our connection. He slides his tongue between my lips, forcing my mouth open. He tastes like citrus candy. Sweet and tangy.

His tongue glides and moves around my mouth, tasting every bit of me he can. His breath is heavy and weighted, as if he were bearing his entire weight into me. My heart rapidly beats, unable to keep up with what he's doing and how he's making me feel.

I'm soaking wet for him. His cock moves effortlessly inside me, and I feel myself already beginning to tighten around him. My walls clench, and his cock swells. I fight the urge to tilt my head back. I don't want to give away what we're doing to anyone who might happen to walk by or come into the store.

I moan against his mouth, my legs shivering with tingles. My orgasm is building inside me.

Jude senses the transition and how close I'm getting. He pulls away from me and wraps one hand around the back of my head, to the base of my neck, all the while keeping up with his pace. In and out. In and out. He twists his fingers around my ponytail, like the way I'm holding his tie.

I'm gasping for air as my impending orgasm builds inside me. Lights dance across the front of the store. From the corner of my eye, I watch a car pull up. The passenger steps out of the car then opens the back to pull out a large laundry bag.

"Jude," I whisper, stifling a moan. "Someone's coming."

"Then, it looks like I better make you come faster." He doesn't bother looking at the person out front. He tugs on my hair, pulling my attention back to him. The corner of his mouth curls into a devious smirk. I want to kiss it right off his mouth, but he doesn't give me a chance.

He wraps his other hand around me, pulling me against him. His muscles are tense, and the pressure inside me builds.

I lean forward, burying my face in his neck. His smell is intoxicating, sending shivers down my spine.

"Oh, fuck, Jude," I moan, biting down on his flesh. I grate my teeth, and he groans. I don't know how much time we have or how much longer until the person outside comes in.

But I don't have to worry for long when Jude's breath brushes against my ear and his pumps quicken. My legs tense around his waist. Combined with the vibration of the washing machine and Jude's cock inside me, I come. My legs tense, holding him to me, and I bite down on his neck again, stifling my moan.

Jude quickly follows, his cock pulsating inside me with his orgasm. He spills into me, and I hold my breath. The sensation both thrills and scares me. I shouldn't be afraid considering I'm on birth control. I remind myself not to dwell on the past. Not anymore.

Jude keeps his arm wrapped around me, holding me to him when the bell above the front door jingles.

It makes my heart skip a beat. I swallow, my nervous heart rattling in my chest. Jude doesn't move from between my legs. I lift my head just as the person who stepped out of the passenger side of the car walks by, their laundry bag hitched over their shoulder.

"Hi," the man says with a wave.

"Hello," Jude returns with a grin. I manage to muster a smile as well.

I bite down on my lip, trying not to laugh.

The man moves to the row of machines behind the one I'm using. My back is turned to him.

Jude leans forward and presses his mouth to my ear. "I have to go," he whispers. "Don't move until I leave."

I close my eyes and take a deep breath. Jude slides himself out of me and quickly tucks himself back into his pants. As quietly as possible, he zips himself up and buckles his belt, then slips his hand between my thighs and fixes my underwear.

When he removes it, he sticks both fingers into his mouth, sucking on them. He pulls them out, and with his eyes pinned to mine, he runs the pad of his thumb across my bottom lip. A slight smile appears on his mouth before it fades. The washer finishes its cycle. The loud buzzing sound fills the room.

With that, he steps back and leaves. I watch him as he pushes through the front door and heads down the sidewalk. My cheeks are flushed, and my heart is still racing. Seconds pass before I bring myself to hop down from the washer. The stranger at the next row of machines looks up and gives me a smile. I know I look a mess, but I don't care. The thrill of what just happened was worth the risk.

I lift the lid to the washer and begin removing my clothes. I want to move on from Jude and forget the past, but even I must admit, a life such as this one would be pretty fucking nice.

CHAPTER EIGHTEEN

Jude

I couldn't stay at the laundromat. I'd already risked leaving the office, knowing my father was due to meet me to discuss a few accounts, including the status of Laurel's family.

After leaving Victoria sitting on the washer with my cum between her legs and her lips swollen from my mouth on hers, I jog to my car parked farther down the street.

I adjust my tie and run my fingers through my hair the second I sit in the driver's seat. The engine purrs to life, and I peel out of my parking spot.

When Victoria texted me earlier, I was set to meet my father in the boardroom. He'd insisted we talk about a few accounts he's hoping to snag. Negotiations are already underway, but he needs me to finalize them or some shit. Every account needs a gameplan. A strategy. My job is to lay out all the benefits the clients would be getting if they were willing to invest their money into our accounts and build their portfolio with us versus the competition.

The amount of detail that goes into snagging every client and persuading them to trust my father makes my head fucking spin.

Honestly, I'm surprised he's bothering to still include me in business deals. My absence at the office has grown. I'd say it was because of my renovations on Victoria's bookstore, but in truth, it has more to do with Victoria herself.

Being with her has awakened a part of me that I let fade away. It's as if I've spent the past four years living in a cave, hidden from the rest of the world. Living the life I thought I was supposed to. Victoria reminds me of what it feels to be alive.

When I pull into the parking garage of my office building, I pop open the glovebox and grab two gummies, then toss them into my mouth and hop out of my car. If I'm going to be dealing with James Harding, I'm going to need a little something to take the edge off.

Dark, heavy clouds roll in. Rumbling thunder vibrates across the city, echoing through the parking garage.

My body is still buzzing with the memory of being inside Victoria only minutes ago when I press the button to the elevator, taking me to the firm's floor.

Our secretary, Jillian, is sitting behind the front desk.

"Welcome back, Mr. Harding." She beams. Her ponytail bobs when she pops up from her chair.

I give her a quick wave, talking over my shoulder as I pass her large, marble desk. "My father still in the boardroom?"

She points behind her. "I think he left about thirty minutes ago."

"Fuck." I screech to a halt, shoving my hair off my forehead. I tug on the ends and drag my palm down the side of my face.

A knot forms in the pit of my stomach. It's a vicious cycle, working for my father. As much as I hate working for him, and the terrible things he's done in the past to those he claims to love, an inherent part of me can't let go. I can't deny the small piece of me that still wants to please him.

"Okay," I breathe out. "Thank you."

"You're welcome, sir."

I leave her at her desk and continue walking down the hall back to my own office. I pass by the empty boardroom. I pass Micah's office and Lennon's, which are both empty as well. Aside from the usual staff, I'm the only member of the family here.

Figuring I'll talk to my father about the accounts later, I grab a few items from my office and head home. I should check my emails or messages, but I don't have it in me. My care level has dropped to a record low. My lack of interest has seeped its way into every fragment of my role in the business: meetings, emails, dinners, conference calls. All of it.

Ever since the night at Eclipse with him two months ago, I haven't been eager to meet with my father. I avoid dinner most weeks, and half the time I expect him to have another woman draped over his lap, ready to pawn off on me.

I text Victoria when I pull into the parking garage under my apartment building. When she tells me she's waiting on the last few minutes of her laundry to finish drying, the gummies I took earlier kick in. My head lightens, and the pressure in my shoulders loosens.

I smile, wishing I'd driven to her place rather than mine. I live in an apartment entirely too large for a twenty-four-year-old man living by himself. As much as I love the way my place looks, it's incredibly isolated, lonely, stifling, and suffocating, reminding me of a life I used to chase but find myself on the fence wondering if it was the right choice.

That's the problem with the choice I made.

I sacrificed everything for this life, but I constantly question the price I paid to get it. It's hard to look at the one I have and not feel shredded by guilt.

I unlock my door and toss my keys into the glass bowl sitting on the entryway table. I flip the light switch to my living room, and the blood drains from my face when I find my father sitting in the dark on the opposite side of the room in the rich, brown leather chair situated in the corner, one leg resting on the other. In one hand, he's holding his phone. In the other, he's swirling a glass of whiskey. The ice clinks against the crystal.

"What the fuck?" I ask, holding back the irritation simmering inside me.

"Where were you?" he asks, his voice calm. Too calm.

I walk farther into my living room, standing feet away from him. He rises from his chair, taking another sip of whiskey from his glass. He must have brought it here considering I don't keep alcohol in my apartment. He probably keeps a bottle in his car for occasions such as these. Occasions such as breaking into his son's apartment.

Traces of white powder are dusted across the top of my end table.

Motherfucker.

I shoot him a glare, narrowing my eyes.

"I had to step out for a bit." I keep it vague, hoping to hell he doesn't question me.

"Don't fucking lie to me," he barks.

"That's rich." I raise my eyebrows. "Coming from you."

"Goddammit!" he yells, throwing his now empty glass at the wall. It shatters and scatters across my floor. The light reflects in the fragments of glass off the pool of amber liquid, and the scent of whiskey filters into the air. It makes me fucking nauseous.

I open my mouth to yell at him, but I'm caught off guard when he stomps toward me and stops in front of me. His eyes are lit with fury. The cocaine he snorted before I came home must be hitting him.

Rain sticks to the windows. Thunderclaps fill the room, followed by flashes of lighting.

"I swear to God, Jude," he spits. "If you don't get your head out of your fucking ass, you're going to cost this family millions of dollars."

I scoff, curling my mouth into a sneer. Heat radiates across my chest. "Family?"

"Yes," he seethes, curling his lip. "Your family built this company from the ground up, and you are single handedly destroying it because of your selfishness."

"My selfishness?" I yell. My body bursts with anger, my skin turning red hot. For years I've listened to my father spout off endless bullshit and lies, but this one pushes me to my breaking point. I think of everything my father has destroyed. Not just his influence on my relationship with Victoria.

My mother's kind eyes come to mind. Her tired, exhausted, kind eyes. The ultimate betrayal my father committed against our family and his marriage to my mother flares the anger raging inside me. I curl my fingers in two tight fists. Now I wish I had a drink to hurl at the wall. Instead, I'm fucking high, and suddenly craving something much stronger. I chew on the inside of my cheek, begging for relief.

"Do you know how much time I've wasted steering you in the right direction?" his voice booms, reverberating off the walls of this sterile fucking penthouse apartment. "Years it took to mold you and make you into a respectable young man." He lifts his hands in front of him and tenses them in frustration, as if he were given the opportunity to choke me, he would. His jaw clenches as he bares his teeth.

"You didn't make me the man I am today!" I shout. "If there's any part of me left that's any good, it would be from Mom, not you." I swallow, my tongue growing thirsty for more than the high floating in my bloodstream. The smell of alcohol taunts me. "Besides, if you took a second to look at anyone but yourself, you'd see that I'm a total fucking mess."

"If your mother could see you now." He growls, his eyes searching my face as if to prove his point.

"But she can't, can she?" My blood boils. My neck grows thick, swelling and overpowering me. I yell as loud as I can, unable to hold myself back any longer. "The chemo stopped working, and you weren't fucking there! She died while you were fucking your assistant in Italy!" I take a step closer, narrowing my eyes. "She was *dying,* and you weren't fucking there!"

"You ungrateful fuck," my father seethes, raising his arm behind him.

I move to take a step back but don't get the chance before his tight fist meets the side of my face. The sound of his knuckles meeting my jaw rings in my ear. Pain radiates across the left side of my face, and I stumble backward. Blood drips from the corner of my mouth. A strong metal taste coats my tongue, and I bend over, pressing my fingers to the blood, letting out a groan. Blood drips in one long stream down to the floor.

I keep one hand pressed to my knee and stare up at my father with hooded eyes. Everything around me is blurry, faded, and distorted. When he steps closer, bending to bring his face to mine, he's the only thing to come into focus.

"You think you're better now than you were then. You might have given up drinking, but I can see you're fucking high. You're no different than us." He curls his upper lip, his usual blue eyes now a stark black. "You're a fool if you think you can escape this. You were meant to be a Harding and nothing else."

I rest both of my hands on my knees and struggle to catch my breath. I stare up at my father, scrounging up the words to say to him. I don't have a comeback because I know my father is right. It doesn't matter the shit he's pulled in the past.

In certain aspects, I fear my past is darker than his.

February 16th

Dear J,

I'd been training months for this. Late night practices and rehearsals. Bruised toes and sore muscles. None of it bothered me. It comes with the territory of being a dancer.

Up on that stage, I immediately searched for you. The curtains opened, and I peeked around the red velvet fabric. I wasn't first to go out on stage. I was thankful, since it gave me time to find you.

I did.

You were sitting in the middle, fifteen rows back, leaning to the side, resting your elbow on the small wooden arm. Still dressed in your suit, you loosened your tie. I smiled, thankful you were able to make it, but my heart sank when I saw the dazed look in your eyes. The auditorium lights had turned off. The stage lights cast a subtle white glow on the audience. But I could see them from where I stood. Two blue eyes glazed over. A clear indication you were drunk. Again.

I brushed aside the disappointment I felt for seeing you this way, and reminded myself to be thankful you were able to make it at all.

Fraternity events and rushing. Parties and classes. It was all temporary. I closed my eyes, took a deep breath, and heard your voice in my head, reassuring me.

Then I went out on stage. You smiled. My heart hammered in my chest, but I know it wasn't simply from nerves. My body hummed with each step I took, feeling your eyes on me, watching me. I loved having you there. Up until college, my parents and Riley were the only ones to ever show up to my performances. Riley filled in the gap when they were absent, but you... you filled a different space in my heart. A space reserved for the person I knew I wanted to spend my life with.

After the performance was over and I changed, I met you out front. You weren't as drunk as I expected you to be, but I could still smell the beer mixed with vodka on your breath.

I figured you had sobered up more than when your driver had dropped you off at the theater. You pulled me in for a kiss, telling me how beautiful I looked on stage. How seeing me dance made you fall in love with me even more.

I let you entwine your fingers with mine as I followed you to your car parked out front. Your driver held the door open for us, and you slid in behind me. Once we were inside, I was reminded of where we were going.

You'd told me the week before that your family

was throwing a celebratory dinner at one of your houses for landing one of the largest accounts in your family's history. This time, it was the house out on the lake. I thought it was strange, but it didn't matter where we were going. I knew your family had a handful of houses scattered throughout Massachusetts. At some point, I was bound to visit each one at least once.

The drive out to the lake house took a bit longer than usual, but I held in my excitement. I leaned into you and rested my head on your shoulder. You traced invisible circles up and down my thigh. I told you about a book I'd finished in a grand total of six hours, begrudgingly stopping because I'd had an exam I couldn't skip out on.

When we pulled up to the house, my jaw dropped in awe. After typing the passcode in, the gate slid open, revealing the long, gravel drive. Golden lit lanterns dotted the driveway. It took an incredibly long time before we finally made it. The water glistened in the moonlight, reflecting in the bay windows along the sides of the house. The gray brick that made up the mansion reminded me of the houses I'd driven past when my parents would take me to Lexington and Concord for the summer. The old colonial mansions built centuries ago.

It was all a dream. You stepped out of the

car, held your hand out for me, and I followed you inside with bated breath.

But the second we stepped inside, I wished we hadn't come at all.

Your father's doorman escorted us to the back deck where him and your brothers sat. They were all circled around the fire pit with drinks in their hands. Micah and Lennon had each brought their dates. They looked different than the women they'd brought with them a few weeks back, but I didn't mention it. I gripped onto your hand tighter as we walked farther out onto the deck. Your father brought a date as well, but the closer we grew to the group, the more I noticed the other woman standing beside him.

Part of me wanted to believe your father had brought two dates—it wouldn't have been out of the norm for him, according to the stories you've told, and from the info I'd gathered in our time together—but I knew that wasn't the case. Your father never once looked in my direction. He didn't acknowledge my presence at all, despite Lennon and Micah's warm greetings. They even went as far as to pull me in for a hug. But it was your father's next moves that had me filled with a sense of dread.

With a devious smirk, he held his arm out, shuffling the woman forward.

He told you her name and her connection to someone he knew through another business similar to your family's. She was tall, thin, and beautiful. Her dark hair was slicked back into a perfect low ponytail. Not one hair was out of place. Her large, gold hoops dangled from her ears, swaying as she held out her hand to you.

You shook hers in return. My stomach flipped.

You eased it by placing your arm around me. Your hand rested on my hip, and you gave me a gentle squeeze of reassurance.

After the initial pleasantries, you stood back. I looked up at you beside me. Your jaw was clenched tight, the muscles twitching. I guess this was the moment your father's intentions became clear.

You knew why he had brought this woman.

"This is my girlfriend Victoria," you said, ignoring him and focusing on the woman beside him.

"Nice to meet you," date number two said with a smile and a hint of disappointment. "I'm sorry," she added. "I didn't realize."

"Of course not," you said, sending your father a glare. "Victoria and I have been together for months now, but maybe my father's been a bit distracted, and it slipped his mind."

"No." He frowned in disagreement. "I brought Rachel here because she was interested in getting to know you. I told her all about your accomplishments in school and figured you two would hit it off."

"You're kidding?" you scoffed.

Tears stung the back of my eyes. I wanted to vomit. I wanted to escape, but I couldn't. We were miles from the city. I felt shackled and suffocated by the glitz and glamour. Suffocated by a life that was constantly trying to purge me from it.

"I'm not." Your father puffed his chest. "I told you before." He pointed to me. "I'm warning you... this woman will ruin you."

Tears sprung from my eyes. I never understood why he hated me. Even as I write this hours later. I've mulled over every second and detail of tonight. I go back to the past several months, wondering where I might have gone wrong. Perhaps it truly is my social standing. My family doesn't earn enough money to stroke your father's ego or fill his pockets. He stands to gain nothing if you're with me.

As tears spilled down my cheeks, you held onto my hand, and pulled me away. We left as quickly as we'd arrived.

I was sobbing as we made our way back to the car. You slid in behind me and told your driver to take you back to your place. But I told you no, I wanted to go back to my dorm. I couldn't go back to your place. I wanted to lay in my own bed, surrounded by my own belongings. Never in my life have I ever questioned my own worth until I met your father and was introduced to your world. How is it possible to be made to feel so insignificant and small when I'd just had the best performance of my dance career less than an hour earlier?

I remind myself of the love you have for me. Your constant reassurance.

Before I stepped out of the car outside my building, you grabbed my hand and pulled me onto your lap. I straddled you, not caring your driver was still sitting behind the wheel, listening to our every word.

"Do you love me?" you asked.

I leaned into you as you tucked my hair behind my ear. It's become a habit of yours. A move you make before you twist your fingers around the tail of my braid. You tugged on the ribbon wrapped around the end, unraveling my braid. My brown waves cascaded down my shoulders. Your touch comforted me and brought calm to my storm of confliction.

"Of course, I do," I whispered. You wiped my tear away.

"I promise I will always protect you. Even from my father."

"I can't." I shook my head and squeezed my

eyes shut. I tried to explain the way I was feeling. "I can't keep playing this role that was never meant to be mine."

"What do you mean?" Worry etched itself into your brow, and your midnight eyes darkened.

I rested my hand on your cheek, fighting the urge to press my mouth to yours. It's always been my go-to with solving any uncertainty or unease I have. My bottom lip shook as I inhaled an unsteady breath. "I love you, J, but sometimes it feels as if I'm living someone else's life. I worry your world will swallow me and leave nothing behind. I worry I'm pretending I fit in when I don't. I'm not sure how much more my heart can take."

"Listen to me," you growled, gripping the side of my face. You urged me to look you in the eye, bringing your mouth closer to mine. The alcohol seemed to have dissolved behind your gaze, but I could still smell it on your tongue. "I plan on loving you for the rest of my life, V. No one before you has ever made me feel this way, and no one after you ever will. There will be no after. You're it. You're all I have, and I will do everything in my power to protect you, and if it takes me the rest of my life to prove it to you, then that's what it takes."

"But what about your dad?" I choked on a

sob, my heart ready to burst. "He's never going to approve."

You wiped my tear again, but this time you placed your lips to mine. Before letting me go, you followed your kiss with a whispered, "Fuck him and his opinions. He'll just have to get over it."

I believed you in that moment, but the second I stepped out of the car, I couldn't help but feel like you'd said it as a veiled attempt to make me feel better, and I don't know whether I should feel thankful or foolish for believing you.

Because as much as I know you hate him, you love him just the same.

CHAPTER NINETEEN

VICTORIA

I WAS NAÏVE TO BELIEVE I COULD CARRY MY LAUNDRY BAG of clean clothes home before the storm hit. Especially when I choose to use the laundromat furthest from my apartment. I consider calling a ride-share but know it'll take longer than if I were to walk home. Thunder and lightning rumble in the sky. My heart skips a beat every time a clap of thunder rolls across the city. I haven't seen or been in a storm like this one since Texas.

Rain pelts my back and soaks my braid. My clothes are drenched. I wish I'd thought to bring an umbrella, or bothered to look at the weather forecast before deciding to trek to the laundromat. I make it halfway home before I decide to give up on trying to keep them dry. I'll have to re-dry them once I get home.

I wish I could run the rest of the way, but the back of my leg twitches any time I pick up my pace. At this point, I give up the fight and enjoy the cool liquid soaking into my skin.

The memory of Jude and me on the washing machine is all I've been able to think about for the past two hours. He left me sitting on the machine with my cheeks flushed and my legs still humming from having him between them. I couldn't bring myself to look at the stranger who walked in on us, or anyone who came in afterward.

Fucking Jude on a washing machine was unexpected and exhilarating. And if I'm honest with myself, I don't know where this leaves us. I've always felt in a constant limbo with him, never knowing what to fully believe and where the truth lies.

There was a vulnerability in his confessions earlier. He'd given me a glimpse into his life now, confessing he'd pulled back from his family's firm. But at the same time, I knew there was still a tie there he hadn't quite brought himself to sever. If the accident and our loss years ago couldn't break him away then, he certainly wasn't free yet. I'm not entirely sure he wants to be free.

The thunderstorm intensifies the closer I get to my place. It vibrates under my feet, tempered only by my footsteps in the occasional puddle. I avoid them the best I can, biting down on the inside of my cheek to distract myself from the ache in my leg. Carrying the weight of my soaked clothes over my shoulder has only worsened the pain.

My phone vibrates in my back pocket. At first, I think it's a notification. I can check it when I get home, but when it vibrates three more times consecutively, I move off to the side, under the awning of a flower shop. I stand beneath it and catch my breath. My shorts are soaked, making it difficult to slide my phone out. When I finally free it, I read the missed call notification and the name of the person calling me again.

I dry my hand off as best I can and answer. "Cain?" I shout above the torrential downpour.

"Victoria." The tone in his voice makes my stomach flip. "Are you home?"

"No!" I shout over the rain. "I'm on my way, though. I got caught in this storm—"

"Have you seen Jude?" he asks, cutting me off. There's a sense of panic and worry in his voice. At first, I think I must be imagining it, but the way my stomach grows more nauseous by the second tells me my gut instinct is right.

"Not since earlier." I blush at my admission. "Why?"

"I think something's wrong. He texted me earlier, but none of it was making any sense. I couldn't make out what he was saying. All his words were jumbled and misspelled. I've tried calling a dozen times, but he isn't picking up."

"Oh my God." I cover my mouth. My throat swells, and the blood drains from my face.

"I thought you might have seen him considering your name popped up in his text."

"Wait..." I swallow. "He mentioned me?"

"Yeah. It was one of the only words I could make out. I called his office, and his secretary said he wasn't there, so I checked his apartment. He wasn't there, either. I figured he might be at your place."

"Okay." I swallow the lump in my throat and nod. My phone shakes against my face, and I realize it's because my entire body is shaking, too. It could be from the rain. It could be from the storm. It could be nerves. My guess is that it's all three. "I'll find him."

I hang up, and with shaky fingers, I attempt to call Jude. When he doesn't answer on the third ring, I step out from under the awning. Sheets of rain pour down on me. I drag my bag behind me on the sidewalk. My leg cries out in pain, but I grit my teeth, pushing through it. Only one block left before I make it to my shop. Through the drops of rain in the dark, I see it in the distance. The new sign Riley ordered for me hangs above it.

Victoria's Book Corner
Opening Soon

I try Jude again. No answer. I pull my phone away from my face and dial again.

I groan, both from the pain and from Jude not answering.

Normally, I wouldn't think anything of him not answering my calls, but considering everything Cain just told me, the worst-case scenario comes to mind.

It's not as if Jude and I are immune to those situations. We've experienced the worst. Had our lives ripped and torn apart by terrible circumstances and bad choices.

Panic settles in my bones, and the blood drains from my face again. When I make it to my store, I limp the rest of the way, only stopping when I hear banging coming from inside. The single chandelier near the back of the store is lit.

Another round of muffled banging strikes up again, forcing me to open the door.

I drop my laundry bag on the sidewalk and stagger my way to the back of the store, following the sounds of shouting and splitting wood, as if someone is breaking through a wall.

"Jude?" I call, shouting as loud as I possibly can.

"Fuck!" he yells. His booming voice gets lost amongst the sound of splitting wood.

"Jude?" I call again. I weave my way around the bookshelves and tables the best I can until I find him. Standing up in the loft, I look up and call his name again. "Jude. What are you doing up there?"

He ignores me.

Too panicked to care, I take the steps up the metal, spiral staircase.

I'm careful with each step, but only because my leg won't allow me to move any faster.

"Jude," I grunt, taking the steps as quickly as possible. "What's going on?"

He's banging again, and it sounds like a hammer breaking into drywall.

The metal stairs creak and sway. I catch sight of a few loose screws and bolts. Swallowing back the bile rising out of me, I push forward. The pain in my leg is almost unbearable. Each step is more difficult than the last. The spiral steps are narrow and unreliable.

When I get to the top, Jude finally comes into full view. He's standing in the middle of the loft, driving his hammer into a large sheet of drywall, just as I suspected.

He lifts his arm with his fingers clenched tightly around the hammer. His arm flies down, striking another hole into the sheet of drywall resting on a different sawhorse from the one downstairs. White chunks and pieces fly into the air. A loud growl escapes Jude's throat. His face is beat red, his neck swollen in anger, the veins under his skin visible.

Tears immediately spring to my eyes. I've never seen him this angry.

He lifts his arm again, and my heart breaks.

"Jude, stop!" I yell, limping toward him. I jog as fast as possible, stumbling on my way over, but I make it to him before he's able to deliver the next blow. I wrap my hands around his, standing on my toes to reach up. My touch stops him. Slowly, he looks up.

Red rimmed, glassy eyes stare back at me. My heart drops to the bottom of my stomach, like a penny tossed into a fountain.

Memories crash into me all at once. I choke on a sob, knowing I've seen this expression before. I haven't seen this side of Jude in four years, but it's unmistakable. It's the same expression I saw on him from behind the curtain, as I laid in the hospital bed, grieving over our loss.

"Victoria," he whispers, his voice cracking on my name.

When I look into his eyes, I think I might shatter right in

front of him. I study his face, taking in the version of him I'm seeing.

Blood is dripping from his mouth, and a large black and blue bruise is spread across his cheek. It looks as if someone has painted his face in watercolors.

I gasp, covering my mouth with my hand. I lower it, unable to take my eyes off him. "Jude," I breathe, taking a step toward him. "What happened?"

I wrap my hands around his face, pleading with him to explain what's happening. I immediately smell the alcohol on his breath, and I feel ill.

"Have you been drinking?" I ask.

The soaking wet ends of his hair stick to his sweat-covered forehead. It might be from the rain, but with his heavy, panting breaths and the damage he's done to the drywall, I assume it's sweat. A tear spills over his wet lashes, and his eyebrows slant in anger.

"Why are you up here?" he asks, ignoring my question. Redness returns to his face, and the fire in his broken stare is aimed at me. "It's dangerous." He gestures lazily and sluggishly to the stairway.

"Stop." I grit between clenched teeth, holding back my cries. I'm worried for Jude. I haven't seen him this way since I've been back in Boston. He hasn't given me any indication of him drinking. Sure, it's possible he never quit, but something is different. Something has triggered him to drink enough to come over here and destroy a sheet of drywall.

"Why are you here?" he yells again, but this time I know he isn't talking about me being up in the loft. He's talking about himself, wondering why I've bothered to seek him out.

"Cain was worried about you," I choke out. "You haven't been answering his calls."

I wrap my arms around myself, yet stay close to Jude. I'm afraid if I put too much distance between us, he'll want to leave.

Jude sighs, pressing his lips together tightly. He breathes in through his nose, shoving his hair off his forehead. His glassy blue eyes search my tear-filled ones. His beautiful mouth tugs downward into a frown, and his chin trembles.

I reach up and ghost my thumb along his blood-stained lip. "What happened?"

Wrapping his hand around mine, he sobs. Tears spill from his eyes, fueled by anger and sadness. He lowers our joined hands and studies them. His palm wraps around the back of mine.

"It's all my fault," he confesses.

"What's all your fault?" I tilt my head to the side, begging him to answer me.

"You." His eyes narrow as if the mere word causes him pain. "And…"

He squeezes his eyes shut and sniffs, choking on a sob. I cry, too. His confession is like removing one single piece of wood from a dam. Water rushes out, destroying all in its path. Waves crash around the four walls of our chests, suffocating us.

"I'm so fucking stupid." He grinds his teeth. "I was so fucking stupid for believing anything could ever change."

"I don't know what you're talking about." I shake my head.

"It's all my fault."

"*What* is?"

"You," he sobs. "Your dance career. The…" He stops himself. "It's all my fault, and I should have known. I've done everything I can to forget what happened, but I can't get it out of my head. That night and everything that led up to it. My mother giving up her battle with the cancer while my father was fucking his tenth mistress."

I swallow, remembering the deepest, darkest secrets of the Harding family. James Harding had an affair while his wife was fighting her battle with cancer. It wasn't the first time, his exploits were common knowledge among the family. One of his affairs resulted in the birth of Jude's baby brother, Micah. They share the same father, but they have different mothers. But Micah's mother was only one of the many affairs James had over the course of his marriage. I learned years ago, after Jude and I started dating, the guilt he carries with him for keeping his silence. For not outing his father and his exploits.

Jude and Lennon love their little brother Micah, despite the differences between them.

"Every single day," he continues, holding his hand to his chest. "I relive it. Images of the car. Seeing you in the hospital bed. Every single day."

Our hearts break together, replaying that night as if we're suddenly thrust back there. Jude's alcohol-soaked eyes, half-shadowed by the hospital curtain. The beeping of the machine above me. The IV in my hand. The hollow feeling in my stomach and chest.

He drops the hammer onto the sheet of drywall and leans on it, hanging his head between his shoulders. They shudder with his sobs. He growls and screams, the veins in his neck popping with anger. I let his rage inflate the room. He's drunk, but I give him a moment to vent. I cover my mouth with my hand, holding myself back from falling apart. I've never seen him this way. Torn and broken. More broken than ever before. I'm no stranger to dealing with Jude when he's drunk, but this is different.

"Jude," I whisper, gently placing my hands around his cheeks, pulling him to face me. I lift his head, and the storm behind his eyes is the catalyst to what's left of my broken heart.

Pain and agony. Torment and guilt. All emotions weaving and intertwining. It's impossible to make out where it begins and where it ends, if it even does. Every bit amounts to a busted lip and bruised cheek.

"Jude, look at me," I beg with a shaky lip.

His eyes fall to my mouth. "I need you to know something, Victoria."

"It's okay." I hush him. "It's okay."

He inhales an unsteady breath. Tears continue to pour from his broken eyes. He gasps for breath, slamming his mouth to mine. I close my eyes, allowing him to soak up my tears. His mouth is hot and fast. He moves his lips against mine, groaning in pain every few seconds. When I open my mouth and allow his tongue to touch mine, I'm overwhelmed by the vodka, metallic mixture. He tastes both bitter and sweet.

He lifts both arms and grips onto the side of my head. My hair is still soaking wet from the torrential downpour. His fingers press into the wet strands. The air is hot and sticky. Jude pours everything into his kiss. His hips lunge forward, pressing into me. I grip his wet shirt, bunching it into my tight fists as I stand on my toes, pushing aside the pain shooting down my leg. Every second of Jude's kiss is worth the discomfort.

I'm relishing in his touch when he pauses, pulling his tongue away. His lips are still pressed to mine, but he parts them as a sob escapes his chest and he rests his forehead against mine, keeping his hands around my cheeks. I place both mine around his, too.

"It's okay," I mutter against his mouth.

"It's not," he whispers back, shaking his head slightly, never breaking our connection.

He sobs again, his shoulders rocking, and his body shuddering with every breath. The seconds pass with him breaking a little more. I'm at a loss what to do. I'm not sure how much more he has left in him. He's drunk. I have no idea who hit him or if he got in a fight with someone at a bar. The guilt and pain Jude is sharing with me is taking a toll on him. He's reaching his breaking point.

"It's my fault," he cries, kissing me again. "It's my fault."

"It's okay." They're the only words I can bring myself to say. I have nothing. There's nothing left inside me.

I let Jude cry with his forehead against mine. He's looking down when he slides his hands down the side of my face. His legs bend, and I fall back against the wall full of empty, broken bookshelves. The edge of a shelf digs into my back, but I don't feel the pain from it. Jude relaxes against me. His hands fall to my sides, and his head lands on my chest. He presses his cheek to my chest and cries. I wrap both of my arms around him, cradling his head in my hands.

We slowly fall to the floor, and he curls his body into mine. At first, he rests his head on my chest, but he slowly inches his head down, close to my stomach. One arm is wrapped behind me, the other rests on my lap, his hand pressed to my stomach.

Each sob he cries bears more weight on me. I tilt my head to the side and stare out into my bookstore with watery eyes. My vision blurs, and my lip trembles.

"I'm sorry," he whispers, dragging his fingers from my knee to my thigh. "It's all my fault." I hold my breath when he doesn't stop. He drags his fingers up my thigh, only stopping when he reaches my stomach to flatten his palm against me. "All my fault."

I rest one hand on top of his head as we both cry in silence. I chew on the inside of my cheek, knowing that no amount of words or seconds of silence will give Jude peace.

Neither of us have been able to live in peace. We walk around pretending as if we aren't broken.

We both sit and cry without speaking another word. I don't

know when it happens exactly, but eventually, he falls asleep on me with his head over my heart and his hand still on my stomach.

February 28th

Dear J,

I thought when we first met, you'd stolen my breath... but I guess you could call me a liar.

My breath was truly stolen the second I saw the double pink lines on the test I held between my fingers.

I fell to the floor and stared at the two lines until they became one. They blended with the tears lining my eyes, delivering a gut-wrenching blow. A million emotions slammed into me at once. I've never felt so conflicted as I did then.

Plagued by shock, I was frozen still. I was thankful Kate was in class. I'd suspected it for a while. Between the constant exhaustion before the day is halfway through, and the tiny knot tugging on the inside of my stomach, I knew. I knew I was pregnant before I'd even peed on the stupid little stick.

I've never been pregnant before, but I guess sometimes you just know. I sat on my floor for who knew how long. I listened to the silence and the muted chatter of my dormmates passing down the hall. Their laughter and screams. The year is almost over. Everyone is gearing up for finals, planning which beach they'll be escaping to the second classes are finished. All the while, I sat on the floor, wondering if I was pregnant with a boy or a girl.

It shouldn't have been the first thought to pop into my head. I'm in no position to be raising a baby. I barely make enough to make ends meet as a part-time barista and full-time student. Then there's my dancing. I knew being pregnant would affect my commitment, but plenty of dancers get pregnant and make it work. I could make it work, too.

Then there was you...

I sat up from the floor and moved to sit on the edge of my bed. We were supposed to meet in thirty minutes for dinner at your apartment. Your father gifted the apartment to you as long as you promised to follow through on the plans he had set out for you.

Go to business school.

Join the fraternity.

Work at his firm.

Getting your girlfriend pregnant wasn't on that list.

I sucked in a sharp breath and told myself I had to tell you, despite how worried or freaked out you might have been. Ever since we've been together, you've been supportive. I didn't have a single reason to doubt you. I knew you loved me, and the minute you found out about this baby, you would love them, too.

I reminded myself of all the promises and reassurances you've given me and headed to dinner with my head held high.

I was nervous to tell you. My palms were sweaty, and my heart raced a mile a minute. I thought it was going to beat right out of my chest and land beside my plate of burger and fries. Worry rested on your brow. Your eyes widened, and you reached across the table. You held my hand.

I took a deep breath and followed it up with word vomit. I couldn't stop the confession from passing my lips. Up until that moment, it was a secret only I knew. But now, you knew as well. Saying it out loud somehow made it feel more real.

I stared at you as your eyes fell to your plate. It was as if you were staring off into space, working out a calculus equation in your head. Your eyes danced back and forth. I held my breath until it became unbearable. The lack of air burned my throat. I took a breath, and you did, too. Finally, you looked up at me.

"We're in this together." A hint of a smile appeared on your perfect mouth. You stood from your seat at the table and wrapped your arms around me. You placed both of your hands around my face and kissed me. "I love you, Victoria."

"I love you, too. But what about your dad?" I hated how I always asked how he felt, as if our relationship consisted of three people instead of two.

"We don't have to tell him," you said. "At least not right away. I'll figure out the time for us to tell him. Besides, this isn't his baby. It's ours."

Uncertainty about your father settled in my gut, though it could have been the tiny bit of nausea creeping up on me, too.

I focused on the fact you said our baby was ours.

I held onto the word, dissected it, and protected it. We may be young, and we may not have everything figured out. But I knew as long as we were together, we'd make it work. We were going to be parents, and the thought made my heart flutter nearly as much as knowing my baby was half yours.

CHAPTER TWENTY

Jude

"Jude." A soft voice above my head wakes me. My stomach turns, and the pounding in my head radiates down to the back of my neck. I twist and look up to find Victoria's face looking down on me.

"We fell asleep," she whispers.

Black streaks stretch down the length of her cheeks. Red lines her eyes, and her skin pales in the morning light.

I lift my hand and gently press my fingers to the corner of my mouth, finding the source of the pain blistering the left side of my face. Dried blood is caked to my lips, and I wince when I press against the bruise on my cheek. The strong taste of old vodka and blood fills my mouth. I fight the urge to vomit.

"How are you feeling?" Victoria asks.

Fuck. It's been years since I've had a drink. I promised myself I would never have another sip of alcohol after the day of the accident, yet here I am, a hungover asshole with sore eyes and a headache from hell.

"Like shit," I blurt out.

"Yeah," She presses her mouth into a thin line.

I turn so I'm lying on my back with my head in her lap. I

reach up and run my thumb down one of the black streaks painted on her cheek.

"I'm sorry." Memories of last night come rushing back to me all at once. Despite the pain of my father hitting me, and the hammer I drove through the wall repeatedly, none of it topped the hurt in Victoria's eyes at seeing me the way I was.

I've kept a tight lid on my emotions over the past four years. I found a way to live alone. I found a way to *be* alone. Eventually, I became numb to the feeling. Until Victoria came back into my life.

Conflict wages a war in her expression. I see it on the tip of her tongue.

"What happened?" Her chin trembles.

I sigh and tilt my head back, staring at the ceiling. My stomach aches. I can't decide if it's from hunger or from the six shots of vodka and three beers I had last night at the bar down the street.

I pull my hand away from Victoria's face and stare into her eyes.

She waits patiently. Her hair cascades around her face, but I can't bring myself to give her an explanation. At least not now when my insides are a mess, and my head feels like it might explode at any moment.

I sit up from her lap and rest my back against the unstable, built-in bookshelf. The light pouring in through the windows blinds me. I wince, needing a few seconds for my eyes to adjust to the piercing light. Sitting up in the loft, above the windows below, provides a bit of reprieve.

I rest my hands in my lap and squeeze my eyes shut.

"I don't know where to begin," I confess. When I open my eyes and roll my head against the wall, Victoria is staring directly at me, sitting in a similar position with her legs stretched out, crossed at the ankle. She's massaging her thigh again. I've caught on to her nuances. She does it when she has a flare up. Her leg is bothering her, but she stays quiet. She doesn't complain. I guess we've both become experts at masking our demons. Funnily enough, though, we haven't been able to hide them from each other.

"Start from the beginning," she whispers, arching her perfect eyebrows. "Or maybe last night would be easier."

The corner of my mouth tugs into a small smile, but it doesn't last.

"When you messaged me last night, I was prepping to go into a meeting." I start small, thinking back to sitting at my desk with the stack of contracts Lennon drafted for me to present to our father. Again, he'd convinced me I was the best at negotiating. Apparently, I wasn't just the best negotiator with clients, I was also the best when it came to presentations with our father. It didn't matter that I'd cut my time down at the office by over fifty percent. Lennon still relied on me to be the prime communicator in the business.

"Oh," Victoria says, pouting her lip. "I'm sorry. I didn't mean to—"

"No." I shake my head, stopping her. "I wouldn't have come if I hadn't wanted to."

A small laugh escapes her before her mouth spreads into a grin. A warm sensation spreads across my chest. It's a temporary balm to the heaviness of last night and this morning.

"Poor choice of words, I guess." I say, remembering how it felt to take her on the washing machine.

"I would have to disagree." She smirks, quirking an eyebrow.

I rub my hands together in my lap. I'm still wearing the same button-down shirt and tie from last night. The now stale fabric has dried after walking six blocks in the pelting rain to get to Victoria's store.

"I'm sorry if I pulled you from an important client," she adds.

I roll my head back to face her again. "My meeting wasn't with a client. It was with my father."

"Oh." She parts her lips, breathing in a small amount of air. I can sense the shift in her at the mention of him. Her and my father never got along. They've never seen eye to eye, and I know that's all on my father.

It's the root to all the problems him and I face. Alongside Victoria, there's the way he treated my mother when she was only given months to live.

"So, you do work for him," she states, as if I've confirmed what she's suspected. She isn't surprised in the least. If I were her, I wouldn't be, either.

"I do." My voice cracks, the words souring on my tongue. Or it could be the fresh blood bubbling from the wound on my lip. It's split back open from talking. "I've pulled back from the company slowly over the years, but more so this year than the last few since I graduated." I run my hand through my hair. "But I still go in every now and then to meet and negotiate with clients. I still go to meetings."

"And dinner at Eclipse?" She raises her eyebrows.

"Yep." I nod. "Despite our family's deep web of secrets, we can be fairly predictable."

She lifts one shoulder. "Too many secrets and you'd draw suspicion to yourselves."

"When you say it like that..."

Victoria nudges me with a grin. "You get what I mean."

I nod, resisting the urge to kiss her. I want to press my mouth to hers, hoping to all fucking hell the bit of happiness inside her rubs off on me. All I feel is darkness. Hopelessness.

"What happened last night, then?" She swallows.

"After I left the laundromat and headed back to the office,

he was already gone. But when I got home, I found him sitting in my living room."

"Really?"

"I didn't tell him where I went," I explain, hoping to put her mind at ease. "Between the work I do here and the odd jobs I do around the city, I figured we were going to hit a boiling point sooner or later."

"So, what? You got into a fight over it?"

I pinch the tip of my tongue between my teeth, and inhale a deep breath. "Wasn't much of a fight," I tell her, pointing to my cheek. "He hit me after accusing me of losing the company out of a multi-million-dollar deal."

"What happened then?" She already knows the answer. She just wants me to say it out loud.

I swallow the thick sensation in my throat. It's suffocating, and my gut fills with shame. I've never considered myself an alcoholic. Rushing to get into Kappa Sigma was like getting sucked into a black hole. The relentless peer pressure and pressure from my father made it easy for me to drink. The motion became a subconscious act I didn't ever question. In the beginning, I didn't set out for it to happen, but along the way, it became a vicious cycle I couldn't escape. One drink became two, and two eventually became ten, until I could no longer count. Drinking made it easier to numb the pain of my past. Drinking made it easier to drown the thoughts constantly in my head.

"I, um..." I clear my throat, gathering up the courage to admit the truth out loud. "I left my place, and I couldn't get the last words my dad said to me out of my head. I found the closest bar and drank my way here." I eye the chunks and pieces of mangled drywall scattered everywhere. The loft is a mess. I roll my head back to Victoria. "I came here hoping to find you."

A smile spreads across her pretty mouth. "You found me."

"I did." I smile back.

Her eyes soften, and her smile fades. She swipes her tongue across her lips, taking in a shaky breath. "What was the last thing he said to you?"

"What?" I ask, knitting my eyebrows.

"You said you couldn't get the last words he said to you out of your head. What did he say?"

"Oh." I close my eyes, remembering the way my father's lip curled, and how the veins popped in his neck. The way the glass shattered against the wall, spraying across my floor.

"You don't have to tell me if you don't want to," she offers, pulling me out of the memory.

"It's okay." I look down at my hands, running my fingers over the back of the other, tracing invisible lines across each vein, noting how the blood running in them is the same as my father's. "He told me I was just like him, and I couldn't escape who I am on the inside."

My stomach twists again. This time I'm sure it's more than the lack of hydration and food. I shove the thoughts of my father down into the parts of myself I keep hidden in the dark, away from everyone else. Tears sting behind my eyes, threatening to build. I don't want to break down again. Not after last night. I let my father's words get to me, and it brought me to a new low.

"It's been four years." Victoria leans over and places her hand on my cheek, lifting my attention off my hands and to her. She stares into my eyes and slowly lifts herself off the floor before she swings her leg over mine and straddles me. Her mouth twitches when she lowers herself on top of me. I rest both my hands on her hips, noticing how she's still wearing the same gray cotton shorts she was wearing last night at the laundromat.

Sitting on my lap, she lifts her hand and runs her fingers

through my hair, then slowly and silently drags her nail down the side of my face, zeroing in where her skin meets mine.

"It's been four years," she repeats. Her eyes dart to mine, and she shakes her head. I've already noticed her rocking her hips against me. "I know less about you now than I did when we met, but I know you are nothing like him, Jude. You never have been."

"But I couldn't protect—"

She presses her finger to my mouth as a tear spills over her dark lashes. My heart breaks knowing I've made her cry again, but it's hard to look at her without remembering what we lost. *Who* we lost.

"You don't have to say anything." She closes her eyes and tugs her bottom lip under her teeth, moaning as she rolls her hips a little harder.

She lifts herself up slightly and slides her hands between us, reaching for my belt. She unbuckles it, then unbuttons my pants. I watch her as she effortlessly frees my hardened cock.

I groan when she grips my length and rubs her thumb over the tip.

"Victoria." Her name falls from my mouth as I wrap my hand around the back of her head, pulling her to me. I want to kiss her, but I know I'm a mess. There's dried blood on my mouth, and half of my face is beaten. I'm about to put a stop to this until after I've been given a chance to clean up, but my eyes find Victoria's. She doesn't speak a word, but she doesn't need to. Her silence and motions are enough to tell me she doesn't care if I'm battered and bruised. Her touch heals me. Her kisses soothe the wounds I carry around inside—the ones others can't see. To the rest of the world, I'm a rich fucking prick. On the inside, I'm a damaged soul, seeking a way to find instructions on how I can put myself back together.

"I don't have the answers," she says, sliding her shorts and underwear aside. She centers herself over me, then slowly sits down. "But I'll do whatever it takes to remind you that you are nothing like James Harding."

I fill her, moaning as she lowers herself all the way down. She's warm and soft, surrounding me with her gentleness, soaking wet already, and ready for me. She leans forward and crashes her mouth to mine. I keep one hand planted on her hip and the other around the back of her head, keeping her mouth to mine.

Our kiss is painful. I grunt as she moves her lips against mine, but the feeling of her moving above me and being buried inside her trumps the stinging sensation.

"How's this?" she asks between kisses.

She tilts her head to the side, putting her mouth to my neck. She rocks her hips back and forth, up and down. Her entire body is pressed to mine. Shivers break out across my skin as she laps her tongue down the length of my neck, bringing her mouth to the hollow of my ear.

"We've all made mistakes, Jude," she whispers.

I squeeze my eyes shut. Adding pressure, I press my fingers into the flesh of her hip. I beg her body to keep me grounded to this floor. I'm afraid if I let myself go completely, I'll wake up and this will all be a dream.

"Tell me a truth," she says on a breath.

"A truth?"

"Yes." Her hot breath dances across my skin, and she brings her face in front of me. "Every time you tell me a truth, I will move faster." She grinds her hips deeper and harder. Her walls tense around my cock. "I want to know," she moans. "A truth that will prove you aren't like him."

She stares into my eyes, grinding her hips harder with every thrust.

My mouth parts as shallow breaths pass between my lips.

It's difficult to think when I'm with Victoria, but I go along with her.

"I hate lobster," I tease.

It takes her a moment to process what I've said. Her head is tilted back. Her eyes are closed, and her chin is tipped up. She's biting down on her lip, moaning with every rock of her hips. When she finally catches on to what I've said, she rolls her eyes and gives me a teasing glare.

"What?" I ask her. "You asked for a truth that set us apart. I hate lobster, and my father orders it every time we go to Eclipse."

"Why do I get the feeling..." She moans, inhaling a quivering breath. "You said this one just to get me to move faster?"

I laugh and tug on the end of her messy braid. She groans, and a shadow of a smile pulls on her pretty mouth.

"I was right," I groan.

"Right about what?"

"You like it when I tug on your hair." Heat radiates across my legs, and my dick pulsates inside Victoria. Every thrust she makes pushes me closer to my orgasm.

"I do." She licks her lips, lifting herself up. She slams herself back down, her beautiful, rounded ass pounding against my thighs. I close my eyes and tilt my head back against the shelving behind me.

"You're distracting me, Mr. Harding. I need a truth."

Her calling me Mr. Harding sobers me. My chest swells with a warmth I haven't felt in years. It's familiar and comforting. Exhilarating and breathtaking.

I yank on her braid again. Her smile falters, and the desire in her eyes grows. They flicker with excitement. Although I gave her a lighthearted truth, she's still picked up her pace. Her breasts bounce higher with every lift. Her moans escape her mouth faster with every drop back down.

I keep my hand wrapped around her hair, keeping her gaze locked onto mine.

"Every day I step into my office is another day I feel is wasted living a life I never wanted." The words spill out of me effortlessly. They shoot straight to my core. They cut me and split me open, wide enough for Victoria to see. Brutal honesty.

"I'm sorry," she whispers. Pain is etched into her voice.

She places her hand against my cheek, and I sigh a breath of relief. She doesn't ask me to explain. She doesn't tell me to expand on my answer. It's a truth. Plain and simple.

"One more," she says, lifting herself faster. Her body clenches around me. She flexes around me and wraps her hands around the back of my neck. With one hand still twisted around the base of her braid, I slide the other between us and press my fingertips to her clit.

She cries out, shocked by my touch.

The intensity in her eyes blooms.

"One more truth," she cries out. "You're going to make me come, and we aren't done. I need one more."

"I fear one day I'll turn into him without realizing I have." It's not exactly a truth that makes me less like my father, but it's a truth, nonetheless. A worry. A fear. Call it what you will, it fucking terrifies me.

What terrifies me the most is the fact that Victoria has never fully believed I was willing to let that part of my life fade into the background. The lavish lifestyle. The power our family name inherited from generations past. Mine and Victoria's relationship stemmed from my desire to follow the path my father had carved out for me. Joining Kappa Sigma. We met that night on the rooftop. I was only there in the hopes of rushing their fraternity. Victoria was seeking an escape from the party, only to find me instead.

She doesn't answer me this time. She doesn't offer another

apology. She simply keeps one arm around my shoulder, the other hand cupped to the side of my face. Every kiss, every rock of her hips, and every confession passed between us is a bandage to our open wounds. We can't have the hope to heal until we've addressed the injuries of our past.

I tilt my head enough to pull her thumb into my mouth. She hooks it inside the bottom of my teeth, feeling every breath rush from my mouth.

"Fuck, Jude." She gasps. "I'm going to—"

I feel every nerve fire off at once. Victoria's pace has quickened. Her thighs clench around me as she tilts her head back, crying out with her orgasm. Her insides vibrate and pulsate along the length of my cock. I tilt my head back and groan, allowing myself to spill inside her.

She rocks her hips back and forth, riding out the rest of our orgasms. She falls against me and takes several seconds to catch her breath before her forehead falls to my shoulder. I untwist my fingers from her braid and wrap both arms around her.

As if I'm waking up from my hangover all over again, the confessions I gave to Victoria come back to me at once. It's been years since I've opened myself up to anyone. The last person I did that to is the same woman sitting on my lap right now. I slide my hand along her back, and she lifts her head from my shoulder allowing me to move my hand along the side of her face and tuck her hair behind her ear.

I stare into her eyes and wonder what all this means. It's impossible to put into words. But then again, so are my feelings for Victoria. I've never been able to explain this hold she has on me. I resisted letting myself get too close to her, especially after what I did. Especially since I'm the one solely responsible for us losing our baby before they were even born.

I swallow the emotion thick in my throat and focus on Victoria's flushed face.

"I have one more truth," I tell her. "But it isn't one that will prove I'm not like him."

"Tell me." She cocks her head in intrigue.

"Up until last night, it's been four years since I've had a drink."

She holds her breath as tears line her tired eyes. She blinks, letting them splash down her cheeks. Her chin quivers as she takes my confession in. The weight of my words is more than the sentence I just spoke. It's months of me showing up at her dorm shitfaced. Months of broken promises and lies.

I don't know whether she's happy I stayed sober as long as I did, or if she's heartbroken at the cost it took for me to get sober. For me, it's the latter.

I can see her question resting at the tip of her tongue. She wants to ask more. She wants to know why it took the accident and the loss of our child to pull me into sobriety. But she doesn't. The pain and anguish are too great for us to handle.

"Tell *me* a truth," I say, wiping the tear from her cheek. "I told you mine. Now I want to hear one from you."

She twists her mouth in thought. Her eyes meet mine. "I spent every day after I left Boston hating you for what happened. I blamed you, and that wasn't right." She sniffs.

I can't say her confession is a comfort. Her truth only solidifies what I've felt about myself. The blow, however, is worse hearing it coming from her mouth.

"It's hard to explain," she continues. "But I didn't think it was possible to hate someone as much as I loved them. Because the truth is, Jude, I loved you. I honestly loved you."

Her choice in using the past tense to describe her love for me isn't lost on me, but I keep my thoughts to myself. I swallow her words and digest them, hoping they'll pass easier than they were to hear.

"I understand." It's all I can manage to say.

Victoria's mistrust in me goes back to me saying I've been sober the past four years. Our relationship was a ticking time bomb. We were tied to the tracks, staring down the oncoming train, waiting for the pin to drop. We were helpless to move, unwilling to admit defeat, until fate stepped in and broke us both.

I see the anguish in her eyes at the life she was living in Texas. An asshole fiancé who never truly loved her. A sister who betrayed her. All on the back of the mistakes I'd made that caused her to flee Boston in the first place.

I wrap my hand around the back of her neck and pull her to me. I kiss her, catching her off guard, and she gasps for a quick breath. I pour every ounce of energy I have left in me. I'm a mess. My cheek is sore and bruised. I'm sure there's still dried blood dotted in the corner of my mouth. My lip is split, and when Victoria's mouth is pressed to mine, I bite back the sting that follows.

If I were anyone else, I'd be hurt that Victoria said she hated me as much as she loved me. But I get it. I understand how it feels to love something so much it aches.

I don't know how temporary this moment might be. Every second with Victoria is a second I didn't know I would be given again. I hold onto this with her. Her kisses are bandages, and her touches are stitches to my open wounds.

It doesn't matter if this is temporary when the truth is laid out for us. And the truth is, Victoria needs me as much as I need her.

CHAPTER TWENTY-ONE

VICTORIA

"Close your eyes." Jude meets me at the last intersection before I make it to my apartment.

It's been months since Riley gifted me the space to turn into my own bookstore, and the grand opening is finally this weekend.

My heart flutters as I cock my head and give Jude a sidelong glance. I step around him.

"We aren't on some famous fixer upper show, Jude," I say, bursting with impatience. "Besides, I saw this place yesterday."

He holds his arm out, stopping me from taking another step.

I stare up at him, crossing my arms beneath my chest, and his eyes fall to them. I'm wearing a purple, cropped tank top and high waisted, black leggings. My body is covered in a film of sweat, and my hair is dripping from the tail end of my braid resting at the base of my neck. I've just finished my first physical therapy session since I returned to Boston. When I first moved back, I was afraid to admit I still needed it. But after the incident at *Lights Out,* and telling Riley about what happened, she convinced me to start them back up again. Deep down, I know my leg will never move the way it did before, but at least therapy staves off the phantom pains that plague my muscles from time to time.

"Quit looking at me like that," I tease Jude. The truth is, I don't ever want him to stop looking at me like this.

His hair looks as if he's run his fingers through it a thousand times since he rolled out of bed. Sweat lines his forehead, and three creases form in the corners of his eyes when his mouth lifts to a smile. His jeans are torn in ten different places and covered in dots of white and blue paint. His black shirt clings to his muscles, sticky from the humid Boston air.

"I don't think it's fair of you to demand I stop looking at you this way." He draws closer, the tip of his boot meeting the toes of my sneakers. "It's impossible when you're dressed like that."

I arch a brow and narrow my eyes. "It's workout gear, Jude. I'm all sweaty and gross."

"Exactly." He steps forward and lowers his face to mine, bringing his mouth to the hollow of my ear. "Let's just say I'm going to find it incredibly difficult to keep my hands to myself in front of Cain and Riley. I can't make any promises."

The blood rushes from my face and spills to my toes. Heat radiates across my body, zeroing in on the space between my legs—the space that consistently and relentlessly begs to be reminded of what it feels like to have Jude between them. His hands. His mouth. His tongue. Any and all of it.

I shove the doubt that repeatedly creeps up in conversations such as these. I'm willingly tying myself to the train track, watching as the certainty of our collision comes into view. I don't know what to make of our reconnection. It's been weeks since I found Jude in the loft of my store, drunk, and hammering his way through a sheet of drywall. The bruise on his cheek has completely faded. The cut in the corner of his mouth has nearly healed. The only wounds leftover from that night aren't visible on the outside.

From what I understand, Jude has kept his distance from the office and his father since the night he confronted his father at his apartment, keeping their communication set to emails and board meetings where there's guaranteed witnesses and an easy escape route.

Gradually, over the course of the past few weeks, I've opened myself up to his world. Learning from my mistakes in the past, I take it in small doses at a time and with a grain of salt.

One week ago today was when I finally gathered the courage to stay at his place. Part of me feared I'd see James Harding again. I'd find him sitting in the corner of Jude's living room, snorting another line of cocaine. He'd look at me with the same signature glare he'd given me the night we met.

The other part of me wondered if it was too big of a step. Most wouldn't assume so. But for me and Jude, it's different. We've broken each other's hearts. Been torn apart by the loss of our child. Then there's the truth Jude spoke that day in the loft. He hadn't picked up a single drink since the night of the accident. I was both heartbroken and pleased at the same time. It's a terrible feeling to be conflicted with one's sobriety. I was happy Jude had finally sobered for those years. I was happy he'd taken control of his drinking and not let it consume him past the point of him staying alive. But I couldn't help feeling sadness at the thought of the circumstances in which it took him to stop. I guess for him, he'd hit his rock bottom. The love I have for Jude has never faded, and despite the fact we aren't technically together any longer, I still wish him the best. I want nothing more for him to be sober and happy, even if it meant losing me in the process.

Then there was the morning after the night in the loft. I saw the shame and guilt in his eyes. I saw how he was just as broken as me. We've both been living our lives surrounded by lies we created ourselves. I hate that his father is enough of a trigger for him to slip back into drinking.

Stepping into Jude's apartment the first day was more than the mere motion of me stepping foot onto the marble floor. It was stepping into a world a thousand times greater and powerful than my own. It was me catapulting myself into his orbit, hoping I'd grasped onto the tiniest shred of tether to keep me grounded.

I took a deep breath and moved inside, determined to focus on Jude rather than the way my body was yelling for me to retreat... until Jude wrapped his hands around the sides of my face and pulled my mouth to his. I melted to him right then. The path wasn't clear, but I knew I didn't want to be anywhere else.

It's been a few weeks since that night in the loft, and I have yet to figure out where we stand. For now, I'm enjoying the simplicity of being around him. It's as if my heart is made of glass, and it's been sitting in a broken pile in the back of my mind. I've only just begun to slowly reassemble the pieces. I take my time. I don't rush it in fear that if I move too fast, it'll break again.

I stare up at Jude's blue eyes glinting in the afternoon sun with a knowing smirk.

"Come on." He crosses his arms over his chest, defiantly. He nods his head to the side, gesturing toward my bookstore. "Humor me."

"Okay." I fill my lungs with air, hoping it'll prepare me for the reveal of my own bookstore. I close my eyes, putting all my faith and trust in Jude, and hold my hand out for him to guide me down the street. When he doesn't take it, I almost crack one eye open but stop when I gasp for breath. Warm lips press against mine. A large hand rests on the small of my back, pulling me forward.

I laugh against Jude's mouth, feeling lighter than I have since I don't know when, and I somehow keep my eyes closed when he pulls away.

"What was that for?"

"Nothing." His thick voice hits the hollow of my ear. "Just wanted to get that in before we head in there."

I hold my breath and force my heart to slow. Jude wraps his hand around mine and pulls me in the direction of the store. I let him take the lead, weaving us in between others walking along the sidewalk. We walk in silence, listening to the sounds of Boston in the afternoon.

"We're here," Jude says as he slowly pulls me to a stop to keep me from bumping into him.

"Finally." Riley's high-pitched squeal startles me. I arch my eyebrows and take a step back but keep my eyes closed.

Her hand wraps around my shoulder, steadying me. "I'm sorry. I didn't mean to scare you." She pulls her hand away. "Why did you have her close her eyes, Jude?"

I find myself grinning.

Silence descends upon the three of us. Or there could be others here and I just don't know it.

Jude laughs. "I thought it would be more fun this way."

"She's already seen the sign," Riley says. "And there's not much she could gather from peeking through the windows from this distance."

I'm not sure whether that's good or bad. I open my mouth to ask, but Jude stops me.

"Fine." He groans. "You can open your eyes, Victoria."

"No," I argue. I want to savor this moment. I want to enjoy standing in front of Jude and Riley, listening to them talk about trivial things.

My life has been anything but trivial, and I won't deny my

heart the chance to feel this. Whatever this sensation might be. Happiness, maybe?

"Come on," Riley begs. I hear her foot stomp on the concrete. "We've been waiting to show you ever since you left."

"We have." Cain's voice draws closer. "There are still a few touch ups that need to be made, but for the most part, it's good to go."

I cock my head to the side, wondering when he came into this conversation. Has he been here the whole time? I haven't seen too much of him since he handed the job of renovating my bookstore to Jude months ago.

"Okay." Riley claps. "We're all here, so let's get this going."

I twist my mouth, wondering why she's in such a hurry. She doesn't have a class today. Maybe she's simply excited to see my reaction to the store.

"On the count of three," Jude suggests.

All three start to count in unison, but I stop them when I decide to open my eyes.

Orange and yellow sunlight hits my vision first, forcing me to take a few seconds to adjust, but once the colors fade, and my storefront comes into focus, I see it.

I no longer see Riley or Cain. Or even Jude. His hand lands on the small of my back, as if he's bracing himself for my reaction. I realize this is his moment, too. Months of dedication and hard manual labor of putting my vision into reality. All of this is on him as well.

The once faded wood framing of the storefront is now painted a rich, glossy, forest green. Old, traditional windows line the front, complete with a black door. Hanging above the door, just below the window to my bedroom on the floor above is the hand painted, wooden sign Riley bought me weeks ago.

Victoria's Book Corner

Tears immediately line my eyes. My breath gets caught in

my swollen throat. I clear it, hoping it'll give me the strength to speak.

"It's more than I imagined." I look at Cain, then Jude. "Thank you."

"The paint is still drying," Cain explains. "That's why we left the caution tape barrier here." He walks forward, gesturing to the yellow tape swaying in the breeze. Each end is tied to an orange traffic cone. I didn't even notice it until now.

"I love the color." I wipe a tear from my cheek.

"Are you okay?" Riley asks, gripping my arm.

I nod and sniff. "Yeah."

Riley's eyes match mine, spread wide and lined with tears.

"Don't you cry, too." I laugh, pulling her in for a hug. I wrap my arms tightly around her and bury my face into her neck. I've spent most of my life looking up to my aunt, even if there are only ten years between us.

"I'm not crying," Riley says unconvincingly.

I close my eyes and take a breath, savoring the warmth her embrace gives me. "Thank you," I mumble into her neck. "This wouldn't have been possible without you."

"Oh, it was nothing."

"Stop." I laugh and pull away from her. I brush a few flyaway hairs and tuck them behind my ear. "It's everything to me, Riley. I came back to Boston practically empty handed. You gave me a second chance at a life for myself."

She rolls her eyes. "I guess you're right." She spins around and hooks her arm through mine, looking up at my store, taking it all in. "This is all you, Victoria. This was your vision. Your passion. You didn't let anything stop you from turning it into reality. You deserve this."

"You're my best friend."

"Come on," Cain says, waving the three of us over. He

stands near the front door with his hand already on the handle. "I'll give you the tour."

The three of us follow Cain inside. Jude drops his hand from the small of my back, and I can sense Riley's side-eye beside me. I ignore her, and when I take in my store, my jaw drops.

Bookshelves stretch from one wall to the next, across the back, to the left, to the right. In the middle sits a large, circular check out desk, complete with a bright gold chandelier hanging over the center.

I step farther inside and drag my fingertips across the top of the glossed, wooden counter. I've seen the bookshelves and front desk already—I walk by them every day—but I haven't seen them like this. Clean and open, ready for me to stock with books and book supplies. It's ready for me to add the finishing touches to transform it into a real bookstore. I swing my gaze to Cain, then Jude.

"This is stunning," I whisper. My voice is weak despite the firestorm of emotions going on inside me. My heart is ready to burst.

Books have always been my escape. A place I could take myself to when life turned into complete and utter shit. I could immerse myself in the lives of others. They were fictional characters, but ones I held close to my heart. My own personal brand of therapy.

That's what I'm hoping my store does for others.

Cain and Riley head toward the back of the store, leaving Jude and me near the front counter.

"So," Jude says behind me. His voice causes shivers to dance down my spine. "What do you think?"

"I love it." I spin around and giggle. "Who knew one of Boston's wealthiest businessmen had a secret talent in construction?"

He laughs and runs his fingers through his hair. He scratches at his chin, holding back a grin. "Yeah, right."

"What?" I tease, pressing my finger to his chest. "Your craftsmanship is unparalleled."

Jude quickly gives a sidelong glance in the direction where Cain and Riley are, and without a second of hesitation, he reaches his hand out and spins me around.

I bite down on my bottom lip to keep from squealing as my back lands against his chest.

He bends his knees slightly, bringing his mouth to the hollow of my ear.

"Look up," he whispers.

I swing my gaze up and read the sign above the finished alcove.

V's Blind Book Corner

Air catches in my throat. It burns and stings in the best way possible. My vision blurs again. Jude took my blind book idea and made it happen. But it isn't just his follow through on running with the idea I'd shared with him months ago. It's his use of my nickname.

Jude moves to stand beside me. I haven't moved, but I can see him staring at me through my peripheral.

"Um..." He clears his throat. "I hope you like it. If you don't like the name, you can change it. I'll make up a new sign."

"No." I snap my head to the right. "Keep it. It's perfect."

A smile slowly spreads across his mouth. I want to kiss him. The dimple in his cheek makes my insides melt. My heart races, but my eyes move past him.

Cain and Riley are still standing near the back, sifting through one of the boxes of books placed in front of one of the bookshelves. It's not that I'm keeping my new situation with Jude a secret from them. I just don't know Cain very well—we're more on the business relationship level—and Riley only knows as much as I've been willing to share, which is mostly everything. She knows Jude and I have been sleeping together, but she doesn't know the depth of the situation. She doesn't know about the night Jude showed up to my store drunk.

She doesn't know the conversations we've had since then. The truths he willingly shared with me.

I hold back my kiss and give his hand a squeeze instead. He gives me a satisfied smile in return.

"What is a blind book corner?" Cain appears at Jude's side with his head cocked to the side and his eyebrows knitted in deep thought.

Jude claps him on the back. "I was confused at first, too. I'll explain it to you later."

Riley drapes her arm around my shoulders and pulls me to follow her. We leave Jude and Cain in front of the blind book corner, and she leads me toward the circular front desk, stopping one foot in front of the flawless wood top.

We both examine the store slowly. She holds me close, and every now and then I swear I hear a sniffle or two come out of her. I examine every bookshelf. My eyes travel up the spiral staircase to the clean loft. It's changed quite a bit since Jude and I were up there last. Now it's safe and up to code.

The memory of that night still lingers, filed into my brain next to all the other significant moments I've shared with Jude.

I can't stop looking at my store, wishing I had my notebook with me. I want to describe this feeling. I want to memorize what this moment feels like. I want to bottle it up, write it down on paper in ink, making it impossible to forget.

"So," Riley sighs beside me. "Let me know when you need a business partner and I'm in."

CHAPTER TWENTY-TWO

Jude

"Tell her I wish her the best, but I'm not sure it's a good idea to go."

I lean back in the large, leather office chair, and stare Lennon down from the opposite side of the table.

We're both sitting in the boardroom, waiting for our scheduled meeting to begin.

It isn't the usual meeting in which our family's partners and assistants attend.

This is a *family* meeting.

One with our father. And our brother Micah.

Lennon taps his finger on the glass tabletop and spins his chair halfway to gaze through the floor-to-ceiling window facing the Boston city skyline.

The grand opening for Victoria's bookstore is tomorrow night. Before I left her this morning in her apartment and told her I needed to head out for a meeting at the office, she extended the invitation to Lennon. I didn't tell her Micah was coming back from his trip to Europe, so she didn't mention asking him.

At first, I was surprised Victoria wanted to ask Lennon to come to her grand opening. Seeing him for the first time weeks ago had been a trigger for her. She confessed seeing him was the reason she'd decided to go out that night to *Lights Out*. She needed a way to escape her thoughts, the same way I try to escape mine all the time.

"I don't agree." I shake my head at Lennon. "Why do you think it isn't a good idea to go?"

"I just don't want to cause any unnecessary drama."

I narrow my eyes. "You mean, you don't want Dad to find out."

"No." He spins back to face me and leans over the edge of the table to rest on his elbows. His dark blue tie hangs between his hands. "Dad doesn't dictate what I do, Jude."

"Right," I scoff.

"Don't," he warns. His expression darkens with a glare. "You know me better than anyone."

"You're right." I sigh, adjusting my tie. I hate this fucking thing. It feels suffocating and isolating. I'm pretending to be someone I'm not. I'm playing a role in a play I never auditioned for. "That's why I also know Victoria has always liked you. She would appreciate you coming to the grand opening."

"I've always liked her, too." He scratches at his clean-shaven chin. His dark brown hair is slicked back perfectly, not a hair out of place. "But..."

"But what?" I ask, popping an eyebrow.

"But—" he starts, inhaling a deep breath, only to be cut off when our baby brother pushes his way through the glass door.

"Well," he yells, stretching his arms out wide. "If it isn't my asshole big brothers."

I roll my eyes and turn back to face the table.

Lennon laughs. "Nice of you to grace us with your presence, Micah. How was Italy?"

"Great. Beautiful food and weather. Made a shit ton of incredible business deals."

Micah is my father's youngest son. Despite the fact he has a different mother than us, courtesy of our father's eighth affair, Micah's resemblance to the Harding family line is undeniable. He has the same quirk to his smile, the same angle to his nose, and the same deep blue eyes. Aside from his mother's light chestnut hair, he doesn't share much with her in the looks department. As for personality, I can't say he got that from our father. Unlike James Harding, Micah has a softer, somewhat vulnerable side. He hasn't outright told me, but I like to believe his mother raised him to stay humble, knowing the family and environment he'd be raised in.

Like any other woman who has fucked our father, Micah's mother knew the advantages of keeping him connected to our family. The good outweighed the bad in her eyes.

As for me, the tipping in the scales has shifted quite a bit over the years.

Starting with today.

Micah's dark blue suit is a contrast to mine and Lennon's black ones. He moves around the table and sits in a seat halfway between us with his back to the city skyline.

"You know," Micah says, digging into the inside pocket of his suit jacket. He pulls out a flask and twists the top off. "I landed the Antonelli family. Ten million in coverage over the course of four years."

"I heard." Lennon nods. He keeps his expression stoic. Impressed but stoic.

Micah lifts the flask to his mouth.

Frustration burns under my skin. I can't explain it, but in this moment, I snap. I abruptly stand and walk over to where Micah is sitting. I snatch the flask from his hand, right before it meets his mouth.

"What the fuck, man?" Micah asks, gawking up at me from his seat at the table.

I sniff the flask and recoil at the smell, wanting to vomit.

I hold it up to him with a scowl. "It's nine in the morning, Micah."

"And?" He pops an eyebrow. "Don't act like you've never drank for breakfast. I've heard plenty of stories about how you partied non-stop in high school and college."

I blow out a hot breath through my nose. "Doesn't fucking matter. You aren't me, and we are not the same."

He spins in his chair to face Lennon, pointing a finger in my direction. "What's up with him?"

Lennon tosses his hands with a shrug and a frown.

"Really?" Micah asks Lennon, stunned. "You have no idea? You're both closer to each other than I am to either of you." There's a hint of bitterness laced in Micah's tone.

I can't say I blame him. Micah was raised mostly by his mother. We never grew up in the same house, apart from summers and every other major holiday. Micah wasn't as present in our lives. At least, not as much as we would have liked. But the choice of having him there was kept from us long enough to make it become second nature. Granted, we've grown our relationship over the past few years, but apparently not enough to lessen the sting of our differences.

"Does this have to do with Victoria?" Lennon asks.

I hate how the three of us have been raised in an environment to believe my decision to back away from alcohol and drugs isn't of my own free will. It's from the influence of someone else.

I love my older brother, but there are times when I see the battle waging in his eyes. Whether he's biding his time with our father until he can take over the company, or if he truly feels he has no way out, I hope he's at least being honest with himself, and he's staying for the sake of the business. Not our father.

"Victoria?" Micah snaps his head in my direction. I'm still towering over him. He raises both eyebrows and stares at me, wide-eyed. "Didn't she move away several years ago?"

"She's back in Boston," I begrudgingly admit. I'm fully preparing myself for a grilling and inquiry, but I won't give in.

My reconnection with Victoria is still fresh. Our past is still painful to deal with, and the last thing I need is to involve my brothers. I already know Victoria's trepidation when it comes to my family.

"Trust me." I sit down in my chair, changing the subject, and place the flask on the table. "You don't need it."

"If it makes you feel better." Micah surrenders with a grin. "I won't drink this early."

"Good." I stare at the flask, remembering the night several weeks ago when I slipped on my sobriety. Guilt ate away at me until I looked into Victoria's eyes, silently promising myself I wouldn't let myself go off the deep end like that again.

No amount of alcohol was worth the risk of losing her. Drinking doesn't hold a candle to the way she can heal me with a single touch.

"So, what's your deal with her?" Micah asks, steering the conversation back to Victoria.

"Who's her?"

The three of us snap our heads toward the door to the boardroom. Our father pushes through the large glass door. Well, more like strides. His movements are dramatic. His hair is slicked clean back, similar to the way Lennon's is styled. His gold watch glints in the morning light.

But what catches my attention the most is his frenzied gaze. His bloodshot, red rimmed eyes land on me before he looks to Lennon, and lastly, Micah.

"Who are we talking about?" he asks, sitting in the chair opposite Micah. He trades glances between the three of us before he pins his glare on me. "Who's her?"

I keep my focus on Lennon, unable to look at my father in fear he'll see right through me, even if he is high as a fucking kite.

"Raquel." Lennon clears his throat, shifting his eyes to our father. "Ran into her in the elevator."

"Oh," he mutters. "Nice girl, but she's a shark."

Lennon's hardened expression shifts back to me. His eyebrows shoot across his forehead. He can tell our father is off, more so than usual.

To be honest, he looks like shit.

Micah adjusts in his seat, sensing the tension in the room. He straightens his back and weaves his fingers together as he leans over the edge of the table. "Hey, Dad," he starts. "I was going to tell you how it went with the Antonellis."

"Oh, yeah." He taps his finger on the table. "Did you score their account?"

"I did." Micah nods. He isn't wearing the same proud grin he was when he first told Lennon and me. He hides his excitement, knowing our father won't be as impressed. In his mind, it's all about the numbers.

That's all his sons are to him: a tool to use to get more numbers. I look between my brothers, wondering if they're happy living this life. It's easy to accept it. We all accept the world the way it's presented to us. As far as money is concerned, we've never struggled, but life is more than just money. At least to everyone except our father, it would seem.

I curl my hand into a fist and focus on the stinging sensation my nails leave on my palm.

"I'm sending over the contract for them to sign later today," Micah adds.

"Are you fucking kidding me?" Our father's sudden shift in tone startles all three of us. His voice is dripping with venom and seething anger. He directs his question at Micah. "You didn't get that shit done when you were with the Antonellis in person?" The harsh sound of his pounding fist meeting the table echoes in the boardroom.

Micah nervously swallows. "I'm sorry, Dad. My mistake."

"It's fine," he sighs, smoothing his hair with his hand before he adjusts his cufflinks. "Next time, you make sure you get them to sign in person. You don't give the client a chance to back out or change their mind."

"Yes, sir," Micah agrees.

My father nods once and pulls a familiar metal tube from his front pocket. The three of us watch in silence as he effortlessly pops the top open and pours the contents out onto the glass top table in one line. He doesn't bother organizing it. He drops the metal tube back into his pocket and leans down, dragging his nose across the glass. The white powder vanishes. He sniffs and dips his finger in whatever residue is left, and massages it against his gums.

Seeing James Harding snort a line of cocaine in the boardroom isn't unusual. No one in the office bats an eye. None of his sons speak a word. We all stay silent, knowing it's better than speaking out.

As for me, my willingness to stay silent is wearing razor thin.

We're all silent when his dilated yet hooded eyes finally make their way to me.

I don't waver. I harden my chest and think of a million other places I'd rather be than here, staring at the man I hate most in the world.

His eyes land on Micah's flask still sitting in front of me.

"I see you're drinking again," he sneers. "Good. Maybe then

you'll start making better deals than the ones you've been presenting me with these past few months."

My vision turns red. I dedicated my entire life to pleasing him. I lost my child and Victoria the night of the accident because I was too busy getting shitfaced drunk trying to satisfy his requirements of me.

And he didn't bat an eye.

When he found out Victoria was in a car accident and lost our baby, he was more worried about how it would look to the press. He didn't give a shit about anything but his reputation.

I tense my jaw. I'm a pressure cooker, ready to burst. My blood boils. I tried. I honestly tried.

When my mother died, I convinced myself it was best to go along with any demands my father made of me because he was the only parent I had left. I'd lost myself in the mindset of it's better to have him around than not at all.

But now, as I look at my brothers who have fallen into the trap of the Harding business, unable to claw their way out, my future couldn't be any clearer.

I want to be with Victoria. I want to explore a career that makes me as passionate as she is about her books. I want to bury myself in her so deeply that she won't ever question where my loyalty lies. I may not be able to bring back our unborn child or rip the guilt I've carried for years knowing it was my fault, but I won't waste any more time feeling as if I can't ever be happy again.

I grab the flask and turn it over in my hand. I consider throwing it, channeling all my anger into the contents inside. I imagine throwing it across the room, shattering the glass walls surrounding us. But I don't. Instead, with a deep, shaky breath, I slide the flask across the table. It hits my father in his stomach and lands in his lap. His dark eyebrows knit in anger. The muscles in his jaw tick.

"Fuck you, Dad," I seethe, standing from my chair. I lean over the end of the table, placing my hands flat on the glass. "I'm done."

"What do you mean, you're done?" he asks, shooting me a poisonous glare.

"It means I'm fucking done." I growl. "I'm done with everything."

He purses his lips, and rocks in his chair. Honestly, I'm shocked he's able to carry this conversation as long as he has.

I chance a look at Lennon and Micah. They both haven't dared to move.

When I look back at my father, he's still mulling over what I've said.

"I would consider what you're doing here, son," he mumbles in a low and slow tone. He lifts his chin and squares his jaw, challenging me. "You're risking everything... and for what?"

I shake my head and pull myself to a stand, then I button my jacket and straighten my sleeves, steeling my attention on my father, making sure he understands every word coming out of my mouth. "I would only be risking everything if I stayed. I'm done."

I quickly scan the room, making sure I catch Lennon and Micah. I try to give them a silent apology for doing this now, and I make it brief because I need to get out of this fucking room. Adrenaline is pumping through me. My heart is skipping beats, and blood is draining from my face like a waterfall rushing down to a river.

I move around the table and am almost out of the room when my father leans back in his chair. He reaches out and wraps his firm grip around my wrist, pulling me to a stop.

I look down at his face, fueled with cocaine, alcohol, and anger. I can smell it on his breath as he shoots daggers up at me.

"Walk out that door and you'll be making a big fucking mistake."

I narrow my eyes. "I used to feel guilty for considering leaving. I used to think you were this way because somehow you were dealt a shitty hand in life. Maybe I never understood you before."

His fingers tighten around my wrist.

"Now I see I was wrong," I continue. "You're just a narcissistic fucking asshole. You're pathetic, and nothing will ever change."

I rip my arm away from his grip and his hand falls away slowly considering how hard I pulled away.

I snap my cuffs back into place and spin on my heel. I open the door to the boardroom and head to my office to begin packing up. When I gather every important item I can think of, I carry the box out of my office and step into the elevator without looking back.

VICTORIA

"Do they taste bad?" I bury my nose in the small bag I'm holding up to my face. When I get a good sniff, I scrunch my nose and recoil. I reach inside and pull a gummy free, pinching it between my fingers.

"Some do. Some don't," Jude explains. "These ones aren't bad, though."

He's lying beside me with his head resting on his pillow and his legs stretched out on top of the covers. He's completely naked. As am I.

My skin breaks out in a shiver as he ghosts his fingers in tiny circles on the small of my back.

I pull another gummy out and drop the bag back onto Jude's nightstand. With a flutter in my stomach, I move around the bed and swing my leg over Jude. I sit back on his thighs, just above his hardened cock. We've already fucked each other twice today. My thighs are sore, and my skin burns from his touch, but I'm immediately wet again the second his erection presses against my fluttering stomach.

"Should I try one?" I examine the gummies again and bring

one to my lips. I open my mouth, ready to pop it in. I haven't been high since college.

"If you want," he teases, running his fingers along the caps of my knees. I break out into a shiver again. "I like seeing you like this."

"Like what?"

"Sitting on top of me with your nipples perked and your pussy wet for me before I've even slid myself inside you."

"Hmm." I rock my hips and lower my free hand. I'm still holding the gummies in the other, but I don't take them. I use my free hand to slide down my chest and pinch my nipples between my fingers, moaning as I rock my hips against Jude.

"Fuck," he groans. "I love seeing you like this."

"You already told me that," I whisper, lowering my hand even further.

"No," he says. "I told you I *liked* you naked and wet for me. I *love* seeing you this way while touching yourself at the same time."

"Huh." I bite on my bottom lip.

Jude wraps his hand around mine and grabs the two gummies still pinched in my fingers. I think he's taking them for himself, but he surprises me when he drops them on his nightstand, next to the bag.

"You don't want to take them?" I ask him.

"I quit." He shakes his head.

"You seem to be quitting a lot of things lately." I smirk.

"What can I say? I'm on a roll."

When my class ended, I found Jude sitting inside my bookstore in one of the brand-new, plush chairs set near the back, dressed in one of his pressed, black, designer suits. Everything about him screamed familiarity of the double life he's been leading until I saw the expression on his face. Sullen and furious. A combination I've seen on him far too many times. Usually after he's seen his dad.

After running a nervous hand through his hair, he told me he finally quit his father's business. There was a quick spark in my chest at the thought of him quitting, but I tried not to put too much stock into his decision. Deep down, I knew if Jude were to truly ever leave Harding Holdings, it would only be because of something catastrophic. I didn't know if Jude's resignation was permanent, but either way, we celebrated by him taking me up to the loft again. This time it wasn't covered in bits of drywall, and it was a bit sturdier.

I rock my hips against him again.

His eyes darken. "Besides, I want a clear head when I watch you lower yourself onto my cock."

Heat blooms across my cheeks. I lower my hand and wrap it around Jude's cock pressed against my stomach. I run my palm down his length, gripping the base. He releases a tight groan from his throat that erupts and vibrates down to my wet center.

"Tell me what you want," he orders.

"I want you," I whimper. "I want all of you." I can't wait much longer before I pull myself up and allow him to fill me.

I open my eyes and watch Jude beneath me. I watch his reaction to my touch and the way he looks at me. I haven't felt this loved and cherished since the last time Jude and I were happy together. It's the way he looked at me, as if I were made perfectly for him.

"Sit on my cock. Slowly... so I can see every change your body makes when your pussy takes every single fucking inch of me."

I lift myself up and center myself over him.

"That's it." He growls. "Let me show you that you're mine."

I swallow. Hard. My heart races, and emotion inflates my chest. I try not to think too deeply into Jude's words. He's never been one to be one hundred percent reliable, but I see the sincerity behind his darkened eyes.

I lower myself slowly as he requested. I'm slick and ready. My skin still aches from having him between my legs several times today already, but I can't seem to get enough. That's always been the thing about Jude. Being with him has always been a delicate balance between the hurt and the good. We can't love one another without feeling loss.

My heart nearly explodes by the time I lower myself all the way and I've filled myself with Jude's swollen cock. I tense above him, gasping for air when he grabs onto my hips, lifting me up.

He guides me back down, never once taking his eyes off the spot where our bodies meet. He watches as I pull him out of me and then back in.

I move faster, rocking my hips deeper and harder.

"Take it," he grunts. "I want your pussy crying out for me long after you've come."

"*Fuck*," I cry out and lower my head. My hair cascades around my face. I lean forward and press onto Jude's chest, rolling my hips. Jude pushes my hair back.

"Do it," he says, moving his eyes downward. "Come all over my dick like I know you want to."

"Oh my God," I moan. "I'm coming." I clench my thighs, feeling myself tense around him. Fire burns, and bursts of electricity dance across my skin. My face tingles as my orgasm slams into me. Jude reaches up and tugs my nipple between his fingers. He pinches and twists it. My orgasm amplifies, causing my legs to vibrate. I'm worn out and exhausted, but I keep going. I keep going until Jude comes and spills inside me.

When he's finished, I lean over, press my mouth to his, and smile against his lips, knowing this is exactly where I want to be. Our future is unknown, but for the first time, I feel a sense of stability and permanence. I turned my dream of owning a bookstore into a reality. And despite the uncertainty I have around Jude's resignation, I feel this time is different. Somehow, since we've reconnected, I've seen a shift in him.

"You were made for me," he whispers. His chest rapidly rises and falls as he catches his breath.

I pop my bottom lip and shake my head, disagreeing with a smile. "No. We were made for each other." I grab onto his hand and press his palm to my lips. I kiss him, then bring his hand down to my chest, allowing him to feel my heartbeat.

After a few seconds, I slide myself off and lay beside him. Our skin is sticky and damp, but I don't care. I need to feel him. I curl up beside him and rest my head on his chest. His heart beats erratically against my ear. He massages his fingers through the length of my hair, and the rise and fall of his chest slows. It isn't long before I fall asleep to the sound of his hushed breathing.

CHAPTER TWENTY-THREE

VICTORIA

When I crack my eyes open, I see flecks of gold dotted across a black backdrop. It takes a moment for my eyes to adjust.

I'm still lying beside Jude with my head resting against his chest. I don't know how long we've been asleep, but when I look up, his face has rolled the other way. Careful not to wake him, I slip away from his body and sit up. I bend my leg and massage the back of my thigh. It's sore, but luckily, I was able to give it some time to rest. The physical therapy has been putting a strain on the damaged muscle, though, the pain is worth the reward. I twist and glance over my shoulder to study Jude, thinking the same applies to him.

Being with Jude has been nothing but grief and heartache, but there's beauty hidden inside, and it's all been worth it.

Every cut and every bruise. Every broken bone and torn ligament. Losing our child has been the most gut-wrenching and devastating agony I've ever felt, but it's also a grief and pain I share with Jude.

I slide my hand away from my thigh and place it gently on

my stomach. I focus on the warmth my hand gives me. Sometimes it's difficult to remember a life used to be inside of me at one point in time. Now there's nothing but a hollow, empty stomach. My heart kinks and coils at the memory.

I thought when I left Jude behind the first time, I was alone in my grief. But he's been there all along, dwelling in his own. We've both been suffering alone together.

I crawl out of his bed and grab the button-down shirt he left draped over the back of the plush, black chair situated in the corner of his large bedroom. I slip my arms into it and fasten the first three buttons, shivering against the cool air blowing through Jude's enormous apartment. Dozens apartments the size of mine could fit inside Jude's. The ceilings are about twice as high, and every surface is spotless. No wall is decorated. There are no family pictures, if there are any to begin with. There's nothing aside from a closet full of suits he's probably only ever worn once.

I glance over my shoulder once more. He's still lying on his back with his head facing the opposite direction. My stomach grumbles, and I fight not to crawl back into bed with him. Deciding my hunger wins, I tiptoe out of the room and head toward the kitchen.

My bare feet land across the cold tile with every quiet step.

It's eerily quiet. Enough to hear a pin drop and the hairs to stand on the back of my neck.

I'm nearly to the kitchen when I stop in my tracks. I let out a squeal, rushing to clamp a hand over my mouth.

Wide-eyed, I stare at the shadow of a man sitting in the corner of Jude's living room. At first, I wonder if I'm dreaming. Maybe I didn't wake up and I'm still back in Jude's bedroom, curled up beside him. But when the man moves, I know I'm not dreaming.

I narrow my eyes and attempt to make out his features in the darkness. The glint of his patent leather shoes, and his gold watch-adorned wrist give him away.

"James?" I croak.

Silence.

My voice disappears into the shadows. I swallow the lump in my throat, trying not to panic. It's ridiculous, really. I've only ever spoken to James Harding a handful of times, but knowing the kind of man he is, those handful of times were far too many.

I take a tentative step back toward the hallway.

"You know," James starts.

I freeze.

"I had a feeling when my son quit our family business this morning that it might have been because of you."

"Um..." My words fail me. Like my body, they are frozen in place, unwilling to budge in the presence of Jude's venomous father.

James scoots to the edge of the chair and digs his fingers into the cuff of his shirt. It's hard to tell from this distance, but the metal piece he's holding in his hand is small. A sharp click echoes in the silence, followed by him hovering it over the table. A stream of powder falls to the table, and he quickly leans over, bringing his nose down to it. He sniffs, then shoves the metal piece back into his sleeve.

He reaches out to take the small glass filled with an amber liquid, and he tips it back and swallows it all in one gulp. I watch every move he makes. The way he effortlessly moves from one task to the next reminds me of when I used to dance. Repetitive and routine. He's done this a thousand times over in this exact same spot.

"Why are you here?" I'm stunned by my own question.

"I could ask you the same." He pulls himself to a stand. His claw-like fingers are still tight around his whiskey glass. He stumbles over to the bar built into the far wall and lifts the glass top to the whiskey bottle, then fills his small glass to the top. He rolls his head to look up at me and sneers. "My son doesn't even have the courtesy to keep any palatable drink at this bar anymore. Seltzer water, I must say, doesn't hit the spot. Thankfully, I had it in mind to bring this over here with me tonight."

Lifting his glass, he tips it back and downs half his drink in one gulp.

I swallow my resolve, and against my better judgment, take a step forward. I've never been one to stand up to James or anyone in the Harding family, but seeing James in Jude's house drinking and using drugs doesn't sit well with me.

"Leave." I fold my arms beneath my chest. The hem of Jude's shirt rises, exposing more of my bare legs.

James eyes travel south, the disgust flickering in his midnight blue eyes.

"Not so fast," he drawls. "Seems like we have a few matters to discuss." He spins around and sits back down in his chair, setting his glass down and reaching for a small book on the end table. He quickly flips through the pages before closing it and tossing it across the room. I jump back when it lands at my feet.

It falls face down. The spine is bent, and the edges on the cover of the book are faded. I tilt my head to the side, examining it in the darkness. With trembling fingers, I bend down and grip onto the spine, picking it up off the floor. The leather against my fingers feels familiar.

Before I'm able to pull myself to a stand, the length of a ribbon underneath the book catches my attention. I pick it up and slide the smooth, purple fabric between my fingers.

My throat swells, and it takes several breaths before I'm able to look back up to James with watery eyes.

"Where did you get this?" I choke out.

A devilish smirk curls his mouth. I cringe, hating the way he and Jude share so many features. Same mouth. Same brown hair. Midnight blue eyes. I nervously glance down the hallway, wondering if Jude has woken up and heard our conversation. Draped in darkness, I can't make out a single thing.

"It's quite humorous, you know." James swirls his glass. Ice clinks, dancing and melting into the brown liquid, and he tips it back and finishes it in one gulp. He wipes the back of his hand across his mouth and stands. "About a year ago, Jude started working a few odd jobs here and there around the city. At first, I didn't think much of it." He sets his glass on the end table and plants his hands on his hips. His eyes glint in the shadows like two diamonds. "Don't ask me why, but I indulged in whatever desire he had to work trades beneath him."

"Beneath him?"

"You've always been a naïve and foolish woman." He tsks, clicking his tongue against his teeth, and narrows his gaze. "Jude is and will always be a Harding whether you agree with it or not."

I shake my head and chew on the inside of my cheek. Speaking with James now brings me back to the conversation we had when he invited me to Eclipse. It was a mistake to go that night. I was a mouse walking into a viper's den. I guess, in some respects, James is right. I've always been naïve and foolish. That night, I was. James begged me to stop seeing Jude. He told me he would pay for the rest of my college and help me find a place to stay if that's what it took for me to remove myself from the picture. After not agreeing to his offer, I stormed out of there having never felt more embarrassed and humiliated.

I hold the book in my shaking hands. Tears spill over my lashes. I quickly read the words scribbled across every single line. I flip a page and do the same to a few more.

. . .

DEAR J,

They were the shade of midnight blue.

DEAR J,

You asked me to name my favorite body part of yours...

DEAR J,

I thought when we first met, you'd stolen my breath... but I guess you could call me a liar.

DEAR J,

It's three in the morning, and I can't sleep. All I hear are the doctor's words over and over again in my head. I'm sorry, the baby didn't make it.

I CAN'T BRING myself to read anymore. My stomach sours, and I want to vomit. I gently run my hand down the page, feeling the indent of the ink I scribbled across each page. The memory of each diary entry floods back to me. I haven't seen this book in four years. The purple ribbon is still wrapped between my fingers.

It's been even longer since I've seen that, but the memory of where it came from slams into me like the train I've seen oncoming for the past several weeks. I'm tied to the tracks, but I can't come undone. I let the train crash into me.

Leaving Kate at the party. Finding my rooftop retreat. The

sound of the spine cracking as I opened the book I'd brought with me. Jude pushing through the door and stumbling across the concrete. The glint of his gold watch. The way he stepped closer to me. How he tugged my ribbon free from my hair and shoved it in his pocket before he kissed me.

"Oh," James cackles.

Lost in the memory, I almost forgot he was here. I look up from the book.

"Don't get all fucking sad on me." He wobbles closer. His leather shoes slip and roll as he walks over to me.

I take a step back.

He steps closer still.

With flaming red cheeks, and my pulse racing, I stare at James with more hatred than I thought possible.

He's grown closer to me now. The scent of whiskey and cocaine surrounds me. My skin crawls, and my stomach wrenches.

"Why are you here?" My voice quivers. I slip the ribbon between the pages like a bookmark and close the book.

"Jude quit the firm today," he states, matter-of-fact.

"I heard."

"Well, last time my son pulled away from the company, it was because you were in his life."

"I had nothing to do with Jude's decision to leave."

"That may be, Victoria. But there's no mistaking the influence you've had on him. History has a way of repeating itself."

"You know nothing." I grit my teeth. I can feel my chin quiver with my words. I try to keep it together. "I loved Jude, and I always have. I only ever supported him, but I knew it never really mattered. I was never going to gain your approval. Neither was Jude."

"My son doesn't give a shit about my approval." He raises his voice.

"All Jude has ever cared about is what you think of him," I say, matching his tone. "I don't know what made you think differently, but all he's ever wanted was your approval."

"All fucking *lies!*" he yells louder. I notice the way his fingers curl into fists. The veins of his neck bulge.

"I don't understand." I shake my head. "I don't understand what I ever did to make you hate me. All I've ever done is love Jude."

"Oh." He shakes his head. "You did more than love him."

I tilt my head and swallow the heat rising in my throat. "What do you mean?" The words burn as they pour out of me.

"You nearly destroyed his life... and when I found out the truth, I thought I'd done what it took to get rid of you."

"I don't..." I hiccup on my sobs. "I don't understand what you mean. Found out what truth?"

"After Jude started seeing you, he was acting out more. He didn't want to come to family functions. He didn't want to participate in the business. He was still in college, but he needed to learn the ins and outs of what it took to run it. Lennon was already headed in the right direction, but I knew if the company was going to last, I'd need Jude as well. I needed him to be the face of the company, and he couldn't do that if he was seen out in public with a dancer who came from outside the city. He needed a woman from our circle. Someone with our social standing. Because if he married a woman of our caliber, he'd have her children as well. But with you..."

I curl my arm around my stomach. I've never felt as horrible as this. I wrap all the pain and torment I've experienced in my life and compare it to this moment. All of it weaves and blends, magnified a thousand times greater.

A poor attempt at best, I try to prepare myself for what I'm about to hear next.

"I couldn't allow that to happen," James says.

"What?" I ask, feeling nauseous. I close my eyes, then open them again. "What do you mean you couldn't *let* it happen?"

The sound of Jude's footsteps coming from the hallway pulls both of our attention away from each other.

James twists his head in the direction of Jude's bedroom.

Jude's standing on the opposite side of the living room, dressed in his loose gray sweatpants and no shirt. His jaw is clenched, and his eyes are burning in the darkness. His gaze drifts between James and me, then falls to the book in my hands.

I follow his stare, my heart breaking along the way. When I look up, he's stomping his way over to James.

"You fucking asshole," he spits. "Get the fuck out of my house."

"I would watch yourself," James warns. If he's afraid of Jude at all, he doesn't show it.

The muscles across Jude's back and arms tense and flex as he fists the lapels of James's suit. Blowing hot breaths and giving one another challenging glares, Jude finally pulls back. He loosens his grip and shoves him. James stumbles, catching himself on the back of Jude's couch.

Jude backs away, moving to stand next to me.

"What did you mean you couldn't let it happen?" I yell with as much strength as I can gather. Anger drips from my tongue, mixing with the sobs I'm choking on.

James snaps his lapels back into place, brushing off the way Jude handled him. I hear Jude's hot and heavy breaths beside me.

We both wait.

"I was suspicious of where Jude's loyalty lay after being with you for some time. One day, while he was at the office, I'd gone through his phone and read the text messages between you."

Jude clenches his hands into fists and steps closer. Reaching out, I stop him. My hand wraps around his arm, pressing into his strained muscles. I need to hear the truth.

James's hooded eyes stay on Jude. "I read a message saying Victoria was scheduling a doctor's appointment for an ultrasound. That's how I found out she was pregnant. It was then I knew."

"Knew what?" Jude scoffs, furrowing his brow.

James hardens his darkened expression. His eyes are lit with fury and drugs. "I knew I had to stop it. I knew I had to find a way to end your relationship." He shifts his attention to me. "I tried the night I invited you to Eclipse, but you wouldn't listen." He shakes his head. "And then to find out you were pregnant... I didn't have a choice." He steps toward Jude. "I quickly typed out a text to Victoria, telling her you wanted to end your relationship."

Confused, Jude furrows his brows. He glances over his shoulder to me. My hand is still wrapped around his arm, holding him close. "Is that why you texted me that night saying you didn't understand why I wanted to break up?"

I nod, unable to say the words out loud. I'm too stunned to speak.

"You asked me what you had done or said to make me want to leave you," Jude says. "None of it made sense. That's why I asked you to come pick me up that night. I was too drunk to text and wanted to talk it out with you in person. But then..."

"The accident," I croak. My eyes are full of tears. Every blink brings on a new set. It's as if the wounds of our past are re-opening, as fresh as the night of the accident.

Jude's expression softens. His eyes fill with sympathy and regret, but most of all, guilt. Guilt for being drunk that night at a Kappa Sigma party. Too drunk to drive back to my place or ask for a ride. He begged me to pick him up and swore we just needed to talk it out.

I agreed, and it cost us everything.

Jude swings his head back to James. "I never saw a text in my phone to Victoria wanting to break up, though."

James lifts a shoulder. "I deleted it after sending it."

"What the fuck?" Jude barks. This time, I'm unable to stop him. His anger boils over, no longer able to be contained. He tears his arm away from my grip and crosses the last bit of space between him and his father. Rearing his arm back, Jude delivers a blow to James's jaw. He flies back and to the side, bending over. James catches himself with his hand landing on the marble floor before falling completely.

Jude towers above him, hunching over and catching his breath.

With tears streaming down my face, I cover my mouth to keep myself from vomiting all over the tile. I force myself to breathe. Air squeezes through my lungs.

"I shouldn't be shocked!" Jude yells. "But somehow, I fucking am."

When James catches his breath, he pulls himself to a stand. He fixes his hair, running his fingers through his brown strands. He straightens his jacket as if Jude didn't just hit him. Flicking his tongue out, he licks the blood dripping from the corner of his mouth.

James's confession tears me apart.

"So," I sob, pulling my arm to my stomach, hoping to hell it keeps me from falling apart. "You're ultimately the reason we lost our baby?"

James cocks his head to the side and flattens his expression so it's blank and void of emotion. "A drunk driver killed your baby. Not me. I sent a text message."

"Fuck," Jude growls, lifting his arm back again. He screams and yells, delivering another blow to his father's face.

I've never heard Jude make a sound as loud and as heartbreaking as the ones he's making now. Blow after blow. Hit after hit. Jude keeps going.

James falls to the floor on his back, and Jude hovers over him. He grips onto his shirt, fisting his tie. He lifts him up slightly off the floor, holding his clenched fist in front of him.

I watch as Jude tears into his father, allowing his deepest, darkest truth to come to light. "I dedicated my fucking life to pleasing you!" he yells. Another hit. "I did everything you asked me to." He punches him again. Blood pours from James's nose, and I hear a crunch.

James's once crisp button-down shirt and clean blue tie is now clenched inside Jude's tight fist.

"You cost me Victoria," he growls, delivering another punch.

"Jude," I hear myself cry out.

He doesn't hear me.

"She lost her dance career because of you." He hits him again. Jude's knuckles are bloodied and bruised, and I can't tell whether it's James's blood or his own.

Jude releases a sob. His anger and torment consume him. Spit spills from his mouth, and he squeezes his eyes shut. Tears line his midnight blue eyes before they stream down his cheeks.

"We lost our baby because of you!" he cries, yelling between his clenched teeth. "You fucking"—another hit—"piece"—another punch—"of shit."

He rears his fist back again. This time, there isn't nearly as much strength behind it.

"Jude." This time he hears me. "Please, stop."

He snaps his head to the side, staring at me with wide eyes. The sight of him is enough to split me in two. I've never seen Jude this way, so broken and lost.

The agony he's bottled up inside has just exploded in a matter of seconds. Streaks of tears spill down his cheeks. I slowly step forward, closing the distance between us.

I glance at James as Jude lowers him to the floor, finally releasing his grip on his shirt.

James groans and rolls to his side, then lifts his hand to cover his nose.

Jude doesn't move above James, though. He rests his hands on his knees and catches his breath before finally speaking to his father.

"I'll send Lennon payment for this apartment, and I'll sign a release granting me freedom from the business. I'll no longer be tied to you in any way, money or name." He runs the back of his hand across his mouth and sniffs. He reaches inside his pocket, pulls out his phone, and quickly taps the screen before sliding it back into the same pocket. "Brian is parked out front waiting for you. Now get the fuck out of my apartment."

James crawls across the floor. He moves several feet, using his arms as if he were army crawling across the tile. After several feet, he gathers the strength to pull himself to a stand. He wobbles and sways, and he spins to face me and Jude. I gasp.

The damage Jude has done to James's face is both terrifying and satisfying at the same time. It's terrible to wish harm to a person, even someone as evil and devious as James Harding. But I can't help remembering all the pain he's caused. James did whatever it took to protect his family's image, all at the price of losing his grandchild.

Only an awful, heartless human being such as James could do something like that.

I don't realize I'm still crying when James exchanges looks between us.

"Jude," he starts, but he's stopped.

"Get the fuck out!" Jude yells, pointing toward the door.

James shakes his head, corrects his tie, and spins on his heel. He stumbles his way to the door, stopping long enough to grab a long sheet of paper towels. He crumples them into a ball and presses it to his nose.

We watch in silence as he walks through the front door, allowing it to close behind him.

We stand side by side with drops and pools of blood at our feet, and I stare at the spots of blood with my diary in my hand and nothing but the sound of our broken hearts beating.

March 29th

Dear J,

It's three in the morning, and I can't sleep. All I hear are the doctor's words over and over again in my head. I'm sorry, the baby didn't make it.

I'm sorry, the baby didn't make it.
I'm sorry, the baby didn't make it.

It's a strange thought to be in love with someone you've never met, but I absolutely was. I always thought I loved you and no one else came before you, but that all changed the second I could feel our baby growing inside me.

I loved them more than myself, and now they're gone. I was never given the chance to find out if they were a boy or a girl. I was never given the opportunity of picking a name.

I never got to feel them kick or move inside me.

I would say it brings me more comfort thinking the baby at least got to hear my heartbeat from inside my chest, but somehow, that makes it worse.

Then I think about you. Losing the baby makes me feel as if I've lost a part of you as well. But I think I already had before the accident.

I tried to think of a reason you wanted to end

this. You told me repeatedly how you were going to protect me. You promised you would love me and our baby. You said it no longer mattered what your father wanted. But I think the time for all those promises passed long before I got in the car and drove to Kappa Sigma's house. You made your decision over and over again when you chose to go to that house.

And the truth and weight of all the choices and decisions made have come to this.

We've lost everything. I've lost our baby. You. My dance career. The doctor says with time I can try, but I know the truth. I've spent the past eighteen years of my life living and breathing dance. Who am I without it?

Who am I without you and our child?

My life has been built around going to school and perfecting my dance. My plans changed the minute I met you, and now they've changed again. Only this time I'm shattered and broken.

It's been four days since they released me from the hospital. The longer I stay in the dorm, the more confused and lost I feel. The walls are beginning to close in on me. Kate tries to comfort me, but she doesn't fully understand the pain I carry inside. The hollow emptiness eating away at me. Being here in my dorm is a constant reminder of

everything I had before. Before the baby.
Before you.

You've tried calling me ever since you saw me lying in the hospital bed. I can't bring myself to answer. The idea of hearing your voice, begging me to stay when we both know it isn't what you want. Deep in the depths of your soul, I know you're better off without me. You'll never let go of your life or seeking your father's approval.

Even writing these words is difficult, but the truth is difficult to face.

Lies are easy. Truths are lethal.

And the truth is that I can't face another day of walking around in the shadow of my former life. I can't risk running into you, knowing if I were to face you all I can see is the face of our unborn child, and all the promises you allowed to fall so effortlessly from your mouth. I can't face you knowing you would only beg for me to stay with you out of guilt. If at all.

Because as hard as the truth is to face, it's staring directly at me.

The truth has always been in your lies.

In all your gorgeous, gorgeous lies.

CHAPTER TWENTY-FOUR

Jude

I curl my fingers in and out, wincing in pain. Victoria's standing in front of me, gently examining my hand with her gentle touch along the skin of my palm and each finger, counting as she goes, as if she's taking inventory of all the cuts and markings.

My lungs are starving for oxygen. I'm certain I haven't taken a breath since my father walked out the door, bloodied and beaten to shit.

The fucker deserved it, and if it hadn't been for Victoria's voice bringing me back down to earth, I could have kept going another twenty punches.

I tilt my head to the side and watch Victoria. Her hair is a mess, cascading around her tear-stained cheeks. Her lips are a pale shade of pink, and she bites down on her bottom one, narrowing her eyes.

"I can't tell if you broke the skin," she whispers. "We should get this under some water." Her voice cracks as she speaks. The words sound distant and detached, as if the reality of my father's truth hasn't fully sunk in with her yet.

My eyes swing to the diary sitting on the arm of my couch.

It's closed, the edges worn and faded. Pressed between the pages is Victoria's purple ribbon I kept after the first night we met.

I look back at Victoria and study her every feature. Her bare chest rises and falls under the safety of my shirt draped around her. It's entirely too big for her small frame, but I can't help the way my insides flutter at the sight. My heart is broken, yet when I look at her, I feel like a life of love and peace isn't far away.

But her silence worries me.

"Victoria," I cautiously say. My own voice cracks, the strain of yelling at my father taking its toll on my throat.

"Yeah?" She's not taking her attention away from my hand as she turns it over.

"Victoria, look at me."

Slowly shaking her head, she squeezes her eyes shut. A tear spills from between her lashes and lands on the back of my hand.

"I can't." She blows a breath out between her lips.

"Why not?"

"If I look at you," she croaks. "It makes everything that just happened real."

"It's always been real," I argue softly. My chest aches seeing her this broken over the truth. "Not looking at me isn't going to make it any less real." I lift my free hand and move her hair away from her face like I'm pulling back the curtain on her expression.

I'm sliding her hair back over her shoulder when she inhales an unsteady breath.

Her shoulders lift before she finally brings her eyes to mine. They narrow, and the corners of her mouth twitch. Her bottom lip quivers. "The truth is too painful."

I tuck her hair behind her ear again and run my fingers along the side of her face. I wish the simple act of wiping her tears away could also take away all the hurt, but it can't. We're two broken people, begging for the moment to come when it won't hurt any longer.

"Tell me."

Her eyebrows pinch. "Tell you what?"

"Everything." I lean forward, imploring her to open up. "Tell me everything you've ever wanted to say. Your fears. Your truths. Your worries. All of it."

I brace myself for her answers, but seeing Victoria the way she is now is enough to leave me broken for the rest of my life. Seeing her after my father made his confession made the reality of our situation more evident.

Victoria shakes her head again.

I hook my fingers under her chin, forcing her to look at me. "You used to write every thought you had in this diary." I pick it up, holding it between us. "Remember how it felt when you wrote your truths."

She hesitates, taking a moment to catch her breath. She's still crying silent tears. Sniffing, she grabs the diary from my hand and flips through it.

Every page is scribbled with ink. Every confession is permanently recorded—a snapshot to the progression of our relationship.

"I..." Victoria clears her throat, bringing her watery eyes to mine. "I don't know if I can." She sighs.

I place my hand on the side of her face, reassuring her. "I don't know what you will say, but it doesn't matter what I think. If it hurts, I'll allow it to hurt. If it burns, I'll feel it. I think we've both spent years keeping our truths to ourselves because we were too afraid to face them. I get it. Living in a lie or in the darkness is easy. This..." I place my bloodied hand on her chest, over her heart. "Keeping this beating, that's the difficult part."

She sobs. Her shoulders rack with her cries, then she takes a moment to catch her breath, licking her lips. She lowers her diary and backs away from me. We're still standing in my living room. Small pools of drying blood lay at our feet. The nauseating scent of whiskey and drugs coats my senses. But all I see is Victoria. All I hear is Victoria and all her confessions.

"I don't know if I can handle this again." Her voice cracks, her eyes widening with the truth pouring out of her. "The heartache. The lies. I can't look at you without thinking what our baby would have looked like. Would it have been a girl or a boy? Would they have your midnight eyes? Would they have become a dancer or a writer or a scientist? I live every single day living a life our baby never got to experience. I spend every minute of every day wondering if they would have liked this color over that one. I wonder if they would have been competitive or artistic. I can't look at you without thinking of what might have been. I look at you and see the future I used to want. And sometimes I look at you and wonder if you'll disappear from this new one."

"V," I whisper, holding a hand out to her. Her confessions slam into me with the weight of a thousand sandbags barreling into my chest. The thoughts she's had over the years are the same thoughts I've carried with me. They're the reason I stopped drinking after the accident. Drinking numbed the pain of losing my baby and Victoria. I didn't want to feel numb. I wanted to remember how it felt that night, standing on the opposite side of the hospital room curtain, listening to the doctor as he told me what Victoria had endured.

I step forward, but she steps back. Her sobs continue.

"No." She shakes her head. "You asked for my truth, and I'm telling you now."

I nod, pressing my mouth into a thin line. I let her continue, but every instinct in my body and mind wants me to wrap my arms around her. I want to protect her. I want to love her.

"I knew being with you again was a risk." She blinks, placing her hand over her heart. "No matter how hard I fought against it, I tried to stay away. Being with you comes with this." She lifts her arms, gesturing toward my entire apartment. "Places like this. Fancy cars and restaurants. Money and greed. Lies and women clawing their way to get to you. I experienced it the first time we were together, and this time is no different. I'm sorry, Jude, but it's hard to be with you and not question the difference between a truth and a lie. You made so many promises when we were together before and even now, I don't know whether I can trust them again. How can I trust you when I can't even trust myself around you?"

She spins in a circle, shoving her hair back off her forehead. She rests both hands on her head as she stares at me. The end of my shirt lifts, exposing more of the smooth skin of her thighs. She's fucking gorgeous standing here in front of me. We're surrounded by destruction, but all I see is beauty.

My heart aches, wondering where she's going with her truths. I wanted to hear her confession, whether it be good or bad, but the fear of losing her is all too real. Her confession stings.

I lost Victoria once before. The possibility of history repeating itself, yet again, is quite real.

"Being with you cost me everything." Her voice breaks again. This time it shoots straight to my heart, delivering a blow I didn't see coming. Her eyes soften as she stares at me. Her hands fall to her stomach. She presses them down, hunching her shoulders over. "I lost my dance career. Our baby. I know now you weren't the one to end our relationship. It was your father's doing. But I can't help looking at everything and wondering when the next break will be. At what point will the price of being with you be too high for me or us to survive?"

"Victoria," I quickly say, closing the gap between us. This

time she doesn't pull away. She allows me to wrap my hands around hers, and I place them to my chest and hold them there. "Every promise I ever made to you was true. I'm sorry I couldn't protect you before, not just from the accident, but from my family. I will carry that guilt with me for the rest of my life. Knowing you lost everything because you loved me. It was never a lie when I told you I loved you, too." I bend my knees, begging her to bring her gaze up from the floor to meet my eyes. "I made my mistakes when it came to drinking. I own those. I know you have no reason to trust me when I tell you I'm done with my father and resigning from the business. But I love you, Victoria, and I will do whatever it takes to make sure you never forget it."

She inhales a shaky breath. "Loving you has been the best and worst thing to ever happen to me."

"I'm sorry." I move my hand from hers and grab onto the side of her face. I bury my fingers through her hair, uncertainty settling in the pit of my stomach.

"I hate that I look at you and see everything I've lost," she confesses as she lifts her tear-filled eyes to mine. "But what I fucking hate the most is how I look at you and I'm still in love with you."

"You still love me?" I ask, unsure whether the adrenaline from earlier is getting to me. Maybe I'm hallucinating, stuck in a reality I've made up in my own mind.

Victoria chews on the inside of her mouth and nods. "If I think about it long enough, I realize I never stopped."

"Me, too." I sigh with relief. "I fucking love you, V. I always have." With both hands, I grab onto the side of her face and pull her to me. I crash my lips to hers. She stands on her toes, pouring her whole body into our kiss.

"I'm sorry," I groan against her lips. Tension builds in my fingers. I already know I'm going to feel it tomorrow, but I don't care. "I'm so sorry, V."

She shakes her head against my mouth, then pulls away. "Stop." She wraps her hands around my neck. "You don't have to apologize for anything."

"I do. I do because I will spend the rest of my life proving my promises to you. I promised long ago that I would love and protect you. This is me following through. Think of it more like an oath than a promise."

"An oath, huh?" The corner of her mouth quirks into a smile. The first I've seen since before the fight with my father.

"Okay," I say, wrapping my arm around her lower back. I pull her back up onto her toes and press my body to hers, pinning her with my gaze. "I amend every promise I ever made."

At first, her eyebrows knit, confused.

"I pledge an oath to stand by you." I place a soft kiss to her forehead. "To be with you." I place another kiss below her eye. "To take every hurt and pain you've ever felt." I hover my mouth over hers, flicking my eyes downward, darkening my gaze. "And make it mine." I don't realize we're dancing slowly until the last words fall from my mouth. "Because you *are* mine. Forever."

A sob rattles out of Victoria. Following through on my first vow, I press my mouth to hers, catching her sob before she releases another.

She doesn't speak another word. She lets me swallow her pain and bury it along with mine. She allows me to dance with her in the living room at her own pace.

Slow and measured. Each step is a stitch closing the wounds of our past.

CHAPTER TWENTY-FIVE

VICTORIA

I snap my eyes open when the smell becomes too much for me to ignore. Rolling over with a groan, I slide my hand across the mattress toward Jude's side of the bed.

Empty.

Sitting up, I clutch the sheet to my bare chest and glance around the room, squinting against the bright orange rays pouring through the windows.

Snatching my phone from the nightstand, I read the time. Five in the morning.

The grand opening of **Victoria's Book Corner** is in five hours.

I place my phone back on the nightstand and crawl out of Jude's massive bed. I don't bother dressing or wrapping myself in one of his shirts. The cool air in his room nips at my skin. Shivers trickle down my spine. I tiptoe out of his room, following the scent down the hallway.

I peek into the living room before stepping into it. The last time I wandered into this room, I found James Harding perched in the chair in the corner shortly before he was snorting a line of cocaine. Flashbacks of my diary being thrown come back at me.

When I don't see his villainous eyes peering my way, I step into the living room fully. My diary is still resting on the end table where I left it last night. I pick it up off the table and finger my way through it. I don't read my own words. It's been years since I've seen these pages. My life was on a different path then, words and letters written by someone living another life. A completely different one to mine now. I stop flipping through the pages when I get to the one with the purple ribbon. It's crinkled and worn but otherwise looks the same as it did the last time I saw it.

I rub my finger along the smooth fabric, remembering the day I'd worn it. Dancing with Kate on stage. Performing for our dance instructor. Going to the party at Kappa Sigma's house. Jude stumbling in on me while I was attempting to read the book I'd brought with me.

I smile at the memory.

"On your desk."

"What?" I snap my head up, finding Jude standing in front of the stove.

He's naked as well. Shirtless, his tan skin and muscles are on full display.

He points to the book in my hand. "I found it on your desk in your dorm when I heard you left the city after they released you from the hospital."

"Oh." My cheeks blush. I close the book and run my hand over the front. "I can't believe I left it."

"I couldn't, either. When you hadn't returned my calls after several days, I bumped into Kate on the way to class one day. At first, she was reluctant to bring you up. She was angry with me for what had happened. I couldn't blame her." His expression softens, sadness settling into his eyes. "When I'd pressed her, she said you decided to quit school. She wouldn't tell me where you'd gone, but she offered for me to stop by your room and grab a few things you'd left behind that she knew were mine. I found that sitting on your desk with a few of your other books."

My eyes swell with emotion. I bite back fresh tears, unwilling to shed any more. Last night was a whirlwind. Between anger and sadness, my body is exhausted. I look up from the diary and give Jude a small smile. "You kept the diary but not the other books?" I giggle, attempting to lighten the mood.

Shaking his head, he laughs and nods toward the bookshelf built into the far wall, beside the stone fireplace.

I cross the room and scan the shelves. Pressed between two gold painted bookends are three books I recognize. Two romance novels, one suspense. I twist my head back and drop my jaw. "You kept them?"

"Yeah." He scrunches his nose. "I didn't care much for the one about the couple who stayed out at the lake house. The ending was unexpected, though."

"You read them?" I ask, stunned.

Casually shrugging a shoulder, he pauses, then frowns. Laughing to himself, he shakes his head.

"What?" I ask.

"Never mind." He shakes his head again. "It sounds silly."

"Try me," I challenge, crossing the room.

He spreads his arms out and uses the heels of his hands to lean on the counter. "I don't know." He hangs his head low, then looks up. The ends of his hair touch his forehead above his brows. His jaw ticks. "After you left, I had this fear that somehow you weren't real. I was afraid that if I let you go, it would be as if you'd never existed. The same could be said for my drinking. Drinking numbed the pain of losing my mom, and the expectations of my father. But after I lost you and our baby, I lived with the pain every day because feeling was better than living as if I were dead."

My lip quivers but I hold back the tears again. I can't cry. Not anymore. I close the distance left in the living room and step up into the kitchen. I'm standing on the opposite side of the island, but I'm close enough to catch the sincerity in his words.

Notorious for keeping his truths guarded, I feel I now know Jude better than I have ever since we met. This is the real Jude Harding. Raw and vulnerable. His heart is no longer shielded. It's displayed clearly on his sleeve.

"So, you read them to remember me?" I quirk an eyebrow.

"Reading the same books you read and knowing you loved them made you real. It proved to me at one point in time that I had the capacity to love someone more than myself or my fucking family."

"Oh." I nod and tuck my quivering lip under my teeth. I watch Jude with a watery gaze. My chest swells, and my insides expand, filling with love for this man I've never been able to let go. And the fact he kept my books on his shelf for the sole reason that I'd read them, as well, makes me fall in love with him a thousand times over.

"So..." He breathes in, clapping his hands. "That's that." I sense the nervousness in his voice. He looks down at the pan he's placed on the stove. The muscles in his arms flex and contract as he moves around the kitchen. I'd almost forgotten that we're both standing in his apartment utterly naked. He digs through the pantry, then the fridge, and grabs a handful of eggs before he gently places them on the counter next to a pack of bacon.

"Jude," I mutter.

"Yeah?" He stops moving long enough to answer, and eyes me slowly. He scans my body as if he's trying to memorize every inch.

"I love you." I smile, stepping into the kitchen. I lift myself up onto my toes, careful not to trigger the muscle in my damaged leg. I kiss him and fall back on my heels. He catches me, placing his hand on the small of my back. Fire ignites across my body.

When he pulls back, he searches my face. "I love you, too."

I grin and step backward until my spine lands against the cool edged surface, and I lean against it, pushing my arms back as I grip onto the edge of the counter. "What are you making?"

He chuckles, looking up to the morning sun pouring in through the windows. His body is veiled in orange and yellow. There's a light to his gaze. He looks happy. *Free.*

It's as if all the weight he's carried with him is suddenly gone.

I feel the same.

The pain of losing our child and the circumstances surrounding how will never fade, but I know that as time goes on, the grief won't feel as heavy or dark.

He turns away from the sun and faces me. "Thought a little celebratory breakfast was in order for your grand opening this morning."

"Oh." I grin brighter. "You don't have to do that. Riley mentioned bringing donuts to the shop before we get there."

"Hmm," he hums, moving to stand in front of me. He grabs onto my hips and lifts me up onto the counter. My bare ass meets the cool marble, and more goosebumps spread across my skin. My nipples peak.

Jude pries my legs open and pulls me to the edge of the counter. His erection presses against my already wet center.

He drags his finger along the inside of my thigh. "I do believe this is my favorite look on you."

"It is not." I tease.

His hand quickly finds my wet center. I gasp, leaning farther back onto the counter. I drop my head back and face the ceiling. My mouth falls open when his fingers find my clit.

"You might be right." He growls. "This is my favorite."

I smile, although he can't see my face.

My smile soon fades, and I'm gasping for air when he plunges his fingers inside me. At first two, then three. He hooks them inside me, landing on the perfect spot.

"Oh my God," I moan, tugging my bottom lip under my teeth.

I look down just as Jude leans forward and brings his mouth to my nipple. He tugs it into his mouth and laps his tongue around my hardened pebble. He pulls my flesh into his mouth on a groan. His thick, heavy voice vibrates across my body. I thread my fingers through his hair.

When he bites down on my nipple, I yelp. The sting intensifies the sensation of his fingers moving inside me.

He pulls away from me and begins lowering himself. With hooded eyes, he bends to his knees.

"You know," he hums against my thighs and places a kiss along the inside. Then another. "I think I'd prefer to have you for breakfast instead." He flicks his gaze up to mine. "Don't you agree?"

He doesn't allow me to answer before his mouth is on me. He slides his tongue up and along my slit. I place both my legs over his shoulders, fisting his hair between my fingers.

"Yes," I beg. "Please." My lungs are starving for oxygen. My entire body burns, and every breath I take is deeper than the next. My head spins as Jude's mouth moves on me. It's different than before. The touch of his tongue is more intense. Every thrust of his fingers is deeper than the rest. My legs vibrate against him.

He lifts his free hand and wraps it over my thigh, pinning me to him. I want to move away, but at the same time, I don't. I want to feel this. Every touch, every kiss. All of it.

I want to remember this moment and never let it go. My

vision blurs. Sparks of electricity burst across my skin, and my orgasm hits. A massive wave trembles over me. I cry out with Jude's tongue still on me, moving effortlessly. When my movements slow, he stands and positions his full cock in front of me. He's hard as stone.

Quickly, he pushes himself inside me. He leans forward and groans, pausing long enough to feel my walls squeeze around him. I lean farther back on the counter. My chest is in line with his face. He bends down, biting on my flesh, harder and sharper than before.

I hiss between my teeth. He pulls back, then slams into me again. Over and over. I'm still feeling the aftereffects of the first orgasm and am quickly approaching another one. My legs burn and tingle all at once. Jude must feel me squeezing around him. After every thrust, he pauses long enough for me to take a breath, then repeats three more times before my legs tremble around him. He cups my jaw with one hand and presses his thumb to my bottom lip.

He stops and stays inside me until he's finished.

"Delicious breakfast." He grins. "If I do say so myself."

His mouth is glistening from being on me moments earlier. I laugh and sit up, wrapping my arms around his neck.

"I agree. You make the best breakfast."

"Huh." He kisses me. "Since I'm without a job now, maybe I should become a chef."

I laugh and pull him to me. I wrap my legs around his waist and lock them together with my ankles. He grunts, feeling my warm center pressing against him again.

"Come to think of it, I think I'd like to keep this chef to myself." I trail my fingers along his neck.

"Yeah?" He hums against me.

"Yeah." I nod. "But I know you have plenty of other qualifications you can put to good use. We have time to figure it out."

"We do?" he asks gruffly. The expression on his face tells me there's deeper meaning to his question. He's wondering how long. How long do we have together? Will we make it longer than we did the last time? Are our hearts healed enough to stand the trials of a relationship as deep and heavy as ours?

"Oh, yeah." I pull him closer. "Time doesn't exist when it comes to us, remember?"

"You're right." The corner of his mouth curls, and the blue in his eyes darkens and intensifies. "You're mine forever. In this life and the next... and the next... and the next."

EPILOGUE

VICTORIA

Three months later

"I've found a few more books I think you'd like for the blind book section."

I spin around as Jude places a large box on the counter. I stand on my toes, peeking inside. There are at least twenty books stacked inside.

"Jude," I giggle. "This is more than a few."

He shrugs one shoulder and digs his hands into the pockets of his dark, torn jeans. Paint is smudged across the line of his jaw. I resist the urge to reach out and run my finger down the length of it. He pushes his hair off his forehead and grins. "What can I say? I got a good deal on them."

My insides turn molten. My thighs tingle at the sight of the man I'm hopelessly and recklessly in love with.

It's been months since our lives collapsed from under us, all at the confession of James Harding.

We haven't seen James since that night. Or I haven't. Jude is insistent he hasn't run into him, and for the first time since the night we met, I don't have any reason to doubt him. Because of all the times Jude chose his father over me, he never chose him once he figured out the truth.

Days after, Lennon drafted up the documents to have Jude formally back out of the business. Jude paid the price of his apartment through his brother, officially cutting all ties with his family monetarily.

The uncertainty of Jude's professional life hung in the balance for all but a week before Cain offered him partnership in his renovation business. Ever since, he's spent his days moving around the city, connecting with small business owners, making their dreams a reality. Much like he did mine.

I have yet to open the store this morning. Aside from the book-lined walls and tables, it's just me and Jude.

After finishing my last course to earn my degree, I finally graduated from the college I was meant to graduate from all along. My dream of becoming a Boston College graduate came true, along with opening the bookstore. Every day is exciting and new. Customers sprinkle in throughout the day, and I didn't realize how fulfilling it would be to surround myself with what I love daily.

The smell of books. Fellow book lovers. Jude.

I begin lifting the short stacks of books from the box, reading the titles of each one as I go. Jude leans over the counter and gives me a kiss. I smile against his mouth. He backs away and aimlessly walks over to the blind book section. He hasn't directly told me, but I know this corner is Jude's favorite part of my store. It's mine as well.

There are countless times I've caught him scanning the shelves, pulling one out every now and then to read the tropes.

Each section is divided by genre, but otherwise, the customer doesn't know which book they're purchasing. It's been successful, and my heart warms any time I see customers in this particular section. Especially when that person is Jude.

I watch him carefully as he scans the rows of brown paper-wrapped books. Like he's done a thousand times before, he cocks his head to the side as if he's deciding which one to choose. He stops to read the three tropes written in black marker on the front, places it back on the shelf, then moves on to the next.

I bite back the urge to laugh. I snort instead.

He snaps his head in my direction. "What?"

"Nothing." I shake my head, biting down on my bottom lip. "I just never pegged you as much of a reader. At least I didn't realize it until you told me you kept those books of mine from my dorm. Now I see you over here almost every day."

"I find it interesting," he says, turning back to the shelves.

He stops in the romance section and pulls another one out to read the front of it with narrowed eyes. His mouth turns down at the corners in thought.

Crossing the room, he moves behind the counter and stands in front of me. "Like this one." He holds the book out for me, keeping his eyes on it. "Second chance. Billionaire. Forced proximity. Soulmates."

I grin and grab the book from him. I'm left breathless when I read the tropes he listed off, but they aren't written on the brown paper like every other book on the shelf.

They're written on a purple envelope, taped to the front. The same shade of purple as the ribbon he'd taken from me the night we met.

I gasp and place my hand on my stomach. Jude does the same, reaching out and delicately dragging his finger back and forth. My stomach flutters knowing the life growing inside me is a piece of the beautiful man standing in front of me.

I tug the envelope from the book, careful to not pull the tape too hard and rip the brown paper wrapping.

Placing the book on the counter, I flip the envelope over to open it but stop when I read the words written on the back.

With watery eyes, I look up and find Jude's midnight eyes staring back at me. "Before you read the letter inside, I have a question for you."

I quickly shift my attention between him and the question written on the back.

"Will you marry me?"

I swallow the emotion thick in my throat and find myself nodding even before Jude has finished asking the question. Because the truth is, I know deep in my soul that there's only ever been one answer.

He pulls a ring from his pocket, reaches for my hand, and slips it on my finger before he presses his mouth to mine.

When he pulls away, I couldn't feel more at peace knowing this is the life we were meant to live all along.

We just took a little detour.

I kiss Jude once more, holding back the tears as best I can, and I tear the envelope open.

I cry tears of joy when I read the first two words written in black ink.

Dear V,

THE END

Want to read Jude's 'Dear V' letter?
CLICK HERE for to read an exclusive bonus!

GET ready for the next Harding brother in *Sweet Nothings*, a Marriage of Convenience/Arranged Marriage Billionaire Romance!

PRE-ORDER HERE

WANT to sign up for my newsletter and be notified of my upcoming releases? Don't miss out on more of the Harding Brothers, coming soon! Sign Up HERE

YOU CAN ALSO JOIN my reader group,

Brittany's Book Lovers.

OR FOLLOW me in all the social media spaces:

Facebook Instagram Goodreads Amazon BookBub TikTok

ACKNOWLEDGMENTS

Wow, what a ride Victoria and Jude's story has been. In my heart, I feel like I owe them so much gratitude and, in many ways, they healed me. They brought me back down to earth and helped me realize I do have worth in this industry. They centered me. I fell in love with them and in the process, I remembered what I love writing the most. Deep, emotional, gripping stories. Spicy romances with tragic pasts. The ones with characters who are riddled with flaws, but you can't help but fall for them anyway. I fell for Victoria and Jude hard. Before writing their story, I found myself questioning my worth and my place. But through the process of writing their story, it became clear I do have a place and I am worthy. I'm so incredibly grateful to them and everyone who had a hand in this book.

Always first, I'm grateful for my husband and my kids. I say this every time, but it still rings true. I do all of this for you. Thank you for lifting me up through the crippling doubt and celebrating every small success. You're my favorite humans in the whole world. Thank you for reminding me every day that I am worthy.

To my sister, Dani for your constant reminder to give myself grace and patience. Your friendship and love are immeasurable. I love you.

To my assistant, Tiffany. Your constant unwavering support means the world to me. Through the late-night messages, last minute scheduling of posts, and my venting sessions where I question every detail, you are there. Thank you for these past few years of being on my team. I appreciate you more than you probably know.

To my editor, Vicki James. This is the second book you've edited for me, and I already know I never want to let you go. Although I've fallen in love with your edits and for your ability to make my books shine, I've found a friend in you. You are kind, funny, and encouraging. Thank you for being my editor *and* my friend.

To Josette and my PR team. Thank you for your support and work on this book.

Sara Massery and Ashley Munoz. For the early morning calls. For the late-night voice clips. For picking me up when I felt the lowest. Your friendship, advice and guidance meant so much to me in the early process of this book. I love you both.

My stunning agent, Nikki Groom. I feel so incredibly blessed to have you in my life and in my corner. Thank you for your willingness to talk me through my creative choices and the direction in which to steer my career. You motivate me and I genuinely am grateful to you for reminding me I belong. Thank you for taking my stories and loving them as much as I do.

My beta readers, April, Amy, Anamika, and Summer. This book would not be what it is without you. Your feedback was invaluable, and I thank you for being a part of this process. April, words can't express the gratitude I have for you. You've been a beta reader of mine for quite a few books but this one has meant more to me than all the rest you've read. Thank you for being there for Victoria and Jude before they were *even* Victoria and Jude. You've not only been a beta reader of mine... you've also become a friend. All four of you have! Thank you for sticking with me.

To every single blogger, booktoker, and bookstagrammer! Thank you for your shares and tags. I love and see you all.

And to you, the reader! Thank you for reading and I am always incredibly grateful for you. I genuinely hope you enjoyed reading Gorgeous Lies and look forward to the next!

All my love.
Brittany

ALSO BY BRITTANY

The Heartbreak Series

The Rules of Heartbreak – Enemies to lovers, next-door neighbors

The Secrets to Heartbreak – Brother's Best-Friend

The Troubles with Heartbreak – Fake Engagement, Sports Romance

Standalones

See Through – Rockstar Romance

Paper Hearts – Second Chance, Billionaire

The Wrong Pitch - Roommates to Lovers, College Sports

What are the Chances – Romantic Comedy Set in Ireland

The Back to Me Series

A Thriller, Romantic Suspense Series

Dissipate

Mine

Back to Me

Without You Duet

Emotional, Second Chance at Love

Without You

Without Me

Harding Brothers Series

Gorgeous Lies - Second Chance, Billionaire

Pretty Heartache - Coming Soon!

Sweet Sorrow - Coming Soon!

ABOUT BRITTANY

Brittany Taylor grew up all over the world including places such as California, England, and Texas. Her love of reading started at a young age. Finally deciding to fulfill her lifelong dream, she took the plunge into the writing world and published her first book when she was twenty-eight. Today she resides in Maine with her husband, two sons, two cats and one dog.